MW01178893

WITHDRAWN

RIDERS OF DESERET

OTHER FIVE STAR WESTERNS BY DANE COOLIDGE:

RIDERS OF DESERET

A WESTERN STORY

DANE COOLIDGE

FIVE STAR
A part of Gale, Cengage Learning

GALE
CENGAGE Learning·

Detroit • New York • San Francisco • New Haven, Conn • Waterville, Maine • London

GALE
CENGAGE Learning

LIBRARY OF CONGRESS CATALOGING-IN-PUBLICATION DATA

Coolidge, Dane, 1873–1940.
  Riders of Deseret : a western story / by Dane Coolidge. — 1st ed.
      p. cm.
    "Riders of Deseret by Dane Coolidge first appeared under the title 'The fighting Danites' as a four-part serial in Short stories (7/10/25–8/25/25)"—Copyright p.
    ISBN-13: 978-1-59414-996-2
    ISBN-10: 1-59414-996-8
    1. Mormons—Fiction. I. Title.
  PS3505.O5697R53 2010
  813'.52—dc22   2010028393

First Edition. First Printing: November 2010.
Published in 2010 in conjunction with Golden West Literary Agency.

ADDITIONAL COPYRIGHT INFORMATION

EDITOR'S NOTE

In a note, Dane Coolidge commented: "This story came to me in 1924 as I was looking out over House Rock Valley." He completed the manuscript on December 23, 1924. He titled it "Deseret", after the proposed state the Mormons organized in 1849, but which was denied recognition by the U.S. Congress. Deseret is also the name given the heroine in the story by the Mormons after murdering her parents at Mountain Meadows. Magazine publishers were still as reluctant in the 1920s to publish any fiction that might be seen as critical of Mormons as they had been in the previous decade when Zane Grey tried to publish his original version of *Riders of the Purple Sage.* However *Short Stories,* a magazine published by Doubleday, Page & Company and edited by Harry E. Maule, because of the historical realism of stories by William MacLeod Raine being published in serial form in its pages and in book editions afterward, was not afraid of adverse criticism from vested interests and bought the story for $4,000, running it in four installments. The title was changed to "The Fighting Danites" by the magazine. Dane Coolidge, at the recommendation of his agent, Harold Ober, rewrote the story in 1933 to make it suitable for book publication by E.P. Dutton & Company. The text here has been restored to Dane Coolidge's original version. The only change has been in the title, altered from "Deseret" to "Riders of Deseret", by which is meant the Avenging Angels of the Mormons who enforced the Mormon settlements beginning in 1849 in what became Utah Territory in 1850. They were intent on protecting the Mormon church from all opposition at any cost.

CHAPTER ONE

It was the evening of Pioneer Day, the Mormons' 4th of July, and the spacious temple grounds were ablaze with pitch-pine torches and the glare of the barbecue pits. From within the shadowy Tabernacle, where the Saints had first worshiped, the mighty organ sent forth its vibrant thunder. The gray temple, half-finished, loomed high, and beneath, in the gathering darkness, there moved a horde of people who had found there the Promised Land. Thirty years before, on the 29th of July, 1847, the pioneers had come to Salt Lake, and on the spot where they had danced, following the admonition of the Prophet, a huge bower of green limbs had been built. Once more the hard-stamped earth was their dancing floor, roofed over with cottonwood boughs, and every pole was decorated with sheaves of wheat and rye, to symbolize the wealth they had won. For in thirty years they had built an empire and called it Deseret.

The horns blared out, the people made way, and with his favorite wife on his arm and a long retinue behind, Brigham Young strode into the bower. He was a big man, with level brows and a keen, resolute eye. As he faced the great assembly, a hush fell on the crowd, for to them he was more than a man. He was the Prophet of the Lord, wearing the mantle of Joseph Smith and talking with God face-to-face. No, more than that, he was a god himself, destined to rule a celestial sphere after death. But when he bowed to their loud cheers he was a man, like themselves—the man who had led them to Salt Lake. On the spot where the temple now reared its massive walls he had driven a stake that first day. His will alone had made them what they were—he was the greatest of all pioneers.

All eyes were upon him as he advanced to the dais and at once opened the festivities with prayer, and then with his wife made merry in the dance as the will of the Lord had directed. Men in homespun and cowhide boots claimed partners in Quaker gray, those in broadcloth sought out ladies of their kind, but to none did they bow with more worshipful eyes than to Tamar, the fair daughter of Brigham Young.

She stood at one side, gay and smiling but inexorable, while young man after young man proffered his arm and craved the honor of a dance. Even to Hyrum Paine himself, the young secretary of her father to whom rumor had more than once reported her engaged, she shook her head and smiled cryptically, and he turned away sullenly as a young man in uniform came hurrying across the floor. This man held out his hand and she sprang joyously to meet him. They were dancing almost before she met his outstretched arm, and the look that she gave him made Lieutenant Zachary Tarrant forget all the world except her.

Her eyes were hazel gray, full of coquetry and fire yet with a trace of sadness in repose, and, as they whirled away together, she spoke eagerly in his ear and he glanced down and nodded assent. Then she questioned him again and the dance was neglected as they fell into animated talk. The music stopped and they hurried off together to escape a fresh rush of admirers, but with the next waltz they were back, swinging lightly across the floor, their eyes bright with the look that spells love. Women turned back to stare. Mormon men exchanged grim glances and scowled at the hated Army blue. Then across the floor there strode the commanding officer's adjutant who tapped young Tarrant on the shoulder.

"By the colonel's orders," he said, "you will repair to your quarters, and consider yourself under arrest."

"Very well," returned Tarrant, after one look at Tamar Young, and went out with his face deathly white.

An hour later, at Fort Douglas, he stood before the colonel who motioned to the adjutant to go.

"Lieutenant Tarrant," began Colonel Valentine, "you are aware of the general order prohibiting fraternizing with the disloyal Mormon populace?"

The lieutenant nodded his head.

"And you are also aware that I warned you particularly to remain away from this young lady, Tamar Young? Now what do you have to say for yourself?"

"Nothing at all, sir. I admit I did wrong."

"And you realized when you went down there that disobedience of orders is punishable by dismissal . . . even death? Then why did you do this thing?"

"I don't know, sir," answered Tarrant.

"Yes you do!" rapped out the colonel. "You know very well and I am going to prefer charges against you. You have violated the first principle of Army discipline, which demands obedience to your superior officer. You know, and I know, the disloyalty that exists in the Territory of Utah today. The Mormon Church and Brigham Young have set themselves up to resist the United States government. They have paraded their militia against the orders of the governor and refused to turn over their arms. That is treason and insurrection and the man who is behind it is the father of this girl that you danced with. Perhaps you do not know that we are being spied on by Brigham Young, and that your association with his daughter has brought you under strong suspicion as the man who is revealing our plans?"

"No, sir, I did not," faltered Tarrant. "I have met Tamar frequently but I have never discussed our plans, nor has she tried to discover them. She . . . she is very unhappy . . . and when we are together. . . ."

"You talk of love. Is that what you mean? Now, listen, Lieutenant, and don't interrupt me. Have you ever heard of Colonel Brandwyn? He came to Salt Lake City with five hundred men and a commission as governor in his pocket, to supersede Brigham Young. But after spending a gay winter he marched on to California and declined to take over the office. Do you know why he declined that appointment? Because this same Brigham Young, the father of the girl to whom you were talking love, deliberately got him entangled with two Mormon women and compelled him to resign or be exposed. That is the man we are sent here to humble, and that is the way he fights."

"You have no right, sir," burst out Tarrant, his eyes suddenly ablaze, "to class her . . . to class Tamar . . . with those women! I would trust her with my life, and my sacred honor. . . ."

"Come with me," said the colonel abruptly, "and I'll show you some papers that may make you change your mind."

He led the way into an inner room, where the secret files were kept, and locked both doors behind him.

"There is the record of her marriage, three months ago," he said, "to Brigham Young's secretary, Hyrum Paine. You can look the papers over, if you wish."

"I don't believe it!" exclaimed Tarrant, pushing the hateful records away. "Is Tamar really married to him?"

"They were sealed by Brigham himself," replied the colonel sternly.

"My God," shuddered Tarrant, sinking down in a chair. "He's got two wives already."

He sat fumbling the papers, his eyes glazed with horror, and the colonel laid a hand on his shoulder.

"Forgive me . . . it was necessary," he said more gently. "You would not take my word without the proof."

"The third wife . . . of Hyrum Paine," groaned Tarrant.

"More than that," added the colonel. "She was working under orders, presumably from her husband and father. Think again . . . did you ever discuss our plans?"

"No, never," declared Tarrant staunchly. "She . . . I cannot believe it. Let me think."

"Here are some papers that may help you," suggested the colonel significantly, and laid a pile of documents before him.

Lieutenant Tarrant looked them over, a line of pain between his eyes, his lip trembling in spite of his pride, and then with a sob he fell forward across the table and buried his face in his hands.

"I am guilty," he choked. "She has played me false. I acknowledge it and I'm ready for my punishment."

"And are you ready," demanded the colonel, "to accept dismissal and disgrace in order to repair this mistake? Then forget about this woman and I will still give you a man's task . . . a task you may be proud to perform. Ever since the Mormon people, fleeing from persecution in the East, established their homes in this land, they have been a law unto themselves. They have set up their own courts, maintained their own militia, even taken up arms against our government, and the very men who resisted the advance of our Army were trained in the Mormon battalion. The Army and the government have themselves to thank for the training of these fighting Danites, but until their power is broken, there can be no loyalty, because the better class of citizens are intimidated.

"The greatest blot on the history of Utah, and on Brigham Young and his church, is the Mountain Meadow Massacre of 'Fifty-Four. And until that blot is removed, until the perpetrators are punished, Utah will remain stiff-necked in its disloyalty. So far the courts have been in the hands of the Mormons and it has been useless to attempt to get justice, but now by an act of

Congress the federal courts have been restored and our orders are to clean up this country. So far every move has been checkmated at the start and the Danites still rule the land.

"In southern Utah, where this party of emigrants was massacred, they are still robbing prospectors and travelers. Wagon trains are being waylaid by men disguised as Indians, the peaceable Mormons are terrorized, and the country about Moroni is as foreign to our laws as if it were a province of Mexico. So much for conditions as they are."

The colonel glanced about and leaned closer to Tarrant, whose eyes were beginning to gleam.

"Our spies have disappeared," he went on, speaking low, "as if they were swallowed up. The probability is they're dead. But it is necessary at any cost to slip a man into that country to report what is going on. And so, if you are willing, I will detail you for that service, which of course is extremely hazardous. Now what do you say . . . will you go?"

"At once," answered Tarrant eagerly.

"Very well." The colonel nodded, and smiled. "I may tell you then, Lieutenant Tarrant, that of all my men you are the one I would choose for this mission. You are Western bred, without the Eastern accent that makes our West Pointers so conspicuous, and in your scouts against the Indians you have shown a courage and dash that will serve you well in this case. From what I gather, the men who have gone before you have fallen into the hands of the Danites . . . it is probable that they have all been killed . . . and in order to protect you from a similar fate I have decided upon a desperate remedy. As a measure of self-protection . . . nothing else, you understand . . . it will be necessary to dismiss you from the Army."

"Dismiss me?" repeated Tarrant, rising suddenly to his feet, and then he bowed his head. "Very well," he said. "After what I have done, I have no right to object."

"No, no," insisted the colonel, holding up a restraining hand, "you don't understand, Lieutenant. This affair with Tamar Young is forgotten, I assure you . . . only don't let it happen again. But for your own protection, if you are taken prisoner by the Danites, it is best that your record should be clear. You were arrested tonight for disobeying orders and fraternizing with the Mormon populace and the affair will be widely known. If you are court-martialed and dismissed, you will appear among the Mormons in the light of a martyr and a friend. You will be an embittered officer, dismissed for an affair with Tamar Young, and that fact alone may save your life. Therefore it is necessary, if you are to undertake this mission, that you should be dismissed from the Army as a traitor."

"I will agree," answered Tarrant, "on one condition . . . that my father be informed of the truth."

"Your father must suffer, too," declared the colonel firmly. "The eyes of the Danites are everywhere. But if you do not return, I will tell him."

"Very well, sir," responded Tarrant with a formal salute, and the colonel held out his hand.

"God bless you, my boy," he said. "And if you succeed on this mission, your services will not go unrewarded. You are to gather evidence regarding this massacre and locate eyewitnesses if possible, but most of all I want a report on the country and whether the population is loyal. If you fail to return or report in three weeks, the dragoons will be ordered south, and if, by the fortunes of war, you should lose your life, rest assured the Mormons will pay. I am placing a great trust in your hands, Lieutenant Tarrant, for this matter may end in a war, but I have never known a man of greater courage or discretion . . . except where the ladies are concerned. We all have our failings and that is yours . . . a weakness for maidens in distress. I may as well warn you at the start."

15

"I will never trust a woman again," answered Tarrant. "But I cannot believe this of Tamar."

"Now, now," assured the colonel, "make no doubt of it . . . you were duped. Read those papers, and remember her words. The third wife of Hyrum Paine . . . there's your disloyalty again . . . practicing polygamy in defiance of our laws. You have suffered, I know, but let this be a lesson and leave these Mormon women alone. Because the man never lived that could outgeneral a designing woman. Take the word of an old campaigner and don't try."

"Very well, sir," replied Tarrant, and went out.

CHAPTER TWO

A cold night wind was sweeping through the sagebrush and dusk was gathering deep on the flats when Zachary Tarrant, spurring out of a side cañon, looked down on Mountain Meadows. Lying between low hills, with higher mountains behind, a broad band of green stretched on to the north until it was lost in the desert twilight, and here, at this narrow neck, where two valleys came together and pinched off into a pass leading south, a whole wagon train of emigrants had been massacred. Their bones had strewn the plain for more than a year, gnawed and scattered by coyotes and wolves, before Major Carlton of the United States Army had buried them in a single grave. Over this a cairn of rocks had been erected to the memory of the emigrants, with a cross on which was written these words:

VENGEANCE IS MINE, SAITH THE LORD.
I WILL REPAY.

Yet nineteen years had passed and no one had suffered punishment. The spoils of the victims had been gathered into the tithing house and auctioned out among the people, the wagons and horses had been divided among the leaders, and the little children parceled out as bond servants, but the bodies of one hundred and twenty men and women lay buried on that plain and vengeance had not been claimed. The children who had been spared on account of their tender years had grown up to manhood and womanhood, but the men who had slaughtered

17

Dane Coolidge

their fathers and mothers still lived and prospered in the church. Some were bishops and high priests, and some still rode the hills as Avenging Angels, carrying death to the apostate and the Gentile.

Tarrant reined in and looked about for the monument and grave, but no sign of the tragedy remained. The cairn of rocks had been leveled, the inscription effaced, and the cross thrown down in the dust. The vengeance of the Lord was mocked.

In the deepening twilight he rode down onto the meadow and crossed to the edge of a deep creek. There, according to the story, the Indians had crept up and fired upon the emigrants at dawn. Seven men had been killed and sixteen wounded at the first treacherous volley from its banks, but the brave pioneers had quickly parked their wagons and made a determined stand. Many Indians had been slain, including two chiefs, and, as the cowardly Paiutes fled, the Mormons, disguised as Indians, had taken up the battle.

For three days, though cut off from water, the emigrants had held their own, until at last by a flag of truce the Mormon militia had lured them out and persuaded them to give up their arms. Then at a signal from their leader the defenseless men and women had been shot down, until only the little children were left. Even the wounded were killed in the wagons, and the returning Indians had stripped the bodies of the dead.

Now, after twenty years, there was not even a cross to show where the emigrants had been slain. Yet Tarrant knew from his maps and the directions he had received that this was the place he sought, and, circling around, he finally found some rough-edged stones, strewn about on a patch of barren ground. He dismounted and turned them over, examining each in turn, until at last on a rock he found the signs of mortar and a woman's name—*Faith S.* Here, then, was the last fragment of Major Carlton's monument, and here must be the scene of the

18

massacre. On this blasted square of earth, where the meadow grass was dead and leprous weeds had taken the soil, the doomed emigrants had made their stand, while from the hilltops on both sides the Mormons, disguised as Indians, had fired down into their camp. Here their rifle pits had been dug and in them, at the end, their dismembered bones had been buried. Now nothing was left but a dead place in the grass and a woman's name on a stone. Tarrant turned away with a curse on his lips.

For a week, riding south through a desert country, he had been dogged by the thieving Paiutes, but now, as his horse snuffed the wind and flinched, he felt a chill of deeper apprehension. More than once that day, as he looked back on his trail, he had seen a dim point of dust—a film of yellower light against the blue of distant mountains that warned him his footsteps were followed. In the gathering dusk, as he had looked off up the meadow, he had noted a bunch of cattle on the flat, and not far to the south were the first Mormon settlements from whence the Avenging Angels had come. Even now the vengeful Danites might be hot on his trail, to kill him for a government spy.

He watered his horse at the spring not far down the dry wash where, during the long siege, the emigrants had run the gantlet to bring back water for their women. There, according to the tale, two little girls had been sent, dressed in white and with buckets in their hands, but the ruthless destroyers had shot them down by the water within sight of their anguished parents. Men and women had perished, too, in the hail of Mormon bullets that had struck up the dust as they ran, and, when they surrendered, they had been led to their doom without a sip of the water they had sought. Tarrant's horse raised his head and stared into the darkening shadows as if he sensed the lingering specters of the dead, and then gave out a sudden snort.

A coyote up on the ridge let out a wild, shrill yell, gibbering and yelping as it pawed at the ground. Once more the sturdy buckskin trembled in his tracks and snorted with fear. A strange tremor came over Tarrant as he dismounted by a bush and hurriedly unsaddled his mount, and, as he twisted on the rawhide hobbles and tied his horse to the bush, he crouched down close to the ground. There was something abroad, more than the coyotes and wolves that howled their farewell to the sun, something that Buck could smell and that he himself could sense, and he dropped down behind his pack.

Trees and bushes seemed to move and take the form of men, the wild gibbering of the coyotes froze his blood, but at last, as night closed down, his horse began to feed and Tarrant made camp for the night. In a shallow depression he dug out a hole deep enough to protect him from stray shots, and, lying behind his saddle, he scanned the outlines of the hills where the wind was wrestling through the cedars. But above its deep roar, as he lay listening intently, he could hear the sound of voices, like an overtone. They came and went, disappearing as he listened for them and singing in his ears when he relaxed, and then of a sudden he seemed to hear two women talking, high up on the brow of the hill. One spoke and the other answered, as clearly as in life, but his horse champed on, undisturbed. It was an illusion, and yet it seemed real.

Then the strange sensation came over him again as he remembered the murdered women who had met their death in that place. They had been separated from their husbands and compelled to march ahead, leaving their babies behind in the wagons, and, at the sound of firing, the Indians had rushed upon them, for the women had been assigned to them. With the knife and the bow and arrow, and the guns with which they had been furnished, they had killed the women and stripped the dead, while the Danites had passed on, carrying back to their settlements the orphans and the spoils of the raid. And, if rumor was true, Brigham Young himself had given the order for their death.

Tarrant stretched out on his blanket with his rifle beside him and gazed in painful reverie at the stars. The woman whose memory was never long absent from his mind was the daughter of Brigham Young, and yet—he could not believe her false. He could not believe that Tamar would betray him, or that Brigham was the author of this crime. The rage and hatred of the Mormons were more than matched by the jealous backbiting of the Gentiles—the truth must lie somewhere between. Yet— Tamar had been married, all the time. The kisses he had won at the cost of his sacred honor had belonged to Hyrum Paine. Tamar had been his bride, his third wife.

"Damn them all!" burst out Tarrant in a fury, and his horse jumped and tugged at his rope.

But as the night wore on and the wind died down, he turned on his side and slept, and the next he knew there was a crash and the thunder of hoofs and his horse went racing past. The bush to which he had been tied came bounding along behind him and Tarrant sprang up to catch him, but as he set off at a run, something warned him to beware, for his horse did not slacken his pace. Fighting madly against the hobbles that bound his front legs, he went dashing away through the night—yet Buck was not a horse to go out of his head at the approach of a coyote or wolf. Nothing less than a waving blanket or the sting of an arrow could make him run as he had, and, knowing his horse to have been stampeded, Tarrant dropped to the ground and wormed back to where he had left his gun.

Nothing stirred for an eternity of aching minutes while he crouched down, waiting to shoot, and then through the darkness he made out a man's form, rising up from the bank of the creek. Another head rose up beside it and they settled quietly down again as Tarrant thrust out his gun. But the time had gone by for stealth and with a bound he whipped out of his hole and plunged through the night for the brush. The heads he had seen wore the slouched hats of white men—he was ambushed by the Danites.

CHAPTER THREE

The dawn found Zachary Tarrant on the summit of a hill that overlooked his evening camp. As daylight came on, he could see his saddle and blankets, just as he had left them on the meadow below. But the midnight assassins who had crept up to kill him were as carefully hidden as he.

As he watched for some movement, all the stories he had heard of Avenging Angels went racing through his mind. They were men who knew no fear, who knew nothing but to obey orders, men to whom murder was a religious duty. Tales of Gentiles and wandering prospectors, shot in the back at some camp ground and despoiled of their animals and goods, tales of apostates, fleeing desperately to escape their ruthless power, but run down and left with cut throats, a hundred gruesome stories came back to him as he waited, but no one appeared below. He had gained the high ground, and, as long as he remained there, the Danites would not dare to approach.

As the sun rose higher and beat down upon the rocks behind which he had made his stand, Tarrant began to suffer the pangs of hunger and thirst and to gaze longingly down at the spring. The half-wild cattle from the meadows above were stringing down to the water, yet he could see they were ill at ease— perhaps they scented his enemies. Perhaps—and what more natural—the Danites were lying in ambush for him, waiting to shoot him down when he returned for a drink or for the food he had left in his pack. Tarrant turned away and fixed his eyes on a distant ranch house, half hidden in a clump of tall cotton-woods. There were children playing about it, and, as he watched their childish games, he wondered what his welcome would be.

No one would be so hard-hearted as to deny him a drink, and, since sooner or later he must cast himself on their mercy, he decided to put his luck to the test. Certainly nothing was to be gained by remaining in hiding, so with his rifle ready to shoot he crept down the hill and walked across the meadow toward the house. It consisted of a series of one-room log cabins, flanked with lean-tos and tumble-down sheds. Every-where were the signs of neglect and decay—sagging doors, broken-down fences, littered yards. Only the front gate was spick-and-span in a coat of green paint, the Mormon sign that their tithings were paid.

The nearer he approached, the more children he could count, standing staring in a huddle on the stoops. Then, as if at a signal, they crowded inside and he heard the doors shut with a bang. But Tarrant was afoot, out of water and out of food, and he kept on till he came to the green gate.

"Hello, the house!" he called as two gaunt hounds that had been baying him circled about and snuffed at his tracks.

"What do you want?" demanded a woman's voice.

Taking courage, he walked up to the stoop. "I'm hungry," he said. "Have you got anything to eat?"

"No!" the woman answered stridently.

"Well, I'll get a drink of water," he announced, and followed down a path to the spring.

Beneath a spreading willow a spring house had been built, on the broad shelves of which stood great pans of milk. As he dipped up the clear water, he gazed at them longingly, but the woman was watching from the doorway. Behind her in a strug-gling mass were the towheads of her numerous progeny, all ey-ing him with frank distrust.

"Who are you?" she asked as he turned back toward the house.

Tarrant answered with a placating smile: "My name is Zack, and I'm clear out of grub. Haven't you got a little something to eat?"

"I've got some milk," she responded grudgingly

Tarrant smiled again. "I'll give you a dollar for a pan of it," he offered.

She shook her head at the money. "No, you're welcome to it," she stated, "as soon as I skim the cream off. Enos, run down and dip him some milk."

She was a tall, slatternly woman with a gaunt, peaked countenance, but, as Tarrant stood waiting, another woman appeared, followed closely by a brood of smaller children.

"Good morning," greeted Tarrant, removing his hat with a gallant gesture, and the second wife responded with a smile. She was still young and comely, although her figure was distorted by the coarse undergarment she wore. It was the muslin endowment garment, cut to cover the whole body and protect it from the devil and all harm, and designed for a shroud after death—but worn by high and low. There was no surer sign of a Mormon than this, although the elite in Salt Lake had compromised with the devil and replaced it by fine linen, cut low. "I was just wondering," went on Tarrant as she stood watching him expectantly, "if I couldn't buy a loaf of bread. Bread and milk make a meal, you know, almost anywhere in Utah. . . ."

"We haven't got any!" spoke up the first wife sharply.

"Well, what do you feed all these children on?" he asked. "I've got plenty of money . . . I'll pay."

"Ve feed dem on milk," explained the second wife with a Danish accent. "But ve haf no vood, to bake bread."

"My husband is away on a mission," added the first wife.

Tarrant nodded his head. All over Utah he had come upon

such families, left to shift for themselves while their husbands without pay were sent to the ends of the world. But no sacrifice was too great for these zealots of the faith and their families were cared for by the church.

"He vill soon be back," volunteered the second wife good-naturedly. "I vill gif you some clabber, if you like."

"Where's your axe?" demanded Tarrant. "I'll cut you some wood, and then you can bake me some bread."

"Ah, the handle is broke," she lisped, and laughed heartily as Tarrant threw up his hands.

"Well, give me some milk, then," he said. "When do you expect your husband home?"

"Oh, right avay," she responded. "He is over with the Injuns. Do you know him, then?"

"No," answered Tarrant, "but I'd sure like to see him. I lost my horse last night."

"Vat, down below here?" she asked mysteriously, and the older wife stepped around the house. A few moments later there was a clatter of hoofs and Tarrant saw a boy galloping off. They knew who he was now, a man fleeing from the Danites, but Tarrant was too hungry to care.

"Yes," he replied, "I was camped down at the spring . . . that's a nice little baby you've got."

"I haf six," boasted the mother with a smile, and the first wife retired with a sniff. She had nearer ten, and all of them raised on skimmed milk. They gathered about him, ready to run at the first move but gazing with wondering eyes. The comely second wife, after filling his cup again, sat down on the stoop and talked. On a high hill to the west Tarrant could see a pillar of smoke, made to summon the husband back home, and along toward noon he came riding in, at which time the second wife slipped away. But as she went, she looked back and smiled, and Tarrant remembered the colonel's advice. He had warned him to leave all Mormon women alone.

The husband was a man poorly dressed and cadaverous, riding stooped over on an old piebald horse. As he reined in at the gate, he fixed Tarrant with a gaze that seemed to search his soul.

"I'm Jake Lingo," he said as he advanced up the path. "And who might you be?" he ended.

"My name is Zachary Grey," responded Tarrant mendaciously, "and I was camped down by that spring last night. But something frightened my horse and he ran away, hobbles and all. I'll give you five dollars if you'll find him."

"Well . . . ," observed Jake Lingo, rubbing his bristly jaw thoughtfully and gazing away at the hills.

Tarrant regarded him curiously. In a country where most men rode fully armed, he had come in without even a pistol and in his deep-set gray eyes there was a look of brooding calm, as if his thoughts were far away. "Of course," went on Tarrant, "if you don't think that's enough, I'd be willing to pay you more. And I wish you'd send your boy down the meadow for my saddle . . . I left it on the flat above the spring."

"Well . . . ," repeated Lingo mildly, and gazed once more at the hills.

"I hear," pursued Tarrant, "you're a missionary to these Paiutes. Perhaps some of them have got my horse. He couldn't go far, with those hobbles, and he was dragging a rope to boot."

"You'd better see the bishop," suggested Jake.

"The bishop?" repeated Tarrant. "What has he got to do with it?"

"I'll go along with you," added Lingo, "soon as I get me a drink of milk."

"But why not go out and get my horse first?" protested Tarrant. "I can't go to town on foot."

"I'll lend you my horse," responded Lingo with finality, and went down to get his milk.

He came back from the spring house, wiping the cream from his lips, and entered the cabin that sheltered his first wife. After a few words with her he paid a visit to his second wife, who followed along behind him as he left. What she had said Tarrant could only guess, but her smile was still kindly and he bowed as he turned away.

"You can ride my boy's horse," directed Lingo, climbing up on the piebald mustang.

Sitting on the sack that served for a saddle, Tarrant rode along beside him down the meadow. But when they came to his camp, saddle and blankets were gone and there were fresh moccasin tracks in the dirt.

"What the devil!" exclaimed Tarrant, dropping down off his horse and starting up the trail at a trot, but Lingo called him back.

"Do not follow them, my friend," he advised. "It is better to see the bishop."

"What has the bishop got to do with my saddle?" demanded Tarrant. "This is carrying petty thievery too far."

"I will lend you my saddle," returned Lingo, speaking slowly, "but if you go, you will surely be killed."

"How do you know that?" asked Tarrant, coming reluctantly back to him.

Lingo fixed him with his brooding gray eyes. "It was revealed to me by the Lord," he said. "I have been baptized for the remission of sins and have received the gift of the Holy Ghost by the laying on of hands in the endowment house. I have been given the gift of tongues, to carry the gospel to the Lamanites, and the power of interpretation of dreams. The spirit came over me as you started on that trail and in a vision I saw you lying dead, and stripped of all your clothes. But if you go with me, all will be well."

"Well, if it's as bad as all that," observed Tarrant with a shrug, "I'll let the saddle go."

He rode along in silence behind the prophet.

CHAPTER FOUR

There was something about the manner of Jacob Lingo that swayed Tarrant against his will, the truth being that his nerves had been more than a little shaken by the prophet's vision of his death. But as they rode on down a broad valley through fields of waving grain, he began once more to have his doubts. In his slow, dumb way the missionary had informed him that they were going to see the bishop, but who the bishop was and why it was necessary to see him were things he had not explained. He rode on down the trail, his head sunk on his breast and his eyes glazed as if in deep thought, but at last, as they neared the brow of the ridge, he looked up with a friendly smile.

"I have had a dream," he announced, "and the Spirit has instructed me to give you all the aid I can. It has been revealed to me that your heart is good, although you are an enemy of my people, and the Spirit has informed me that you will do us a great service, though at the time it will not so appear. But I saw in a vision you and me standing together on the banks of a swift-flowing stream, and the wagons of my people were passing up over a ledge of rocks on their way to the Promised Land. Of the rest I cannot tell, but you were there to help us and the people nodded and smiled as they passed. So from now on Jake Lingo is your friend."

He stretched out a bony hand and Tarrant took it, though he wondered, for he had no great faith in these dreams. And if Lingo was his friend, it would seem more to the point to help him recover his horse. But instead the lank missionary was taking him to Moroni where three men before him had disappeared. Yet he was afoot and alone in a friendless country where every man's hand was against him, so for better or worse he followed along over a ridge, flanked with black extinct volcanoes on both sides. Underfoot there was sharp-edged lava and barren beds of cinders, but, as they topped the divide and looked out over the valley, Tarrant was astonished by the beauty of the scene.

"The blessing of the Lord is on my people," observed Lingo, halting his horse and sitting at gaze. "This is all the work of His hand."

"Is that so," murmured Tarrant politely, and the prophet nodded aggressively.

"God has given us this land of Deseret," he pronounced, "for our Zion, our Promised Land. Do you think we fear the Gentiles, or the whole United States government? No! The God of battles is with us. We are few and they are many but we will never be conquered, as long as we keep the faith. 'My hand is with you always,' saith the Lord."

He ran on with such a homily of disjointed quotations that Tarrant began to think he was cracked, and then, as he made an end, his head fell forward again and he was wrapped in another dream. They passed down a narrow cañon, where a roaring stream of water was led to the ditches below. Checkered fields spread out before them as they caught glimpses of the wide lowlands and smelled the fragrance of newly mown hay. Then suddenly they turned the corner of a high, buttressed hill and Moroni, the Mormon stronghold, lay before them. There was a sweep of green fields, long streets edged with trees, and, in the midst of it, a towering temple, white as snow. It loomed up among the trees and the lesser houses of the town like a dream temple, not made by hands. Yet as Tarrant looked closer, he saw men swarming like ants and teams driving up to the doors.

"What is that?" he demanded, bringing his horse to a halt, and Lingo straightened up and smiled.

"That is the temple of the Saints," he said. "When this valley was a wilderness and no settlers could enter into it on account of the roughness of the way, Heber C. Kimball, the Apostle, made a wonderful prophecy, every word of which has come to pass. He prophesied that a road would be built over the Black Ridge and a temple would be built in this valley, where the Lamanites from east of the Colorado River would come to get their endowments. That white building that you see is the great Moroni Temple . . . and the Lamanites will soon come, as Apostle Kimball prophesied. I am a missionary to the Indians . . . the Lamanites of the Book of Mormon who wiped out the Nephites on this continent . . . and God has given me the promise that before this temple is finished their hearts will be opened to the gospel."

"Oh, I see"—Tarrant nodded—"these Lamanites you speak of are the Indians."

"Why, yes," answered Lingo impatiently. "The Indians are Lamanites, of course. Haven't you read the Book of Mormon, my friend?"

"Only slightly," confessed Tarrant, "but tell me about this temple. How did they come to erect such a beautiful big building away down here in the desert?"

"This is no desert," defended Lingo, "this is the land we call Dixie, the home of the cotton and corn. All that white that you see is fields of cotton, and we make it into cloth ourselves. We have fig trees and pomegranates and all manner of fruits and flowers, for the Lord has given His blessing to this land.

"Five years ago," he went on, "we had a great drought in these parts. The dams in the Virgin River and also the Santa Clara were washed out by terrible floods and the people had nothing to eat. But President Young always sought some means of giving support to his people and he hit upon the plan of building this temple, where we could come and receive our endowments while the great temple at Salt Lake was being finished. He called upon the people of Dixie, and all the other counties in the south, to bring in their tithing to Moroni . . . their flour and hay, their wheat and oats, their cheese and beef and fruit . . . to furnish food for the workers on the temple. He also called upon each town or ward for so many men and teams who were to bring their own supplies and work free of charge, only getting credit for their labor on the temple. They were allowed so much credit per day, and anyone who needed anything from the Lord's storehouse could get it and have it charged against his work. So the Saints built their own temple and the people were fed and everybody was prosperous and happy."

He paused, well satisfied with his long explanation, and Tarrant gazed at the temple again. It rose up in the midst of almost tropical verdure, long rows of flaunting poplars, vineyards and orchards and fields of hay, like a building from some other world. By its side, but dwarfed to nothingness, there rose the spire of the Mormon tabernacle, a typical New England meeting house, but the temple displayed the architecture of another age and land—broad parapets, heavy buttresses, and crenellated walls with a tower rising point above point, and all gleaming white in the sun.

"It is beautiful," he said again.

"So even you like it?" observed Lingo, showing his long teeth in a slow superior smile. "You thought we were ignorant, now, didn't you? You didn't believe we could build such a church. The plans of that temple were drawn by Brigham Young, the man who built the tabernacle at Salt Lake."

"Oh, Brigham Young, eh?" repeated Tarrant. "So he's an architect, too."

"He is everything," declared Jacob Lingo warmly. "But the plans were made by the Lord. He gave them to Brigham, his revelator to the people, and Brigham sent them down to us. The foundations of that church are twelve feet under ground and made of solid black malpaís, the walls are made of sandstone, and the timbers for the roof were hauled down by ox teams from those peaks."

He pointed to some mountains, standing out blue against the horizon, and Tarrant shook his head and sighed. "It is a great work," he said, but his real thought he kept to himself. *How could such a religion, producing temples that entranced the eye and gleamed like jewels in the sun, produce also the brutal men to whom the Mountain Meadows Massacre seemed a work well pleasing to God? How could Brigham Young, the architect, who had planned this great church, plan also the death of innocent men and women . . . and little children, unable to do harm? Yet he was given the credit for both.*

"It is a great work," stated Lingo with decision, "and Bishop Drake is driving it, day and night. He is the man I am going to see, for we must consult him about everything."

"What? Lot Drake?" cried Tarrant, astounded, and Lingo suddenly glared into his eyes.

"Yes, Lot Drake," he challenged. "What then?"

"Why . . . why he was the man . . . ," began Tarrant weakly, and then he remembered his part. Lot Drake was the man who had led the company of Danites in the ill-omened Mountain Meadows Massacre—he was the major of militia who had sent forward the flag of truce—he was the man who had ordered the soldiers to fire.

"Say, who are you?" demanded Lingo in low, measured tones. "You kind of act like a government spy."

For a moment Tarrant stared back into his straining eyes, and then he shook his head. "No," he said, "I'm a prospector. But a man would be ignorant, never to have heard of Lot Drake, the Danite."

"Yes, you've heard of him," sneered Lingo, "but have you ever heard the truth? Have you heard of the big mills he's built in this country, to weave our cotton and grind up our flour, have you heard of the ditches and towns he's laid out, and of the good that he's done for our people? No, all you've heard is the black lies of these Gentiles and apostates, but I tell you Lot Drake is a great man. Look at that temple . . . he built it himself. When nobody else could push the work along, he took over the job himself, and I want to tell you he makes them boys jump. He may be rough, but he gets the work done. And if you're a government spy . . . he'll know."

"All right, let's go and see him," answered Zachary Tarrant blithely, and Jacob Lingo scratched his head.

"You don't act like no spy," he grumbled. "But spy or no spy," he went on with a stubborn smile, "the Spirit has commanded me to help. What you do may seem against us, but in the end it will prove a blessing. All things work together for good for those who fear the Lord. Have you ever looked into our faith?"

"No, I never have," confessed Tarrant, and Lingo's eyes lit up with proselytizing zeal.

"When the Prophet Joseph Smith went out into the woods and asked the Lord which sect he should join, the Lord appeared to him in a vision and said he should join none of them, for every one was false. All the churches in the world were wrong and conceived in abomination, and the professors thereof were corrupt. They taught for doctrines the commandments of men and they had fallen away from the true faith. But the angel Moroni, after whom this town is named, appeared to Joseph in a vision and showed him where a book written on plates of gold was hidden. That book was the Book of Mormon, upon which our faith is built. It was written on gold in the reformed Egyptian language and with it were deposited the two peep stones, Urim and Thummim, through which the plates could be read. Joseph Smith read them off behind a curtain in his room and Oliver Cowdery wrote them down. Would you like to have a copy of that book?"

"Yes, I would," answered Tarrant.

As they passed down into the town, Lingo expounded his faith like a zealot. Along both sides of the road, in the shade of the giant poplars, streams of water flowed in gurgling ditches that led out into the fields. Rows of mulberries and honey locusts overshadowed square brick houses, each set back in its garden of fruit trees, and from the vineyards the thrifty Mormons were hauling loads of purple grapes to be pressed into Dixie wine.

It was a land of prosperity, of corn and wine and the plenitude of the earth, but, as Tarrant rode by with his rifle across his lap, he felt certain that for him it was a trap. Not for nothing had Jacob Lingo mounted him on this horse and taken him into town. Despite the talk and cant, Tarrant knew he was under arrest—and Bishop Drake would decide his fate. He was to appear and plead his case before the man he had come to convict—Lot Drake, the chief of the Danites.

They turned down a broad street, lined with pomegranates and fig trees. Beside the Zion Store with its all-seeing eye and the church motto—*Holiness to the Lord*—there was another and larger storehouse with the words *Bishop's House* above it—the place where the tithings were paid. Every man who lacked the money or a ready market for his crops could pay his taxes in kind, delivering fruit, hay, or eggs to the all-seeing, all-powerful bishop, who would later convert them into cash. But the load of hay for the Lord's storehouse must be clean and free from weeds, the butter and eggs of the best, else the bishop and his councilors would call the brother before them and bring him to strict account.

Beyond the stores stood the Tabernacle, with its walls of red sandstone and its windows and cornices done in white, and above the neat clock tower there rose a slender spire with a gilded ball and wind vane at the top. Here in this oasis of the desert, sheltering an alien faith, it was still the smug meeting house of Puritan New England, and the clock chimed the hour as they passed.

Beyond it, on the broad lot that the church had reserved, was a building of a different sort, the huge Mormon temple that dominated the whole valley and struck the true note of their faith. When its roof was finished and the massive doors hung, no Gentile foot would ever cross its threshold, no unbeliever would witness its mysteries. Strange rites would be practiced, Elohim and Michael the Archangel would converse with Jehovah behind a veil, and immigrants from foreign lands would be baptized to save them from hell. It was beautiful—a thing of power.

Down the long, dusty road that led in from the south, lines of wagons drawn by oxen were toiling in from the far mountains, bringing timbers for the vaulted roof. Men were hurrying to and fro, chipping stones, squaring planks, pouring in and out the open doors like ants. They dismounted and tied the horses. As the two passed through the doors of the temple in search of the bishop, Tarrant found himself a man apart. In his buckskin shirt and leggings, his broad hat and well-made boots, he stood out among them like a man of a different race, for they were clad in homespun and hickory shirts. Their cheap wool hats had slouched in the rain and wind and their boots were big and coarse, and in their eyes, or so it seemed, there was a strange, foreign look, the stolid gaze of the peasant. They were freed from the United States and the domination of the Gentiles; Lot

Drake was their ruler instead.

Still inquiring for the bishop, Lingo passed on from group to group, and then, as Tarrant turned a corner, he was conscious of a pair of eyes that seemed to bore him through and through. A huge man stood there, watching him, his mouth drawn to a grim line. Without being told, he knew it was Lot Drake, the man who was both bishop and judge. But if that was the case, he was tried and sentenced already, for there was no mercy or kindness in that face.

"Who are you?" demanded Drake, suddenly taking a step forward and looking Tarrant boldly in the eye, and Jake Lingo stammered and stopped short.

"My name is Grey," answered Tarrant quietly. "I'm a prospector and. . . ."

"You're a liar," broke in Drake, "you're a government spy. I knowed you the minute I saw you. More than that," he went on, wagging a threatening finger that made Tarrant blink and step back, "you're an officer in the United States Army."

"No, sir," denied Tarrant, "you're mistaken."

"There's no use trying to lie out of it. I can tell by the way you walk. There's a hereafter for fellows like you."

"Please correct me if I am wrong," replied Tarrant defiantly, "but you've been a soldier yourself. Since when has that been a crime?"

"Since when?" bellowed Drake, smashing his fist into his palm and waking the echoes with his roar. "Since the soldiers killed Joseph Smith in Carthage jail. Since Albert Sidney Johnston marched his army into Utah and got turned back by five hundred men. I was one of them myself, and I burned off the prairie until their cattle and horses died for feed. And I don't care who knows it. I burned their wagon trains, too, and left them to starve through the winter."

"That is neither here nor there," answered Tarrant shortly. "I was brought here by this man to complain to the bishop about my horse and saddle that were stolen."

"Your horse," mocked Drake. "You ain't got no horse . . . you're lucky to be alive. And let me tell you right now you're talking to the bishop and also to the probate judge. So you'd better sing low or I'll throw you into jail. That's all now . . . you git out of the country."

"But what about my horse?" demanded Tarrant. "I hear you're in charge of these Paiute Indians. . . ."

"Haven't got a thing to do with them. Jake, take this man away. What d'ye mean, bringing a Gentile in here?"

"Why, he . . . I. . . ."

"Take him away," raged Drake, "and tell him to keep away. I don't want him around here. Now git!"

He waved them out of the temple, and, after looking at him a moment, Tarrant turned and followed after Lingo. "I'll stay here as long as I want to," he said.

Jake frowned and shook his head. "Don't talk so loud," he whispered.

CHAPTER FIVE

With the parting words of Bishop Drake still ringing in his ears, Zachary Tarrant passed out of the shadowy temple like a man half dazed by a blow. He had heard strange tales of the power of the Danites, and of the wonderful system by which they kept track of strangers and nosed out the enemies of the church, but to be recognized on sight and denounced as a spy both astounded him and touched his pride. His life had been spent in the wildest parts of the West, for his father had been a soldier before him. He had hunted and trapped, even traveled with prospectors, but his pretense had been unmasked at the start. Without waiting for a word or an accent to betray him, Lot Drake had known him at a glance.

Yet perhaps, after all, it was not so wonderful. Tarrant had recognized in Drake the bearing of a soldier, for it is something almost impossible to conceal, and Drake had done no more than perceive by his stride that for years he had marched in step. But the bishop had gone further—if indeed he had guessed at all, for Tarrant's coming might have been made known to him in advance—he had recognized the bearing of an officer. It might even be that he knew Zachary's name and station and the errand that brought him to Moroni, although Tarrant had so stoutly denied it. He might, even then, be planning his death.

Tarrant straightened up proudly as he strode past the gaping workmen, for now he had nothing to conceal. It was easy to perceive by what magic touchstone Drake had picked out the former spies. Having been a soldier himself in the Mormon Battalion—which had been forced into service during the Mexican War—he had learned the unconscious mannerisms by which a soldier is marked for life and applied his knowledge with vengeful cunning. He had watched the walk and gesture, the set of the shoulders and head, of every man who entered his ward, and his loud accusations had been no more than rough bluster to frighten Zachary into a confession. But to admit he was a spy was to sentence himself to death and Tarrant had held his tongue.

It was true he was a soldier, it was true he had been an officer, but Drake did not know that he had been court-martialed the week before and dismissed from the Army as a traitor. If Tarrant could evade the murderous hands of the Avenging Angels until his true identity became known, he might have a chance to escape, and the safest place to stay was right in town. If he fled in the night, the Avenging Angels would follow after him, and all accounts agreed that, once they took a man's trail, they never stopped till they left him in his blood. They were ruthless, and killing was their business. Like the fox who had stood at the mouth of the lion's cave and noticed the tracks all pointing one way, Zachary now perceived that he had come into a country that was easier to enter than to leave. He had slipped into the Mormons' stronghold, just as the other three soldiers had done, but he was a marked man now. If he attempted to leave, the Avenging Angels would put him to death.

"Let's go over to the hotel," suggested Tarrant to Lingo, pointing to a big, rambling house across the street, but the prophet shook his bowed head. There was sweat on his forehead, and, as he struck it from his eyes, Tarrant could see the tremor in his hand.

"I must git home," he mumbled. "It's coming on to storm

and my family hain't got any wood. But I'm sorry I brought this on you."

"Oh, that's all right," said Zachary. "No harm done, I'm sure. How much do I owe you, for the horse?"

"The horse?" repeated Jake, looking up at him in a daze. "Oh, that's all right, not a cent. But, say, I'm kinder weak, seeing this come out the way it has. Could you buy me ten cents' worth of snuff?"

"Why, certainly"—Tarrant smiled—"why didn't you mention it before? I didn't know you had such a vice."

"Well, I have," confessed Lingo, "and many a night I've knelt and prayed for the Lord to take it away, but times like this, when I'm kinder weak and faint, I've jest got to have my snuff. The Mormon people are commanded to give up whiskey, and tea and coffee, and tobacco in all its forms, or we won't come to the fullness of our kingdom. We won't be found worthy, when the thousand years come, to dwell in the celestial world, and someone else will be exalted in our stead, unless we pay for it with fasting and prayer."

"You've got a hard religion," said Zachary soberly, and bought him the snuff at the store. "Now how about some grub, for the folks?"

"We got plenty," declared Lingo, helping himself to a pinch of snuff. "But I got to git home and chop some wood. It's the Lord's work first, and always has been, with me, but my wives they're patient . . . they don't mind."

"No, I suppose not," observed Tarrant, and, turning to the storekeeper, he called for a hard-wood axe helve. "There's a present," he said, "I'd like to send back to your wives. Their axe handle was broke when I was there."

"Well, sure enough." Lingo smiled. "I remember now, it was. Thank you kindly . . . I've got to be goin'."

He shambled out the door and Zachary followed after him

until he came to his gaunt, piebald horse.

"Better stop and have supper," he suggested.

Lingo shook his head as he conceded: "Well, I will go over and git a drink of milk, and make you acquainted with the folks. Brother Mayberry keeps the hotel."

He led the way across the street and peered into the vacant parlor, after which he struck a bell on the rickety center table and took another pinch of snuff.

"Nobody here," he muttered, starting down the long hall that was full of the odor of cooking, and, passing on through the dining room, he came at last to the kitchen where he pushed open the door and stopped short. Tarrant looked over his shoulder and saw a girl by the stove, carefully lifting out a pan of freshly baked bread.

She was the last girl in the world he would expect to find in such a place—not a Mormon type at all, for they for the most part were large and fair and built like a peasant woman, while she was slender and dark. Although she was dressed in Quaker gray, she wore it with such a grace that the homespun seemed in some way transformed. She had what the French have—style. Her black hair was gathered in a chic knot down over a neck that was straight and poised like a swan's, and for all her hard work her hands were as slim and white as if she were the daughter of an aristocrat. Tarrant wondered—perhaps she was.

She set down the pan of bread with its fragrant loaves and turned a flushed face to the door. As her eyes met Tarrant's, the flush grew deeper, while her glance fell modestly to the floor. But in that one swift moment he had surprised a look of fear in the depths of her large, dark eyes—a look of fear, and wonder, and appeal—and then they were steady and calm. He took off his hat and bowed gallantly, but Lingo shoved him roughly aside.

"Howdy, Deseret." He grinned. "Where's Brother Mayberry

today? I've brought a guest for your hotel."

"He's out getting in the hay," she responded quietly, and stole another glance at the guest.

"Where's Mary, and Sister Caroline? Are they out haying, too? Well, well, it does look like rain."

"Yes, they all went," she said, "except me."

"I'd like to get a room for a few days," spoke up Zachary, and Lingo turned in dismay.

"You going to stay here?" he demanded almost angrily.

"Why not?" inquired Tarrant. "I can't leave till I get back my horse."

"Yes, but Bishop Drake. He ordered you to leave the town."

"I'm going to stay," announced Zachary firmly. "That is," he added with a smile, "if the young lady will give me a room."

"Why, certainly," she replied, a sudden flash in her black eyes.

Lingo stood aghast. "But Deseret," he protested, "do you think Brother Mayberry . . . ?"

"He left me in charge," she answered curtly, and took down a bunch of keys.

"Give me that front room . . . upstairs," suggested Tarrant politely. "It has such a wonderful view."

"It costs a dollar a night," she warned as they tramped up the stairs.

Zachary fetched out his purse. "I'll pay in advance," he said, and handed her a $5 bill.

"Oh, you've got money!" she exclaimed in surprise. "All we use is Zion Store scrip."

"And that shows me up for a Gentile. I suppose that's what you mean? But I reckon the money is good."

"Yes, it's good," she admitted as she opened the door and showed him into the big front room, "but you'd better pay Mister Mayberry. Uncle Jake doesn't seem to approve."

"No, I'll pay you. Five dollars for five days. Then, if I leave, he'll have his money. This gun is all the baggage I've got."

He set his rifle in the corner and glanced out the window and in the glass he saw Lingo jerk his head.

"All right," agreed the girl, and went pattering off down the stairs while Jake closed the door behind her.

"My friend," he began, "I want to warn you, right now, not to make eyes at our Mormon girls. That is something that ain't allowed. It'll only git you into trouble, and it ain't called for in no case, Mister Grey."

"Why, what's the matter?" Zachary laughed. "Was I making eyes? Well, she is a mighty nice girl."

"Young man," warned Lingo solemnly, "you don't know what you're doing. Didn't you hear what the bishop said? He told you to leave the country."

"I'll leave," answered Tarrant, "when I get good and ready . . . and when your bishop sends back my horse. I know who it was that stampeded my pony. There's no use talking Indians to me. From the way your bishop acts, I'd believe almost anything of him . . . about the Mountain Meadows Massacre, for instance."

"I wouldn't talk that way," advised Lingo earnestly. "The bishop is a dangerous man, when he's roused."

"You go back and tell your bishop that he'll find me right here, and I'll stay here until I get back my horse. I saw the heads of the two men that crept up to my camp. They weren't Indians. You know that yourself."

"I am a missionary to the Indians," stated Lingo gravely, "and they never stole nothing from me."

"Of course not," agreed Tarrant. "They're good folks. Treat 'em right and keep your word and they'll always be your friends. Let's go down and get something to eat."

"Now, my friend," protested Lingo, laying a hand on his arm, "I want to warn you again about this girl. There's a special reason, in fact, why you should not be seen talking to her or paying her the least attention. The inner voice has told me that your heart is good and that in time you will be the friend of the Saints, but you are too rash and headstrong, and in the case of Deseret I am warning you for your own good."

"I thank you kindly," responded Tarrant, bowing mockingly, "and I promise to remember your words. But in my famished condition I can't stop to argue the question. I'm going into that kitchen right now. Better come along, and get something to eat."

"No, no," shrilled Lingo, brushing the young man's hand away. "But remember, you are risking your life."

"I'm starving to death," answered Zachary over his shoulder

With a sigh Lingo shrugged and went out.

It was really the smell of the newly baked bread that had drawn Tarrant back to the kitchen, but, as Deseret opened to his knock, he forgot for a moment the hunger that was gnawing at his vitals. Tamar Young had been charming, but events had proven her false—and Deseret was prettier by far.

"What is it?" she asked, and, when he explained, she paused and considered a minute. "You'll have to eat here," she said. "I can't leave my baking to wait on you." Then, going to the cupboard, she set out honey and hot bread, with a pitcher of creamy milk. "Will that last you till suppertime?" she asked.

"You bet." He grinned, and, after washing at the sink, he sat down and began to eat. "This is good," he mumbled at last. "I'm hungry . . . nothing to eat all day."

"Where have you been?" she ventured to ask.

"Camped at Mountain Meadows, but somebody stole my horse. Then they brought me down to the bishop."

"Mountain Meadows," she repeated faintly. "Why . . . what were you doing there?"

He shot a keen look out from under his black eyebrows. "I'm

a prospector, passing through," he explained, but the scared look had come back into her eyes.

"What did the bishop say?" she asked.

"He said I was a soldier and a government spy," replied Tarrant with a reckless smile. "So you want to look out," he warned.

"Yes, and you want to look out," she returned on the instant. "Don't you know what he can do, if he wants?"

"What's that?" inquired Tarrant, still eating, and she peeped out the door before she spoke.

"He can have you killed," she whispered. "You'd better be careful how you talk."

"Well, it's all over now," he grumbled. "How long have you been in these parts?"

"Oh, always. Or nearly always."

"You're no Mormon girl," he said with conviction, and once more she peeped out the door. Then she drew near with a sudden, mysterious smile.

"What makes you think so?" she asked.

"Well, you don't look like one," he stated bluntly.

"Why, how do you mean? In what way?" she questioned.

He answered with a sweep of the eye. First he glanced at her hair, massed so artfully on her head, then at her face with its delicate coloring. His eyes dwelt on her slim hands and swept down to her feet, which were exceedingly small. He spoke only with his eyes but Deseret read their message and blushed a rosier red.

"I . . . I shouldn't have said that," she faltered, and became very busy with her bread.

"I beg your pardon," said Tarrant, blushing in turn. "What I meant was, you look different from the rest. And that's a pretty name . . . Deseret."

"Yes, it is pretty," she admitted. "Mother Mary found it for me. She just opened the Book of Mormon and there on the first page was a verse from the book of Esther. 'And they took with them also Deseret, which is by interpretation a honey bee.' I'm not their child. I'm just adopted, to work."

"Oh, I see," he murmured, and fell silent. She was an orphan whose parents, perhaps, had perished on the desert or fallen the victims to frontier warfare—but she was not of the Mormon breed, that he knew. He finished his meal in silence, while outside the wind swooped by and the first raindrops tapped on the roof. Blinding clouds of dust arose and the front door slammed violently, but still the thunderstorm held off.

"It's going to rain," he said, and rose from the table to go.

"Oh, wait!" she cried, rousing up from her brooding. "Wouldn't you like some of our Dixie wine?"

Her mood had suddenly changed, and, as she came back with goblet and pitcher, the old, radiant smile had returned.

"It's just at its best now," she said, and poured out a brimming glass.

"May I drink to your health?" he inquired with a bow.

She replied with a low, formal curtsy. "You are not a Mormon, either," she stated. "And you have been a soldier, I know."

"That is what the bishop says," he answered dryly.

"The Mormons don't bow that way," she explained.

"You have a very nice bow of your own," he returned. "Allow me to thank you for saving my life."

"Oh, you mean with the meal." She laughed. "You were kind of hungry, weren't you?"

"Nothing to eat since yesterday noon, except some skimmed milk at Uncle Jake's. Is he your real uncle, or what?"

"No. He . . . he just kind of adopted me at first."

Her eyes, which had been so merry, suddenly contracted to a look of pain and her breast heaved as she met his startled gaze.

"Oh, I'm sorry," he said contritely. "I didn't know."

"Never mind," she said, and pointed to the door that had opened slowly behind him. Upon the threshold, huge and menacing, stood Bishop Drake himself, his eyes squinted wickedly down.

"I'll do all the sparking here," he said to Tarrant. "You leave her alone . . . understand?" He jerked his head insultingly in the direction of Deseret and his bull neck seemed to swell with jealous rage. For the moment he looked almost like a maniac.

"Why, what do you mean?" demanded Zachary, aghast. "It was nothing but a friendly conversation."

"You Gentile whelp," yelled Drake, "git out of this kitchen! What do you mean, making up to my gal?"

"I wasn't making up to her," defended Tarrant hotly.

"Oh, you warn't, eh?" railed the bishop. "I heerd you, talking and laughing. There's a hereafter for fellows like you. I've seen pretty boys before, making eyes at Deseret, and somehow they all came to a bad end."

"Well, by the Lord," flared back Zachary, "this is a free country, isn't it? I'll make eyes at her as much as I please."

"Oh, you will, hey?" sneered Drake, backing away with venomous calm. "Well, go ahead then. Have a good time."

"Oh, no, no!" burst out Deseret, clutching Tarrant by the arm, but the bishop had closed the door.

"You'll be killed!" she wailed, burying her face in her hands, but he patted her consolingly on the shoulder.

"He was going to kill me, anyhow," he said.

CHAPTER SIX

There was an ominous drumming of raindrops as Tarrant ran back to his room, and, just as he caught sight of Drake in the distance, the first fury of the storm was let loose. It ripped up the dust in the angry scudding clouds that were seized by the wind and swept past, then with a crash of thunder the downpour commenced, only to die out as quickly as it started. A hush suddenly fell, and at the temple across the street Tarrant could see the weary workmen coming out. They had taken shelter from the storm, glad to break their killing pace and enjoy a brief respite from the labor, but, striding among them like a taskmaster among his slaves, the bishop was driving them back. Bigger than any man among them, it was not by size alone that he dominated the scene as he did. Every move that he made was pregnant with power—he was their ruler, a veritable king. But he was angry now and at the least sign of shirking his voice roared out like a bull's. And this was the man who had laid claim to Deseret and predicted for Zachary a bad end.

Of all these peasant converts who bent their backs at his bidding and jumped when he gave the word, not one dared oppose his will, but Tarrant had bandied words with him from the start—perhaps he had gone too far. He had defied him to do his worst, forgetting everything in his anger, for the 3rd Dragoons were hundreds of miles away and powerless to protect him. Tarrant was a spy in a hostile camp, a broken officer, dismissed for treason, and his devotion to Tamar Young that had brought him to disgrace would avail him nothing now. He had dared to hold speech with Deseret Mayberry, and for that his life was held forfeit.

Things that before had seemed cryptic were very clear now— Jake Lingo's veiled warnings, Deseret's fearful eyes, the silence of the empty hotel. They were all of them afraid of Lot Drake. Twenty years before he had led the band of Danites in the massacre at Mountain Meadows—could his power be any less now that he was bishop and judge to boot, than it had been on that fateful day? He was agent for the Indians, and priest and captain as well, and behind him were the Danites, the Avenging Angels. Tarrant had overlooked all this when he had answered back so hotly and now it was too late to retract. He must stand up and fight to the end.

With the slash of the pouring rain the hotel had suddenly been invaded by a rush of returning hay hands. The three wives of Mayberry, flushed and sweating from their work in the field, hurried back to their places in the kitchen; the halls seemed to swarm with children. As Tarrant came down the stairs, he spied Mayberry, the hotel proprietor, in anxious consultation with Deseret.

The Mormon women, as he had imagined, were big-boned and competent, well-fitted to be the mothers of men, and the children who stood staring were towheaded and freckled and swaddled in their coarse endowment garments. Nor was Mayberry greatly different from the rank and file of Mormon farmers, although now he kept the hotel. He was gaunt and stoop-shouldered, clothed in the cheapest of jeans, and in his deep-set eyes was that mingled arrogance and fear that Tarrant had learned to expect.

"This is Mister Grey," said Deseret as Zachary approached, and hurried back into the kitchen.

"How are you, sir," greeted Mayberry, looking his guest over purposefully. "Now about that upstairs room. . . ."

"I've taken it for five days," said Tarrant.

"But my daughter had no authority to rent the room," complained Mayberry. "I'm expecting a party of guests tonight."

"Very well," said Tarrant stiffly, "you must put them somewhere else then. I paid for the room in advance."

"But the bishop . . . ," protested Mayberry, and Zachary cut him short.

"What the bishop says is nothing to me."

"What? Nothing to you? Well, my stars," murmured the hotelkeeper, and shuffled off into the kitchen.

Tarrant returned to his room and, throwing open the dripping windows, sat back where he could watch the street. Across the road at the temple the men toiled on wearily, dead-beat with their labors in the heat; wagons drove in from the country and drew up before the tithing house or stopped at the Zion Store; the sweet-toned clock on the tabernacle chimed out the hour of 6:00 and a triangle sounded below. Then the workingmen quit and came hurrying across the street to wash up before the evening meal.

Zachary scanned their rugged faces as they tramped up the path and there was one that seemed vaguely familiar, though he could not place the man. He was stooped, with a long, slouching stride, and a face strongly pitted with smallpox, and yet in some way he reminded Tarrant of a soldier. It was not his bearing or gait, for they were far from being soldierly, but something personal to the man himself, and, as he glanced up, he saw Zachary watching him.

At the stroke of the second gong there was a rush for the long dining room, and, when Tarrant had taken a seat with his back to the wall, he noticed this same man, eying him. He was gaunt and emaciated, as if from some long sickness, and, as Zachary watched him covertly, the man glanced up again with a flash of recognition in his eyes. Then he gazed into his plate with a stony, hangdog stare and Tarrant racked his brain to remember him. Often before on distant scouts he had met men who had eyed him furtively, deserters from the Army or privates honorably discharged who would not venture to address an officer. But this man had nothing to mark him—Zachary would swear he had never been a soldier. And yet he had met him, somewhere.

But there were other and less friendly faces in the long line of Mormons who sat stolidly munching their food, for many of them had heard the bishop when he had denounced him for a spy and the others had been told by them. Every eye was upon him, and, after making a hasty meal, he rose up and returned to his room. He was a marked man among them, a man to be shunned, and, when at last he walked down to enjoy the cool of the evening, he was given a bench to himself.

The brief dash of rain had washed the dust from the tall mulberry trees and freshened up the wilted lawn, but the two-story brick hotel still radiated the heat that it had drunk in all day from the sun. No one stayed inside, except the women and the little children who were by way of being put to bed, and yet of all these workingmen there was none who would demean himself by sitting on the same bench with a Gentile—or, as they looked at him, a government spy.

It seemed curious to Tarrant that, within the borders of the United States, there should exist a country where loyalty to the government was a crime, punishable even by death. Yet such was the condition in what the Mormons called the State of Deseret, as he had been brought to know, and these men, speaking his language and many of them born under the same flag, looked down on him as an intruder and a spy. He had been branded a traitor twice but now he felt the shame that comes to a man without a country.

A Mormon dance was to take place in the Social Hall across the street, and, as the hour approached, the girls of the town strolled out, escorted by attentive swains. On the broad benches in the churchyard, where the courting of the young people took place, they sat and waited idly for the dance, and soon from the Mayberry lawn impatient shouts arose, directed at the girls inside. Of these Elder Mayberry had several of marriageable age besides the dark-haired Deseret, and, while the dishes were being washed and the tables set for breakfast, there was much rivalry among the boys in claiming a dance. Then in groups of three and four the young folks came trooping out and hurried across to the Social Hall.

It had been commanded by Joseph Smith in one of his first revelations that the people should make merry in the dance—and no injunction of the Prophet was more religiously lived up to by Latter-day Saints, young and old. Since the dance, with them, was a religious observance, every Mormon town had its Social Hall, built on the same lot with the Tabernacle and the schoolhouse. Sometimes the three were combined in one, but the dance was never omitted, especially on Friday nights. The music was striking up before Joel Mayberry left the hotel, in company with his youngest wife, and with them Zachary noted the slender form of Deseret, the last of all to go. He somehow imagined that she went with them reluctantly, although she followed meekly along with Mother Mary, and, fighting off an impulse to slip over and watch the dance, he fell into silent musings. All the noisy young men who had been sitting on the benches or sprawling on the broad front lawn had followed in the wake of the other girls—not one had lingered to offer his arm to Deseret, and yet she was the fairest by far. But Lot Drake had attended to that—all the pretty boys who had made up to her had somehow come to a bad end.

The fiddles were playing an old-time country jig and

Zachary's foot was beating time when he spied a lone man, pacing past the hotel and craning his neck to look in. Tarrant moved back into the shadows, where the lights from the Social Hall would not make him a target for bullets, and watched as the stranger paced back. It was the deserter, the man who had recognized him, and suddenly he came down the walk.

"I want to see you," he said mysteriously.

"Come over here," answered Tarrant quietly. "But remember, I've got you covered."

He tapped the barrel of his pistol on the edge of the bench and the deserter edged toward him doubtfully.

"Ain't nobody around here, is they?" he asked. "Let's move over closer to this hedge."

He led the way to a seat at the corner of the house, where a row of rank pomegranates threw black shadows, and Zachary followed quickly after him. The deserter was not the type of a Danite or assassin—he was a mild, slow man and from the very tone of his voice Tarrant knew he was safe to trust.

"You remember me, don't you, Lieutenant?" he began. "I'm Porter . . . used to be in the awkward squad. I seen you watching me this evening, and I've come to make a trade. I won't tell what I know if you won't."

"How do you mean?" inquired Tarrant guardedly. He remembered the man now—the rawest recruit in the awkward squad, a man who could never keep step—but what was he doing in Moroni?

"Well, it's this way," explained Porter, drawing closer by degrees and talking low in his ear, "when the colonel sent me down here, I was to spy on these Mormons but . . . well, to tell the truth, I've joined them."

"You've joined them," repeated Zachary. "What for?"

"Well, I'll tell you, only don't talk so loud . . . these people don't know who I am. If they did, they'd kill me like a rat."

"I believe it," responded Tarrant.

"Yes, they're bad that way," admitted the deserter, "but at the same time there's good people, too. It's these Danites, and the bishop, that are doing all the killing. The rest are scared of their lives. When I first came down here, I went to work on a ranch, and I reported to the colonel every week. They never suspicioned me . . . the colonel was right, there . . . but the other two before me was killed. That made me awful skeery about mailing any letters, and the next thing I knew I got sick. Turned out it was the smallpox, but the widow woman where I was working took care of me like I was her son. She's an awful nice woman. I'm fixing to marry her. That's why I don't want you to tip my hand."

"Oho," said Tarrant, "you won't tell who I am if I won't report you as a spy? Well, now, that's a fair trade, except for one thing . . . they know who I am already."

"Who knows?" demanded the deserter with a start.

"Bishop Drake . . . and he's told the rest. But hold on, I'm not through yet. If I understand correctly, you were sent down here as a spy. Have you ever considered what your punishment would be if the Army should occupy this country?"

"They'll never do it," asserted Porter confidently.

"Don't be too sure of that," warned Tarrant impressively. "Now I'll propose a trade to you. If you'll tell me what you know and what's going on in this country, I'll undertake to square you with the colonel. Until then you're a deserter and a traitor to boot, and they'll send you to prison for life. But you're still under cover, and you can be of great assistance, so if you'll make your report to me. . . ."

"Well, I'll do it," agreed Porter reluctantly, "but, Lieutenant, this spying ain't right. I never wanted to do it, but the colonel put it up to me and I hadn't no choice but to go. He told me I'd never make a soldier, not in a hundred years, because I never could learn to keep step, but, if I'd come down here and make a report once a week, he'd give me double pay and no drill. That's why I agreed to come, them sergeants was killing me and cursing me like a dog. But I say it ain't right to come and spy on these people . . . their government is better than ours."

"You don't say," observed Tarrant sarcastically.

"Yes, it is," declared Porter. "I don't care what you say, they treat us poor people right. I been kicked around all my life, but when I come down here, they treated me like a man. Every house where I'd stop, they'd set out their best for me, and give me a bed for the night, and then they'd begin to preach and brag up their fine ranches and ask why I didn't join the Saints. One feller I met had been a mill hand over in England, working for fifty cents a day, and here he had a ranch of a hundred and twenty acres, all cleared and planted to crops. When he came over from England, the church advanced his passage money and the neighbors helped him clear and fence. They loaned him their tools and their horses and their plows and showed him how to build a house. But, hell, in the Army I was worse than a dog . . . and so I joined the Saints."

"I reckon this widow had something to do with it," suggested Tarrant shrewdly. "But what do you think of these Danites, killing every man that comes into the country?"

"Well, keep out, then," returned Porter defiantly.

"By the Lord, I can't get out," returned Zachary. "You know that as well as I do. And before we go any further, which way do I travel if I happen to escape from this town?"

"You go south," directed the deserter, "right down this straight road, and in six miles you're across the line. The other side is Arizona, only they ain't no government there . . . it's a kind of a no man's land. Arizona can't govern it because it's north of the Grand Cañon, and there's no way of getting across, and Deseret can't run it because it's filled up with outlaws, men that will fight at the drop of a hat. But if you ever slip away, go down the road to Hurricane . . . that's a Mormon town, jest across the line."

"By grab, Porter, I appreciate this," said Tarrant warmly. "Now tell me what I can do for you. That's the first I'd heard of this no man's land."

"It ain't much of a country," protested Porter. "Trouble is, they's no place to go to. You can't go west because there's two hundred miles of desert, and the Paiutes will git you, sure. You can't go east because the Navajos are on the warpath and won't allow no white men to pass. But if these Danites take after you, hit the wind for the line and them outlaws will feed you, anyway. If any Mormon should feed you, he'd be killed."

"That's a fine, cheerful religion," commented Tarrant dryly. "Now what about your report?"

"What report?" demanded the deserter sullenly.

"I want you to turn over all the information you've got, concerning this Mountain Meadows Massacre. Isn't that what the colonel sent you down for?"

"Yes, but. . . ."

"No buts," broke in Tarrant sternly. "Either you report or you don't . . . and take the consequences."

"Well, they were all in on it," confessed Porter, "every man in the country, because they all belonged to the Mormon militia. They was ordered out, like any other soldiers, and, when the bishop told them to kill those people, of course they had to do it. They feel mighty bad about it, some of them, but if they'd refused, they'd undoubtedly have been killed. They don't like to talk about it, but, as near as I can git, they figgered first on the Injuns doing the killing. Lot Drake organized the Injuns and gave 'em the guns, but the emigrants whipped 'em off. Then the Danites chipped in and kept it up for three days until the wagon train ammunition was gone, and then finally the whole regiment of the Nauvoo Legion came down and finished the job. You know . . . with a flag of truce. They got scared then, and Lot Drake called them together and made every man take an oath. They swore they'd never tell and they swore a bigger oath to kill the first man that did. The Danites look after that, yet. Well, that's all. I've got to be going."

"Hold on," spoke up Tarrant, "you haven't told me anything. I knew all that already. Haven't you located any witnesses or got any papers to prove this on Bishop Drake?"

"I've got one paper here," responded Porter, feeling despondently inside his shirt. "If I give you that, will you let me go? It's a letter those emigrants wrote when they seen it was the Mormons and not the Injuns that was attacking them, and they sent it by two men to California. The man that had the paper was wounded getting away and an Injun found him asleep and killed him. The Danites chased the other for two hundred miles before they finally got him. But this Injun that killed the wounded man stripped his body of all the clothes, and found this paper sewed inside them . . . and one day when he was hungry he traded it to a Mormon for some grub."

"But how did you get it?" inquired Tarrant.

"Well, I stole it," confessed Porter sheepishly. "That was when I first came down. But this man, while he was wounded, wrote a description of the white man who was the leader of the Injuns . . . he even knowed his name. It seems they had a parley and this emigrant went out to meet him. It was the bishop here . . . Lot Drake."

"Say, give me that paper," demanded Tarrant eagerly, but the deserter backed away.

"If they knowed it, they'd kill me," he said.

"Yes, and if they found it in your shirt, they'd cut your throat all the quicker. Hand it over," said Zachary peremptorily.

"Well, take it," stuttered Porter in panic. "By grab, I never thought of that."

"Now tell me one thing more," went on Tarrant. "How does Drake stand among these Mormons? Are they loyal to him or just afraid?"

"They're afraid," declared Porter in a tragic whisper. "This man that had the paper was afraid. But he hated Drake so bad for taking one of his women that he kept the letter, anyway. The bishop was tried once . . . nearly twenty years ago when they sent down the U.S. soldiers and that judge . . . but this Mormon didn't dare to show his hand. And it wouldn't've done no good, because they had a Mormon jury and the Danites was as thick as flies. They're all afraid to testify, but if the soldiers would protect them. . . ."

"They will," Tarrant assured him. "What more?"

"The young fellers don't like him," muttered Porter, drawing closer, "because he wants all the women for himself. They call him a man among men and a devil among women, but he's the bishop and what he says, goes. He's brave, he'll fight, and they're afraid to oppose him, but they wouldn't be sorry if he was hung. Because every time they happen to spark the wrong girl, he puts Ammon Clark on their trail."

"Ammon Clark," repeated Tarrant. "Who is he?" But Porter only clutched him by the arm. Two men, appearing from nowhere, were coming up the walk, and the deserter rose up with a curse. Then with the impact of a battering ram he smashed through the pomegranate hedge and went running away through the dark. Zachary drew his gun and stood waiting in the shadows—but the men spoke together and withdrew. After that all was silent except for the chirp of crickets and the sawing of the fiddles at the dance.

CHAPTER SEVEN

Standing under the pomegranates with his pistol ready to shoot, Tarrant listened and waited for the returning footsteps of the Danites, the two men from whom Porter had fled. That they were Danites he did not doubt, although the deserter had not said so, but whoever they were, they did not come back, and he slipped his gun back into its holster. The music of the fiddles drowned the eerie chirp of crickets as the orchestra struck up "Money Musk", and at the call—"Git yore pardners!"—he forgot the midnight prowlers and his foot began tapping the dirt. Making rhythmic blinks of light as they glided past the door, he saw the dancers go flitting by, and suddenly it occurred to him that he was inviting an attack by lingering in the dooryard alone.

How much safer it would be, and pleasanter to boot, to mingle with the carefree throng. What was gained, after all, by this dodging and hiding when he was absolutely at the mercy of his enemies? If they wished to accomplish his death, they would get him, sooner or later, and in the meantime he might see Deseret. Again drawing his pistol from its holster, Zachary tucked it carefully out of sight beneath his waist band, and then with eager steps he bade farewell to fears and shadows and went striding across the street to the dance.

There was a crowd of boys around the door, playing hide-and-seek in the black shadows or standing to gawk in at the girls. To avoid the beam of light that was projected into the night, Tarrant approached at one side in the dark. Then, gazing in enviously, he moved closer and closer until at last he stood just outside the threshold. The Mormons were waltzing slowly, according to their custom, the ladies in white muslin and the men mostly in shirt sleeves, for the night was hot and close. On a stand in the rear the two fiddlers stamped and played, hoeing it down with true rural zest, but look around as he would Tarrant could not see Deseret, although he watched for her dance after dance. Could it be that she was a wallflower, while these big, blowsy Mormon girls had partners and to spare? He craned to the left and right, and there in the corner was Deseret, sitting alone.

She was the first of all to see him, for the dance was in full swing, and, as he caught her eye, she smiled at him mournfully and turned her face away. But the scraping of the fiddles had got into Zachary's feet, and, when he beheld the fair partner who might be his for the asking, he threw discretion to the winds. Stepping boldly through the door, he strode across the room and stood before her, bowing.

"Good evening," he greeted with a gallant flourish of his hat and a smile that had fluttered many a heart, "how does it come that you are a wallflower?"

She shrugged her shoulders prettily, glancing about with fearful eyes, and made a place for him at her side.

"Is this a Mormon custom?" he inquired.

Her answer was a faint-hearted laugh. "It is in Moroni," she confessed.

"What?" he protested. "Let the queen of the ball sit it out, dance after dance? I'm a stranger here, but this isn't right." He rose up impulsively and offered his arm. "Will you favor me with a dance?" he asked.

"Why, certainly," she assented with a mischievous smile, and in a moment they were whirling across the room. But hardly had they started, or so it seemed to Zachary, when the music came to a halt, and with every eye upon them he escorted her to a seat, not without a qualm. For suddenly, as he did so, feeling the hostile stare of the Mormons, he remembered Tamar Young. When he had danced with her on that ill-fated day, he had felt the same hateful glare—and then the colonel's adjutant had appeared. But he thrust the thought aside, and, when the next dance was called, he rose up again and offered his arm.

"May I have the great pleasure?" he asked, and once more she surrendered to his smile. Though he was garbed in buckskin and she in a homespun gown, they made a handsome couple as they waltzed, but when he led her back, she suddenly turned pale and he felt her hand clutch at his arm. Mrs. Mayberry, the first wife, was coming toward them.

"Let's go for a walk," he proposed impulsively, and the next moment they were out under the stars.

The crowd of boys by the door had disappeared and no one saw their hasty flight as they took shelter behind the trunk of a giant mulberry.

"What shall we do now?" he asked as she stood trembling beside him, and Deseret burst into tears.

The Mayberrys had come out and hurried across the street, where they could hear them calling her name, but she made no attempt to answer.

"Let's go back here, and hide," she whispered at last, and led the way into the churchyard.

"Now what is the matter?" he inquired tenderly as she sank down on a bench beneath a tree. Her answer was a stifled sob.

"I can't go home, now," she said. "Mother Rachel will scold me terribly."

"But what for?" he protested. "You've done nothing wrong."

"They . . . they've forbidden me to dance . . . except with the bishop. And, oh, I just hate him." She straightened up angrily, pounding the bench with her fist, her breath came hot on his cheek. "I'd like to kill him!" she said.

"Yes, but why? Why can't you dance?"

"He wants me to marry him . . . and he's got nineteen wives already. Nineteen . . . and over sixty children. I told him I never would, and so, just to punish me, he . . . he acts like he did today. And Mister Mayberry won't let me dance with the boys any more, because . . . because it gets them into trouble with the bishop. But I do love to dance." She sighed. "Nobody asks me now."

"So do I," he confessed, "and when I saw you sitting there. . . ."

"Oh, I know," she answered. "We forgot all about it. Wasn't it wonderful . . . just to dance?"

"I never thought," he went on penitently, "it would get you into trouble."

"I don't mind that," she confided, "but what about you? When the bishop gets angry, he's terrible . . . he'll try to have you killed."

"I don't care," he said, "as far as that goes. But what about you . . . will you marry him?"

"What, that awful creature? No, and, if he does make me do it, I told him I'd kill him . . . and I will. But I just won't do it, that's all. I couldn't." She shuddered, and, drawing closer, she whispered: "He killed my mother . . . that's why."

"Why, what for?" he demanded, startled.

"At the Mountain Meadows Massacre," she replied.

"My God," breathed Tarrant, "and you?"

"I'm one of those seventeen children that they spared because they were little. But I know . . . I saw him do it myself."

She shuddered and drew away, and, as he sat there in the darkness, he heard her stifled sobs.

"But, Deseret," he said at last, "does he know that you

remember this? Because if he does. . . ."

"I know . . . he'd kill me," she finished. "But I've never told anybody else."

"You can trust me," he responded, "I won't tell." And he took her hand in his.

They sat then in silence, and, as the bitter tears came, she leaned against his shoulder and wept.

"I'm so lonely." She sighed. "With all these people around me, the people that killed my father and mother. I just hate them, all the time. They only kept me because I could work."

"But this man, Uncle Jake . . . what about him?"

"He took care of me, at first . . . he kept all seventeen of us, until they gave us around to the folks. No, I don't hate him . . . very much. But he's a Mormon, just like the rest. And he knows that Bishop Drake is the man that killed my mother and yet he wants me to marry him. They're crazy over their religion, and their women are nothing but slaves."

"And you're a slave, too, then," he said.

"I always was," she answered, "but they treat their own daughters the same way. Oh, I look at them sometimes when they're talking and preaching that way, and they don't seem human to me. All they think about is marrying and having lots of children, to enlarge their celestial kingdom. I don't believe in it, at all."

"Then what are you going to do?" he asked.

"That's it . . . I can't do anything." She sighed again.

"Do you want to get away?" he inquired, and suddenly she caught him by the hand.

"Will you take me?" she begged. "I'll go anywhere."

"Yes, I will," he promised, "but not now. You just stay here and be careful . . . and be sure you don't marry Lot Drake."

"I'm afraid," she pleaded. "He looks at me so terribly. I don't care what happens . . . take me away."

She pressed his hand against her cheek, and for a moment his brain seemed to whirl, then he remembered the Danites, the skulking forms in the dark, and drew her into his arms.

"I'll take care of you," he whispered, "but I can't take you away now. The Danites are on my trail. I saw them the other night when they stampeded my horse . . . they did that to put me afoot. And now that I'm in their power, I expect it will come to a fight. I wouldn't dare take you now."

"Did you come for me?" she asked, her face very near his. "Did something seem to tell you I was waiting, or were you just passing through?"

"I came down to save you," he assured her eagerly, and Deseret gave him a kiss. Perhaps not purposely, but their lips met in an ecstasy, blotting out the words each would have said, and Deseret bowed her head on his breast.

"I'm so glad," she said. "I was tired. There was no one to help me fight."

"Only wait," he promised, "and I'll come back and get you, with a regiment of cavalry at my back. Lot Drake will be punished yet."

"Oh, what was that?" she demanded, struggling feebly to escape his arms, but he would not let her go.

"Never mind," he soothed, "I'll take care of you, Deseret. What was it you thought you heard?"

"I heard horses coming," she said, and Tarrant raised his head. Above the squeaking of the fiddles and the shuffle of feet he heard a noise like sudden thunder—or horses crossing a bridge. Then as they shrank back out of sight, a band of riders appeared, galloping furiously up the road. The ground trembled as their horses' hoofs struck the earth. There was a clatter of flying hoofs, and, as they flashed into the light from the door of the Social Hall, their leader rose high in his stirrups. He was a tall man, superbly mounted on a star-faced black, and, as he rode into the wind, his long, red beard whipped behind him like the tail of a fox. Then with a rush they thundered past and were swallowed up in the darkness from which they had come volleying forth.

"Who was that?" queried Zachary, "that man with the long, red beard?"

Deseret clung closer, crying. "That was Ammon Clark," she sobbed, "the captain of the Avenging Angels. He's come to kill you. I know."

Chapter Eight

Riding like centaurs out of the night, Tarrant had seen with his own eyes what before he hardly believed to exist—a band of Avenging Angels, the Danites of the church, galloping recklessly through the town. The broad ray of light from the open door of the Social Hall had revealed them in one flash as they passed, every man on a blooded horse with a carbine beneath his knee and a black hat pulled low over his face. But Ammon Clark, their captain, had had his hat rim thrown back, and his long, flowing beard made him appear a veritable Thor, riding the wind as invincible as a god. He had come at the command of Lot Drake.

Zachary felt the high courage that had carried him so far suddenly leave him, while his heart turned sick. With so much in the world to live for, with Deseret to protect, he must fight for his life with these Avenging Angels. They were not like the skulking creatures who had frightened away his horse; they were men, as he could see, armed and equipped for their business—to carry terror to the Gentile and apostate. They were officers of the church, the left hand of Brigham Young, men who knew no law but his will and the will of the bishops who obeyed him.

"Run and hide in your room," urged Deseret in a panic, and Tarrant obeyed without knowing why. Rushing across the street, he felt his way down the hall, where assassins seemed to lurk on every side, and not until the door was locked behind him did he recover from his unreasoning fright. Then with rifle in hand he crouched by the window and gazed up and down the road.

Everything was as quiet as before. From the hall across the street the light still poured forth and the fiddlers had not slackened their pace, but farther up the street were the red lights of a saloon and before it stood the Avenging Angels' horses. Zachary laughed to himself, but tremulously, and turned back to barricade his door. They had come into town to get drunk.

He woke the next morning to find the sun well up and everything below him astir. There was a fragrant smell of coffee and home-smoked bacon and the gong was summoning him to breakfast. But before he went down, he took his pistol from his belt and spun the cylinder thoughtfully. From all he had heard, it was not the custom of the Avenging Angels to carry out their work in public. They operated by night or in the silence of the desert, where nothing would be seen or heard. Still his offense had been great, and, remembering the anger of the bishop, he glanced down into the street. There, standing at the horse rack with his head hung low, was Buck, his stolen horse.

Zachary gave a whoop of joy and went bounding down the stairs. As he passed through the hall, he came face to face with Mayberry, who detained him with an outstretched hand.

"Mister Grey," he began, his face working with passion, "I will thank you, while you are here, to mind your own business and leave my daughter alone. You are not of our faith and. . . ."

"We'll talk that over later," responded Tarrant impatiently, and hurried out to see his horse.

Buck had traveled far that night, but he was still sound and strong. As he recognized his master, he gave a joyous whinny and sucked his bit, begging for a drink.

"Why, you poor old plug," cried Zachary, "you're gaunted to a shadow!" But as he was leading him toward the stables, Lot

Drake came striding over, accompanied by a Paiute Indian.

"There's your horse, Lieutenant Tarrant," he said, and Zachary eyed him warily.

"My name is Grey," he replied.

"Grey or Tarrant, it's all the same to me, only don't think for a minute you can fool anybody. I telegraphed to Salt Lake City and my orders are to release you, so I sent over and got your horse. But if you'll take my advice, you'll git out of this town as quick as God will let you. I don't like your style . . . understand?"

"Yes, I gathered that yesterday," responded Tarrant with a smile, "when you called me a government spy."

"Well, I call you that again," declared the bishop hotly. "I don't care what Brigham says. And, say, don't git so smart." He lowered his voice and his desert-squinted eyes seemed to bore Zachary through and through. "I've taken enough," he ended, and turned away with a muttered curse.

Tarrant went on to the stable where he fed and watered his horse. Then, still pondering on this new turn in his affairs, he started back toward the hotel. Some time during the night Drake had telegraphed to Salt Lake and in some astounding manner he had received orders from his superiors to release Tarrant and give back his horse. Could it be that Brigham Young had at last been deceived, after outwitting the Army for years? Could it be that the colonel's ruse in dismissing Tarrant from the service had worked out to save his life? It was possible, but Zachary was doubtful. Yet somewhere in Salt Lake he had a friend at court, a friend who had saved his life. Who else could it be but Tamar?

He paused outside the door, his blood pounding at the thought, and like a shadow he saw Deseret pass. How was it, then? Which did he love? He had put Tamar from his heart, and, somehow, in one night, Deseret had slipped into her place.

In a day and a night he had met her and loved her, and pledged himself to be her protector. And yet, there was Tamar, still his friend. She might have interceded when Drake's telegram had come—reporting his presence and the sentence of the Avenging Angels—for she was deep in the confidence of her father. Brigham trusted her—and used her, too—and through her he used others, like Tarrant. Were they saving him, to use again?

"Young man!" called a harsh voice from the dining-room door. "You'd better come in to your breakfast!"

It was Rachel, the first wife of Mayberry. As he hurried in, she showed him to his place. Then with her lips, pursed and forbidding, she served him in stony silence. Deseret had been banished to the kitchen and he knew he would not see her again. Yet the memory of their parting wrung his heart. How lonely she was, how unprotected and helpless among these people who had killed her parents. How her thoughts must rise up and haunt her day and night when she saw their brutal bishop striding past. With her own eyes, as a child, she had seen him kill her mother, and yet she had never dared to tell. Only to Zachary, although he had come as a stranger, had she confided the anguish of her heart. And he had promised to save her from Drake.

He hurried through his meal to escape the Gorgon-eyed Rachel, whose stare threatened to turn him to stone. As he retreated to the bench beneath the mulberry tree, he met Mayberry, returning from the store. But here suddenly was a different Mayberry from the man he had met in the hall—a Mayberry all smiles and servile greetings.

"Well, well," he observed, "got your horse back, I see. That's good. I knowed you would. Our bishop is short-spoken but he's a wonderful man, a great man, lots of influence with the Indians. Yes, Brother Drake is a great man in many, many ways. Only a year ago that temple was nothing, and look what he's made of it now. He's a driver, I'll admit, but he gets the work done, and he builds for time and all eternity. He's a wonderful manager of men. Got several fine ranches and businesses, besides a big gristmill and sawmill. And over east of here, on the desert, he has charge of all the church cattle, a matter of some twenty thousand head. He's a big man, is what I mean. Besides being our bishop, he's the judge of the probate court. But he's never too busy to get back a man's horse for him, or attend to a widow and orphan."

Mayberry paused and beamed expectantly, his shallow eyes fairly glistening, but Tarrant curled his lip and said nothing. If the bishop had restored his horse, it was only because he had stolen it, and what man in Utah Territory had made more widows and orphans than Lot Drake in his Mountain Meadows Massacre? But Mayberry was not easily discouraged.

"We Saints," he continued, sitting down in the shade and pushing back his battered old hat, "think we have the best religion in the world. Of course others disagree, but the time will soon come when everyone will recognize its worth. Our social conditions prove it. Every man pays his tithing, one-tenth of all he makes, and the poor are all provided for without any color of charity. The bishop collects the tithes and he and his councilors look after the sick, and the families of those off on missions. 'Do unto others as you would have them do unto you!' That's our motto, and we try to live up to it. Well, good morning, a good morning to you."

He rose up and shook hands with a tall man with a flowing beard who Tarrant instantly recognized as Ammon Clark, and, after a few nervous remarks, Mayberry excused himself hurriedly and the captain sat down in his place.

" 'Mornin'," he said after a long look at Zachary. Drawing out a Bowie knife, he hacked a sliver off the bench and began to whittle a toothpick.

"Good morning," answered Tarrant politely, and waited for him to go on. In the glaring light of day the captain of the Avenging Angels was not such a heroic figure—his nose was short and snubbed, his complexion was coarse and freckled, and tobacco juice had stained his long beard, but he had the upright bearing of a soldier and his brows suggested the eagle in their arch.

"I understand," he said at last, speaking in a harsh, truculent voice, "you've been an officer in the U.S. Army."

"Yes, I was in the Army," admitted Tarrant. "How many years did you serve?"

"I served one," snarled Clark, jabbing his knife into the bench, ". . . the most miserable year of my life. They made us march afoot from Santa Fe, New Mexico, across the desert and clear to California. Out of water half the time and our wagons came to pieces, so we had to pack our grub on our back, and all the time that damned Gentile doctor was trying to kill us with calomel." He stopped and spat in deep disgust, then launched into a tirade against the government and the Army in particular. "Well, what do you think?" he demanded at last as Zachary sat in silence. "They drummed you out of the Army for making love to Brigham's daughter . . . what do you think of the government now?"

"I'm not talking about that at all," answered Tarrant. "I came down here to get away from it."

"Well, you won't," declared Clark, "you won't git away from nothing." He stabbed his huge knife into the bench.

"Just what do you mean by that?" inquired Zachary, moving away and jerking his holster to the front.

Ammon Clark surveyed him coldly. "I mean," he said, "you're a damned government spy, and we know jest exactly why you're here. I've backtracked on your trail and I know where you camped. Now you git out of town. Hear me?"

73

He put his knife back in its sheath and glowered malignantly at Tarrant before he rose and strode back to the saloon, and Zachary sat like one in a trance. It was easy to see what Clark and Drake were aiming at—they were trying to frighten him into riding out of town, where the Avenging Angels would have him at their mercy. Even the bishop's supposed kindness in returning his horse was no more than a ruse to tempt him forth.

The orders from Brigham Young, if he had sent orders at all, were not meant to spare his life, merely to release him from arrest and encourage him to ride where the Angels of the Lord could shoot him down. Yet Zachary was half tempted to yield. Once up on the back of Buck with his rifle beneath his knee he could fight for his life, like a man. But if he lingered about town, he would be arrested and searched, and, if the deserter's papers were found, they would prove his death warrant. They would prove beyond doubt that he was a dangerous spy, for they implicated Lot Drake in the massacre, and that wicked Bowie knife with which Clark had stabbed the bench would serve its dread purpose again.

Zachary wondered dimly why, if they had decided to kill him, they had left his rifle in his room, for out on the open desert a man with only a pistol would be helpless against men armed with rifles. Yet, if he went back to get it, the deceitful Mayberry would see him and immediately give notice to Ammon Clark. Tarrant sat idly on the bench, glancing up and down the road and laying his plans to escape. While he was deep in thought, he was roused from his reflections by the patter of sand on his hat.

He looked up quickly and, peering out from the window, he beheld the smiling face of Deseret. But when he sprang up to join her, she shook her head warningly and held up his rifle inquiringly. He nodded his head vigorously, and, thrusting it out the window, she dropped it into his hands. Then with a farewell smile she drew back out of sight and Zachary blew her a kiss.

It seemed almost unreal, this exchange of smiles and kisses while Angels were all about, but so it had seemed when he met her, only yesterday, and promised to protect her with his life. It was the Avenging Angels, galloping past, the fear of Bishop Drake, that had made those brief minutes like months. Now, still facing death, he paused for one more glance before he began his long flight. But Deseret had fled, and, holding his rifle out of sight, he hurried back and saddled his horse. Across the street at the temple the Mormon workmen passed to and fro, long teams came slowly in down the road. As their dust rose, thick and high, a lone horseman whipped into it and went galloping off to the south.

CHAPTER NINE

Down long, dusty lanes where lofty cottonwoods lined the ditches and cattle stood drowsing in the shade, Tarrant went at a slashing gallop. When he realized that no one was pursuing him, he reined in to a trot and so came to the edge of the desert. Behind, all was fences and flamboyant greenness, corn in rows, fields of hay and sleeping farmsteads, but at the edge of the last ditch that brought water from the mountains there was nothing but baked soil and salt brush. Yet not so far distant, at the base of other hills, there was a similar spot of green and the road led in a straight line toward it.

Beyond these southern hills there rose a long, red mountain clothed with cedars and crowned with pines. To the north and east a high white cliff extended on until it was lost in the haze. It threw a half circle, barring the way to the north, and eastward across the desert and the cañons of the Colorado lay the land of the hostile Navajos. But behind lay Moroni with its gleaming white temple and its men to whom murder was God's will.

The rugged country beckoned to Tarrant—it was rough but its cañons would hide him. He topped some low hills and below him lay the town of Hurricane, rich with greenness, shaded by trees. Everything was calmly serene and beautiful in this vale among the desert hills. There was no hint of disorder or of impending strife, and yet here was no man's land. At the foot of the hill, on the bank of the first ditch, Tarrant saw a sign with the one word *Utah,* and across the ditch on a similar sign was the single legend *Arizona*. A beehive, symbolic of the State of Deseret and of the industry of the Mormon people, was sketched on the Utah signboard, but across the ditch there was no symbol for Arizona except the huge word *Saloon*.

Zachary rode down and crossed the bridge into no man's land, where every man was a law unto himself. Not liking its looks, he jogged past the saloon and down the long road toward town. Tall cottonwoods overhung the rushing stream of water that flowed along the side of the street, and, as Tarrant was riding in their shade, his horse suddenly flew back and a man rose up from the bushes.

"Throw up your hands!" he demanded. "I am a robber!" He leveled a half-empty whiskey flask at Tarrant's head. He was a huge, raw-boned fellow with a wrinkled, clownish face and a half moon of straggling red whiskers. With a grin Zachary threw up both hands.

"Have a drink!" commanded the robber, suddenly reversing the bottle, and Zachary touched it to his lips.

"Have another!" ordered the robber, measuring the liquor with his thumb and cocking his eye at him sternly. "You're in Arizona now, where the giant cactus grows, and you're drinking with a white man . . . understand? I'm Jerry Wamsutter, of Rustler Mountain." He again handed up the bottle.

Tarrant took a drink, after proposing his very good health.

"Did you come from Moroni?" demanded Jerry, crowding the flask back into his hip pocket. "Well, now, I want to ask you a question. Did you, or did you not, see a one-eyed Mormon hanging around that corner saloon? You did not. Very well, I thank you."

He took a drink himself, swaying uncertainly on his feet, and Zachary slumped down in his saddle. For, although this knight of the road had held him up with a bottle, he had a big pistol in the slack of his overalls.

"Very well," he said again. "You have answered my question, and I thank you kindly, my friend. That Mormon-faced whelp must be hiding around here somewhere . . . he's afraid to arrest me, by grab." He assumed a heroic posture and straddled out into the sun while he gazed up and down the road. "He's *afraid!*" he yelled with a wild, reckless laugh. "I don't care if he is the constable, he's afraid to arrest me! I'll cut his heart out, the heenie-kneed whoopus!" He whipped a long Bowie knife out of the leg of his boot and waved it till it gleamed in the sun. "Bull chips and bear sign!" he whooped defiantly. "Panther tracks and the ground tore up! *Yeeee!*" He shouted his war cry again and again, and staggered back into the shade. "He's afraid to arrest me! I'll *kill* 'im!"

He nodded his head at Zachary and his rugged face lit up with a smile of drunken approval. "Shake hands," he said, "you're my friend. And you're a Gentile, or I'm a danged liar. But, gentlemen, I can tell a Mormon, too."

He threw back his head and began a ribald song, coming out strong on the roaring chorus:

> *I can tell what you are by the color of your hair,*
> *I can tell what you are by the clothes that you wear,*
> *You're a Mormon, dod-blast ye, git back to Utah!*

"Well, good luck, my friend," said Zachary as the song at last came to a close. "I've got to go down to the store."

He reined away and the robber stood staring after him.

"Hey!" he yelled at last. "Stay away from that deadfall! If you enter that store, you're a goner!"

"All right," answered Tarrant, looking back over his shoulder, and rode off, laughing, down the road. Here was no man's land with a vengeance—a strapping big Gentile, holding up strangers with his bottle and defying the Mormon constable to arrest him. And yet, coming from Moroni and with the fear of the

Avenging Angels upon him, Zachary decided that he liked the country, although not well enough to stay. Already he had seen a way that would take him to the high mountains, whose wooded summits he could see to the south, but first it was necessary to replace the provisions that had been stolen when his camp was robbed.

It was noon and the single broad street of the village was deserted, except for the dogs. As Tarrant tied his horse at the rack in front of the store, he saw inquisitive faces looking out. He stepped into a place that was more saloon than store, since the hardware and provisions were relegated to one side and the rest was given to billiard tables and bar. Four men were in the saloon, engaged in a game of pool, but, when he entered, they laid down their cues. Then a small man with one eye rushed forward to meet him, his face twisted to a false, sly smile.

"Why, hello, Charley!" he hailed. "By George, I'm glad to see you!" He held out his hand to shake. But Tarrant had seen men deprived of their pistols while their right hands were held in a handshake, and he stepped back and shook his head.

"My name isn't Charley," he stated. "You've made a mistake, my friend."

"No, I know you!" insisted the man, still holding out his hand. "I know you, but I can't recall your name. Didn't I see you over in Moroni?"

"You may have seen me," retorted Tarrant, "but that doesn't make me your friend. Where's the man that keeps this store?"

"Here I am," announced the bartender, waving them up to the bar. "What'll you have, boys?" he asked expectantly.

"I don't drink," spoke up Zachary as they all turned to him. "All I want is a little grub."

"Well, you are a short sport," sneered the one-eyed man. "Ain't you going to buy the drinks? Here, I'll buy you a drink . . . how's that?"

"No, gentlemen," declined Tarrant, "I didn't come to trade drinks. What I want is some grub, right now."

"Pah!" exclaimed the one-eyed man, going off in a pet.

The barkeeper strode over behind the counter. Zachary laid in a supply of bacon and flour and coffee and threw down a $20 bill. But as the barkeeper picked it up, the one-eyed man came running over and grabbed it out of his hands.

"Where'd you get that bill?" he asked, and deliberately tore it in two.

"Here! What do you mean?" demanded Zachary angrily, and the one-eyed man bristled back at him.

"That bill is no good," he declared. "It's bogus!" And he threw it on the floor.

Tarrant stepped back, astounded, and, stung to the quick, he struck out and the meddler went down. But his fall was only the signal for the others to rush in—and, as Zachary stepped back, the saloonkeeper vaulted the counter with a bar bottle raised to strike. Tarrant leaped to one side and avoided the blow. Then, seeing that a battle could not be avoided, he rushed in and knocked the saloonkeeper back against the counter. The others backed away, and Zachary stood with his hand on his gun.

"This has gone far enough," he warned.

"Go after him!" bellowed the saloonkeeper, reaching recklessly over the counter, but Tarrant scorned to shoot. They were four to one, but in a rough-and-tumble fight he did not ask odds from any of them. With a dexterous movement he knocked the bully backward and jumped out of his reach.

"I'll fix you," cursed the saloonkeeper. "I'll blow your damn' head off." And he raced around behind the bar. But Zachary, instead of drawing his own pistol, leaped up and balanced on the bar. Beneath he could see his man, snatching a revolver from the shelf, and with a plunge he rode him to the floor.

There was a scramble as they fell, both grabbing for the gun, but Tarrant wrenched it loose. As the ruffian came up fighting, he smashed him over the head with the barrel. Then he swung the loaded gun on the rest. They had snatched up their billiard cues but, seeing him armed, they hesitated and stood at bay.

"Panther tracks and the ground tore up!" yelled a voice out in the street, and a huge man came riding in, spurring his horse through the swinging doors. It was Jerry Wamsutter, his eyes on fire. Flinging himself to the floor, he made a rush at the three toughs while his fists rose and fell like trip hammers. Before they could flee, he had overtaken them like a whirlwind, and, once in his power, they were heaved and tossed about until at last he kicked them out the door.

"Where's that barkeep?" he yelled to Tarrant. "Did he invite you to have a drink? Lemme show you what happens when you drink with these Mormons! Didn't I tell you this place was a deadfall?"

He clapped Zachary on the shoulder and, with his moon face grinning, reached back and dragged out the groaning saloon-keeper.

"Now here you are," he expounded, propping his victim against the bar, "lined up for a drink on the house. 'Have one with me, boys,' and whingo, you're gone, plumb down into dead man's hole!"

He pulled a rope behind the bar, and like a flash the floor opened. The bleeding barkeeper was precipitated to the cellar beneath, and the trap door swung back into place.

"How's that?" demanded Jerry in drunken triumph. "But, sa-ay," he went on, "who have we got over here?" And he nabbed the one-eyed man just as he was making a break for the door. "Well, if it ain't Bill Crump!" he proclaimed, and the one-eyed man began to tremble and beg.

"Don't hit me, Jerry," he pleaded. "I'm hurt . . . I can't hardly move."

"You was moving for that door when I caught you," retorted Jerry. "Don't you know this man is my friend? You're a hell of a constable, an officer of the law, playing dirty tricks like this!"

He swung him around in the air as if about to slam him to the ground, then he lowered him in front of the bar and shook him like a dog that has a snake.

"Now you stand there!" he directed, placing Crump on the trap door, "and if you make a move to run, I'll kill ye. Here, have a drink, my friend . . . no, have one on me!" He set out a glass of whiskey. "Now . . . all set? Then go!" And, jerking the hidden rope, he sent him to the bottom of the cellar. "How's that?" he inquired with a jovial nod and smile. "Ain't that the way to treat 'em? Have a drink!"

He knocked the neck off a bottle, poured out two glasses, and flung the rest of it across the store.

"Here's to hell," he proposed, "where all good Mormons go. I can lick the whole bunch, with one hand."

CHAPTER TEN

"Have another one," urged Jerry Wamsutter, leaning hospitably over the bar and regarding his guest with an amiable smile, and he knocked the neck off another bottle.

"No, thanks," responded Tarrant, "I've got to be going."

Jerry tossed off the drink himself and wrinkled his forehead anxiously. "What's your hurry?" he complained. "Hang around a little while and maybe they'll come back for more. The drinks are free, and who wouldn't wait for another fight like that last? You was doing well, for a man of your weight, but it takes Jerry Wamsutter to clean 'em. I'm pisen for Mormons and they don't dare to kill me, on account of my three brothers in the hills. Because the first man that kills a Wamsutter will have to kill three more . . . which way are you traveling, my friend?"

"Oh, back into the hills," answered Zachary vaguely. "I'm out on a prospecting trip."

"Heh. Prospecting, eh?" Jerry grinned, reaching down into his pocket and fetching out a buckskin sack. "What do you think of that for gold?"

He poured a handful of coarse nuggets on the bar and fixed Tarrant with shrewd, twinkling eyes.

"I've got the best placer north of the Grand Cañon," he boasted, "and there ain't Mormons enough in Utah to take it away from me, no, sir. My brothers and me will fight till we die first, and these dog-faced Mormons know it. I can come down here bare-handed and turn the town upside-down and nobody dares to shoot me. If they do, there's Jack and Dick and my brother Arthur to boot, that can all shoot a sparrow hawk on the wing. There's lots more men back in these hills that would like nothing better than to wipe this town, Hurricane, off the map, and then what would Brigham do, and Lot Drake and all the rest of them, for a place to keep their sealed wives? Hell, yes, the town is full of them . . . all those houses over there. We're jest across the line, in Arizona."

"What difference does that make?" asked Zachary.

"All the difference in the world. All the difference between being jailed under the Edmunds Act and coming down here to live like a danged Turk. It's polygamy, sure, but there's no courts here to try them, either federal or any other kind. But it's all right with me, I'm heartily in favor of it . . . these poor women get lonely at times. Ain't it perfectly natural they should? The most natural thing in the world . . . and a big, upstanding fellow like me, coming down out of the mountains, looks mighty good to some of them."

He shook his head and chuckled, but Tarrant had suddenly remembered something. The name of Lot Drake had brought him back to the real world and he stepped out to look down the road.

"I've got to be going," he said.

"Wait a while," pleaded Jerry, "and I might go along with you. What's your hurry, here's lots of good liquor."

"Well, I'll tell you," explained Zachary, "there's a man named Ammon Clark. . . ."

"Hell's bells," yelped Jerry, vaulting over the bar and running out to look for himself, "is that the man you're looking for? You come along with me. I know the country better than you do. Old Ammon is a hard man to lose."

He led his horse out of the barroom while Zachary was gathering up his supplies. With the dogs running after them, they went galloping out of Hurricane, leaving a cloud of dust behind. Up the valley to the east they continued at a high trot, turning off across the barren desert. After looking back a few times, Jerry reached into his hip pocket and fetched out his half-empty bottle.

"This calls for a drink," he observed with a sober smile. "What does Ammon Clark want to get you for?"

"Well, you see," said Tarrant, "in traveling through the country I happened to camp at Mountain Meadows. That gave them the idea I was a government spy and they told me to get out of town."

"By grab . . . here!" cried Wamsutter, shaking his horse into a gallop. "We got to make tracks. They'll be coming. I know that Ammon Clark. He runs cattle over on the desert, and he rides the best horses in the country. So they took you for a government spy?"

"I couldn't talk them out of it," admitted Zachary, and Jerry eyed him shrewdly.

"I knowed it, the minute I saw you," he said. "You set in the saddle like a soldier."

"I'll have to break myself of that habit," observed Tarrant, and Jerry nodded vigorously.

"Yes," he agreed, "or bring down a few more soldiers and put the fear into their black Mormon hearts. See that house over there?" He pointed to a stone house, out on the point of a distant hill, and reined in closer to Tarrant. "That's Brigham's Castle, jest south of the line. He's got it all loopholed like a fort, says he does it to fight off the Injuns, but the damned Avenging Angels are thicker than fleas around that place, every time he comes down for a visit. The boys up in the hills call it Brigham's lambing grounds, they're so many of his kids running about, but that fort was built strong to stand off the government, if they ever try to make him a prisoner. An Avenging

Angel told me that himself. Couple of Brigham's wives over there now, and maybe a few of them Avenging Angels, so we'll turn off and take this old trail."

He reined away to the right, following a rocky path that led up over a high, red ridge, but, seeing Tarrant's eyes on the stone house at the point of the mesa, he returned to the subject of Brigham.

"That house," he said, "is built right over a big spring that runs out and fills up them little lakes, and down this way is another . . . where you see all them cattle. They'd come in pretty handy for beef. They's grub enough in that castle to last an army of men, and, when Brigham comes down here, the Avenging Angels swarm in until it looks like a regular fort. And when I say Avenging Angels, I don't mean these low-down toughs that you find all over Utah. These are the fire-eating kind, that have got into trouble and come south to get away from the soldiers. They use 'em for cowboys, to handle the church herd, and stand off the war parties of Navajos. But if it ever comes to a showdown, you'll hear from these fellers. They'll fight the whole Army to save Brigham. And Ammon Clark is the fightingest one of all."

Jerry glanced back over their trail and spurred his horse to a faster gait.

"Notice that beard of his?" he queried. "Kinder long, eh, like it had never been cut? Well, sir, Ammon Clark was Joseph Smith's Number One Angel, when they had all that trouble back in Missouri. He'd go anywhere and kill anybody, and, jest before Smith died, he gave him his Prophet's blessing. That's big medicine with these Mormons, being blessed by the Prophet, and Joseph Smith told him, as long as his beard was uncut, he'd never be killed by a Gentile. The result is, he ain't afraid of a thousand soldiers . . . or nobody else, for that matter."

He looked back again, stopping his horse under the brow of a hill and sweeping the desert with squinted eyes.

"See that dust?" he said at last. "Somebody's coming out of Hurricane. I'll bet it's them."

He spurred his horse into a mad scramble up over the rocky slope and along the far side of the ridge, but every few miles he would ride up near the summit and peer over the crest of the hill.

"That's them!" he declared at last, when, as the sun was sinking low, they gazed back from a clump of cedars.

Tarrant could see a bunch of horsemen crossing the desert at a gallop and undoubtedly following their trail.

"Now watch me fool 'em," said Jerry confidently, and rode on several miles through the cedars. Then he circled back over the rocks, where their tracks would not show, and took shelter within sight of the trail.

The sun had tipped the peaks, painting the red hills a bloodier hue and hanging a gorgeous canopy in the west, before the first of the Avenging Angels appeared. It was Ammon Clark himself, jabbing his horse at every jump, and behind him followed six men on winded mounts, flogging and spurring to keep him in sight. He rode upright in the saddle, leaning down from time to time to scrutinize the tracks in the trail. Behind him like twin streamers flowed his long, red beard, which had been blessed by the Prophet Joseph.

Jerry Wamsutter, lying low behind a pile of boulders, shifted his rifle and rumbled in his throat, but they had doubled back a mile and the Angels still pressed on, whipping and spurring over the rocky trail.

"I'd like to take a crack at Ammon with this Forty-Five-Ninety," remarked Jerry as they passed out of sight. "Something about those Mormon shirts and long, sweeping whiskers . . . it don't seem reasonable, somehow. Don't you reckon a bullet would go through 'em?"

"I certainly do," assented Zachary, "and I'd be willing to stake my life on it. Now what do you plan to do next?"

"Oh, sure," responded Jerry, "I got to thinking about them shirts. We'll ride right across the trail on this flat ledge of rocks, and that gives us a whole night's start. And tomorrow morning at sunup I'll show you the grandest placer that ever laid outdoors in Arizona. More'n that, my friend, I'll show you Dick, Jack, and Arthur Wamsutter . . . three of a kind and a hard hand to beat. And if them Avenging Angels track us somehow, we'll find out for certain whether them shirts will turn a bullet."

CHAPTER ELEVEN

Daylight came at last, after long hours of dreary plodding when their horses balked again and again, hours when they lay down among the rocks and dozed uneasily until their mounts were able to proceed. But in the first pale light of dawn Tarrant saw a saddle in the mountains toward which Jerry was evidently riding. As they crossed the divide, he looked down on a windswept mesa, barren of everything but stunted cedars and sagebrush. Yet at sight of this desert waste Wamsutter's horse pricked up his ears and stepped off at a brisker pace. A flock of sage hens rose before them, deer and antelope bounded away, and at a turn of the trail they looked down on a lonely cabin, standing guard at the mouth of a gulch.

"Here we are," announced Jerry, who had been dozing in his saddle, and at his shout three men stepped out. They were all giants in size, clad in red shirts and canvas overalls and heavy miner's boots.

As Jerry rode down the hill with his chance companion, they stood watching in somber silence. There was something in their pose and the grim looks on their bearded faces that told Tarrant he was far from welcome.

"Well, boys," said Jerry as he drew rein at the door, "I brought home a young feller . . . er, what's your name?"

"Tarrant, Zachary Tarrant," replied his guest.

"Yeh . . . -Zack," went on Jerry, unabashed. "This baldheaded feller is Dick and these two others are Jack and Arthur. Where's that chink? I want some coffee."

An old, weazened Chinaman in the sloppiest of Chinese trousers came shuffling to the door, and, as Jerry shouted a rough greeting, he squinted his bloodshot eyes and regarded him malevolently. "Wha' for you no blingee gin?" he demanded.

"Plumb forgot it, Sam." Jerry grinned. "Started to bring you a bottle of whiskey but we drank it all up on the way. Say, make me some coffee, quick."

"No makee coffee!" shrilled the Chinaman in a tantrum. "You pay me money. I go. Me no likee this place. Allee time you fo'gettee buy gin."

"Aw, whassa malla you, Sam?" replied Jerry good-naturedly. "You want them damn' Mormons to kill me? Me get in fight, savvy? Saloonkeeper no good. Allee time fight, send seven men to kill me."

"Been drunk again, eh?" spoke up Dick, rubbing his bald-head reflectively and glancing at Arthur and Jack. "Did you whip all seven yourself?"

"Hell, no," disclaimed Jerry, "that's another bunch entirely. But Zack and me cleaned up that Hurricane Saloon and like to broke every bottle in the place."

"Well, what about these seven, then?" demanded Dick.

"That's the question," admitted Jerry, "what about 'em? It's Ammon Clark and his Angels that are on our trail now. They followed me . . . or rather Zack . . . clean from town."

"Why, you dad-blasted fool!" burst out Jack. "What you want to tangle up with them for?"

"Well . . . ," began Jerry, and then he glanced at Zachary. "We was drinking there together, and these Avenging Angels took after him, and . . . I didn't want to leave him to be killed. What's the matter with you, Jack? You afraid of Ammon Clark? Think that Mormon shirt of his will turn bullets?"

"Why didn't you bring that gin?" broke in Arthur impatiently.

"If this danged Chinaman quits, you've got to wash the dishes. Ain't that so, Dick and Jack? I'm tired of it."

"Me quittee, light now!" shrieked Sam in a passion. "Allee time you go to town, come back drunk. No blingee me nothin'. Allee time dlinkee, dlinkee."

"Hey, who are you talking to?" demanded Jerry arrogantly. Seizing the little Chinaman by the slack of his trousers, he gave him a swift run around the house. "Now," he said, "you cook me some breakfast. Hurry up, now. Don't talk back to me."

The old Chinaman stood trembling, his bleary eyes wild with rage, then with an animal-like cry he rushed back into the kitchen, and they could hear the stove covers rattle.

"That's the last time you go to town," declared Dick Wamsutter bitterly. "Now this long-tailed chink will quit."

"He can't quit," came back Jerry as the other brothers joined the chorus. "How the devil can he git to town? Raise his pay . . . we got plenty . . . but any time he says . . . 'Quit!' . . . Jerry Wamsutter is here to say . . . 'No!' "

"Aw, shut up," retorted Dick. "I'll handle that Chinaman. And the next time, by grab, I'll go to town myself. Git down, Zack, and come in to breakfast."

He spoke this as a mere aside, and in fact rather grudgingly, but Tarrant was too hungry to wait for a warmer welcome and he followed into the smoky cabin. This was kitchen and dining room and bunkhouse, all in one, and by the stove in the corner the recalcitrant Sam was sullenly preparing the breakfast.

Except for one window the cabin was unlighted, but in each of the four corners there was a pair of loopholes, and four heavy rifles on the racks. But what caught Tarrant's eye first was a long row of pickle bottles, set on a shelf high up on one wall. Every bottle was full of gold.

"Interested in mining?" inquired Dick politely, and, as he met his eye, Zachary saw the first gleam of mistrust.

"Well, yes," he said, "although I don't know much about it. But why do you leave all your gold in those bottles? Aren't you afraid that somebody will steal it?"

"Not a bit," declared Dick, who seemed to be the spokesman. "If they do, they're welcome, that's all. Any time any *hombre* thinks he can get away with our dust, there it is, right up on the shelf."

"Oh, I see," murmured Zachary, and said no more until the flapjacks and coffee were served. That he had fallen into the company of desperate men was something that could not be denied, but after Jerry, between mouthfuls, had told the story of their battle, the brothers seemed to regard him with more favor. Jack and Arthur in turn made some polite general remark, and, when the hasty meal was over, Dick beckoned to Jerry and they held a long conference outside.

"It's all right, boys," announced Dick as he strode back into the room. "Mister Tally here, or whatever his name is, ain't trying to jump our claim. He's jest hiding out from Ammon Clark. Had some trouble with Lot Drake . . . they kinder took him for a spy . . . and now of course they're trying to kill him."

"And, judging from the way he sets a horse," put in Jerry, "I reckon Zack's been in the Army."

"Oho!" exclaimed Jack, who so far had said the least, and now extended a friendly hand. "Glad to meet you, Zack," he said. "Any show of the soldiers coming down and taking this country?"

"Well, yes, gentlemen," answered Tarrant. "If I can get back with these papers, I believe you can look for them soon."

"We'll take care of you," promised Arthur, shaking hands in his turn, but Zachary still doubted his welcome.

"Thanks," he replied, "I don't need to trouble you further. Just put me on a trail that will take me out of the country."

"You stay right here," spoke up Jerry heartily, and Dick

beckoned Tarrant outside the door.

"Now, look here," he said, "don't git in such a hurry. Them Angels are watching the trails. You jest hole up with us until the excitement is over. You're welcome . . . as far as that goes, glad to have you for company . . . but we're having a little trouble ourselves. We have to be careful with strangers."

"Oh, that's all right," responded Zachary, but Dick had not finished his speech.

"We're looking for a fight here," he ended.

"Well, count me in, then," answered Tarrant, and Dick nodded approvingly. "It's this way," he explained, "them Mormons down at Hurricane are trying to jump our claim. That one-eyed constable, Crump, is the leader of the gang, but they ain't got the nerve to fight. What they're trying to do is to starve us out by cutting off our grub and whiskey. What we're trying to do is to hold down the diggings until the soldiers come into the country."

"They'll be here very soon," Zachary assured him.

"All right, then," exulted Dick, "all hell can't whip us now. But if it wasn't for the Navajos raiding through this country, they'd've jumped us long ago. You see, Brigham has given his orders to keep out all prospectors, because the first time they's a big gold strike, the miners will rush in and take the whole country away from him. I reckon that's one reason they were so rough on you . . . they don't want any prospectors in the country."

"No, they spotted me for a soldier," replied Tarrant. "And with them, that means a government spy."

"Well, that's your business," Dick answered bluffly. "I don't care whether you're a spy or not. But I started to tell you about these Hurricane Mormons, the cowardliest pack of whelps in the world. We slipped into this country while the Injuns was so bad that they'd drove the Mormons out. Came in from

Colorado and first thing the Mormons knew we'd located this ground, and this water. They came rushing in then and staked down below us, although Brigham had warned 'em not to mine. But after the excitement was all over they found out we owned the water, and of course there wasn't enough. Then what does Bill Crump do but come up here with his outfit and demand half the water as his right. To hell with him. Brigham Young himself couldn't git enough to wash out a shirt. So then they got ugly and we run 'em off the mesa, but the odds are against us, of course. We're jest holding on by the skin of our teeth until the soldiers come down and tame 'em."

"I understand"—Zachary nodded—"but won't it get you into trouble if I'm found here, hiding from the Avenging Angels?"

"Well, of course," admitted Dick, "it will. But out in this Western country we white men have got to stick together. We'll do our best by you, and, if you git out alive, maybe you can do something for us. But you'll never git away by yourself. All the passes are guarded. You can't make your way north, and over to the east the Navajos are on the warpath, killing Mormons and running off stock. That's what gave us the chance to slip into this country. A bunch of Mormons up north killed three sons of old Kuchene, the war chief of these western Navajos, while they were over in Utah trading. But the fourth son got away and swum the river at Ute Crossing and Kuchene picked him up. Been shot twice through the back and had laid down to die when this war party cut his trail. Well, sir, since then all the Mormons have been hunting their holes and trying to blame the killing on the Gentiles, but that boy of Kuchene's, he swears it was the Mormons, and the old man takes his word for it. So if you meet any Navvies, you tell 'em you're an American, if you don't want to lose your hair."

"They might not stop to ask me," suggested Tarrant.

"Yes they will," asserted Dick. "They're mighty particular not to git into trouble with the Americans. It was only fifteen years ago we rounded up the whole bunch and kept them at Fort Sumner four years. They won't kill an American, but Mormons are different. They've always taught the Injuns they're a different breed of cat and now they're taking the consequences. But say, you lay down and take a good sleep, and we'll look after your horse."

He led Zachary into the cabin and put him to bed in his own bunk, and, when he woke up, it was evening. The Chinaman had been placated by a couple of ounces of gold and was cooking a very good supper, and after a friendly meal Tarrant retired to his blankets and slept the clock around until daylight. Then, while the Wamsutters went up the gulch to feed gravel into their sluice-boxes, he remained out of sight in the cabin.

At noon they came back with half a pound of coarse gold that they had picked from the riffles before they quit, and that evening they brought down a buckskin sack of amalgam that yielded a pound or more in dust. Their mine was a bonanza, but every day they worked it, they did so at the risk of their lives. Yet the moment they left their claim, the Mormons would jump it and they would lose all the unmined gold.

For several days after Tarrant came, the Wamsutters took their rifles with them when they went up the gulch to work, but as no Avenging Angels appeared, they left the cumbersome weapons behind, carrying only their pistols and knives. With Zachary in the cabin they felt safe from any surprise, but one day, as he lay reading, Tarrant was brought to his feet by the smashing impact of a volley of bullets. For an instant he stood staring at the holes in the wall. Then, as he dropped to the ground, the Chinese cook dashed past him and went flying out the door.

"No killee me!" he screamed, holding his hands up as he ran.

From the ridge to the west there came a chorus of whooping

laughter while bullets smacked all around him. As for Zachary, he lay quiet, his rifle in his hand, until the Chinaman disappeared up the gulch. More than the others he had expected this, for he knew the malice of Lot Drake and remembered the threats of Ammon Clark. Yet he, too, was surprised, and, while the bullets were striking the cabin, he crouched down where he could look out the door.

The assaulting party of Mormons had taken shelter behind the ridge, as he could tell by their mocking yells, but, being alone in the cabin, he deemed it better to wait before he gave them any notice of his presence. A shot from one of the loopholes would only invite a hundred more, and meanwhile he was comparatively safe. The four rifles of the Wamsutters, still resting in the rack, comprised an arsenal in themselves, while they, being armed with only pistols, were out of the fight as far as long-range shooting was concerned. They could defend themselves in the gulch if they were attacked at close range, but to run back to the cabin would mean death.

Tarrant crept along from one corner to the other, scanning the open country through the loopholes, and then in a volley the rifles opened up again. He dropped down against the wall. But this time the bullets were going over the cabin, being directed at the mouth of the gulch.

Zachary watched the spot and presently he saw Jerry as he rose up and ran from rock to rock. But the bullets came too thick, and after a long wait he leaped up and darted back. There was a yell of derision from the ridge above, and the next minute Tarrant heard horses, plunging and sliding over the rocks as the Mormons charged down to take the house. The time had come at last for him to make his presence known. He rose up and peered through a porthole.

Down the trail from the divide a band of Mormons were riding, waving their rifles hilariously in the air, and in the lead of them all was—not Ammon Clark the Avenging Angel, but Bill Crump, the one-eyed constable. Zachary thrust out his rifle and drew a hasty bead. At his shot, man and horse went down. He jacked up another cartridge and fired at the following man, who went off of his horse into the rocks. Before Tarrant could shoot again, the whole band of Mormons was spurring back up the ridge.

They hung low over their horses, too panic-stricken to look back. While Zachary was sending bullets to hasten their flight, Crump rose up and followed on foot. His right arm was dangling loosely, flapping about as he scampered up the trail, but he ran as if the devil were after him. Meanwhile the other man had abandoned his horse and slinked away up the hill. In one magazine of shots the Mormons had been routed and the Wamsutters came rushing from the gulch.

"Gimme my rifle!" cursed Jerry, and, snatching it down off the hook, he went plunging up the hillside after his enemies. Jack and Dick and Arthur followed, but they soon came running back and went pelting down the gulch to get their horses.

"You stay here!" directed Jerry as he went by the cabin, leaving Tarrant to guard their treasure as they spurred away up the trail. But shortly before dark they came back down the ridge, spurring as savagely as when they had left.

"Git for cover!" panted Dick as he snatched for the bottles of gold. "We ran into Ammon Clark!"

Chapter Twelve

There was a scrambling for cartridges and provisions and gold as the Wamsutters swarmed into the cabin. Then, dragging their horses behind them, they hurried up the gulch where they took shelter in the pit they had sluiced out. In this ready-made fort they were safe for the time being. When darkness came on, they ran back and forth like ants until the cabin was emptied of its supplies.

The volley of bullets from the ridge had pierced its walls through and through, thus demonstrating the weakness of their defense. Up the gulch they were assured of a good supply of water as well as shelter for their stock. Zachary did his part by making breastworks out of sandbags, after which they waited for the dawn.

The Wamsutters had pursued the claim-jumpers to the edge of the desert where the trail led down off the ridge, and, except for an accident, they would soon have caught Crump who was riding double, having lost his own horse. But as they spurred down the red hill, they met Ammon Clark himself, riding back into the desert with his Avenging Angels. The bullets had come thick and fast as both sides took to cover, but the fear of losing their horses soon induced the Wamsutters to retire, and their retreat had been the signal for pursuit. Even the cowardly jumpers who had been fleeing for their lives had turned back and joined the chase, and only by hard riding and making a stand at every pass had the brothers made good their escape. But now, back at their diggings and with Tarrant's breastworks for defense, they waited confidently for the Mormon assault.

"We're all right," declared Jerry, as the false dawn tinged the east, "them Mormons are jest like dogs. If you run, they'll run after you, but if you stop and make a stand, they'll turn around and git for the house. They ain't a man in sight, and won't be."

"But let's lay low, all the same," argued Dick. "Maybe they'll ride down to the cabin if we hide. Lay low and say nothing until we git 'em in the open. . . ."

"And then try out them Mormon shirts," put in Jack.

"Yes," spoke up Arthur, who was the best shot of the family. "I've always wondered if them robes would turn lead."

They smiled grimly at the jest and in a matter-of-fact way began getting a makeshift breakfast, but Tarrant knew that the chances for their escape were very slim, for the Mormons would swarm to the fray. For them it was not merely the wiping out of five Gentiles. There would be loot—bottles of gold—and, for the first man who reached the ground, the possession of a very rich claim. Even the gold already mined was worth thousands of dollars—and the Mormons had seen the bottles of nuggets. It was the dare that the bold brothers had hung up before Bill Crump and all the rest of his gang, and this battle that was to come—for them, at least—would be a fight for the gold.

But in this broad pit, where in stripping the bedrock the Wamsutters had broken down the banks, there was food enough to last several weeks. There was water in the sluiceway, and, if it came to a flight, five horses ready to ride. Nor were they overawed by the terrible name of the Avenging Angels, since most of their killings were from ambush. They did not, as a rule, come out into the open and give their victims a chance to fight back. Their resort was to treachery under cover of the night or pursuit across the desert wastes. But before they conquered the Wamsutters and Zachary Tarrant, more than one robed Mormon would bite the dust. Like the shirts of the Indian ghost dancers, their robes might make their hearts brave, but they would not give them immunity from bullets.

As he sat behind his sandbags looking out through a neat loophole at the cabin and the barren ridge behind, Zachary had a sudden sense of the unreality of it all, a disbelief in death. Something told him as surely as if he actually heard it that he would live to escape from this place, yet what could intervene to save him from the Mormons was more than he could surmise. Certainly not from five men, no matter how valiant, would the Avenging Angels take flight, but, while he watched for the lurking forms that he knew were there somewhere, he smiled at the ways of fate. For making love to Tamar, for being the Mormons' friend, he had been dismissed in disgrace from the Army, and now, as he watched and waited, his thoughts were not of Tamar but of another woman—Deseret. He loved her in a different way than he had loved the passionate Tamar, with her eyes that had said "Yea" and "Nay". Deseret's eyes were honest; they held no allure but the mirror of her own gentle soul. They told of no conquests, no well-concealed amours, but of maidenly purity and a longing to escape from the curse of a plural marriage. They were steady, quiet eyes, and, if Lot Drake forced a marriage, she would kill him herself without waiting for any lover's tardy hand. But while she watched for his coming, even now while he was beleaguered, her fate might be upon her at last.

He was roused from his meditations by the sharp voice of Jerry, calling angrily to the Chinaman to come back, and, as Tarrant looked around, he saw the half-crazed cook scuttling frantically off down the gulch.

"Let 'im go," said Dick. "He's left his money down there somewhere and all hell won't stop him now."

Ever since daylight when, belatedly, Sam had discovered his

loss, he had sat crouched against the bank, rocking to and fro and muttering to himself. Now, out of his head with fear for the safety of his savings, he was running down to dig up his gold. Their eyes followed him curiously as he scampered across the flat and entered the open door. As Tarrant was scanning the hillside, Jerry nudged him in the ribs and pointed to the sand wash below the house. A black hat had bobbed up from the cover of the cutbank, but Jerry held up his finger to wait.

Every gun was trained on him as the skulking Mormon looked again, then crept forward to cut off his prey. Glancing up at the hillside, Tarrant caught a sudden movement where other forms crept down from rock to rock. The Mormons had been concealed, watching the apparently deserted cabin, and the Chinaman had made them break cover. Seeing him run back alone, they had taken it for granted that the white men had long since fled. Heads popped up here and there, only to dodge down instantly as their owners writhed nearer the house, but the defenders of the fort had eyes for only one, the man who was crawling up the wash.

Like most of Clark's Angels, he wore a black hat, which now revealed every movement that he made, but so intent was this hunter on the game he was stalking that for the moment he forgot everything else. Near the corner of the cabin he rose to a crouch. As Sam came out, he charged. One terrified shriek told that the Chinaman had seen him and the Bowie knife he held in his hand, and then every rifle was trained on the Mormon who was gaining ground at every jump.

"Let me have him," insisted Arthur, and the others held their fire until his .45 roared out like a cannon. The Mormon stopped short and went over backward, bored through and through by the bullet, and suddenly every head on the hillside ducked down. All was silent save the gibbering of the cook. He came running like the wind, his sloppy slippers long since lost and his queue trailing out behind, but not a man in the fort looked back. They had seen the peering heads and now, in their absence, the ridge seemed peopled with enemies. But out on the flat the Mormon lay motionlessly, with a red spot forming on his breast.

"What'd I tell ye?" Jerry chuckled. "Them robes are no good." And the rest of the boys nodded grimly.

The day wore on to noon and no more heads appeared. Finally, up on the divide, they saw a group of horsemen gathering about a man who had just ridden in.

"Some feller from town," grunted Dick. "I wonder what he thinks of that?"

He jerked his thumb toward the body of the Mormon, laid low by a single shot, and after a long wait the crowd of Mormons opened up and a lone man rode down toward them. Above his head on a stick he bore a white flag and Jerry whooped derisively.

"Look at that, now!" he jeered. "Don't that remind you of the Mountain Meadows Massacre? When these Mormons git licked, they always try a flag of truce, but here's one *hombre* that don't show a head."

"No, nor me, either!" answered Dick, feeling the same. But Zachary had recognized the horse—it was the same gaunt piebald that Jake Lingo had ridden when he had taken him in to the bishop.

"I know that man," he said. "You boys watch the rocks and I'll go and see what he wants."

"You'll do nothing of the kind," answered Jerry peremptorily. "What do you think you want to do . . . git killed? Never trust a damned Mormon. It's part of their religion to send all us Gentiles to hell."

"But this man is a missionary . . . Jake Lingo."

"I don't care who he is. If you step out into the open, some

Mormon will pot you for a certainty. Let him come down here with his flag."

"Well, all right," agreed Tarrant.

Lingo, after waiting, finally rode up to the mouth of the gulch. "Is Lieutenant Tarrant up there?" he shouted.

"Tell 'im no," directed Jerry, but before they could stop him the lieutenant had answered for himself.

"I've got a message for you here!" called Lingo eagerly. "Don't shoot, boys . . . this is all a mistake."

"I guess it is," blared back Jerry, "as far as you folks are concerned. What the hell are you fishing for now?"

"Zack's wanted in Moroni," explained Lingo. "Here's a safe conduct from Brigham Young."

"Keep away from that feller," advised Jerry, turning to Tarrant. "You're a danged sight safer with us."

"I reckon you're right," agreed Zachary, and settled down beside him while Lingo waved his paper and shouted.

"Let 'im holler." Jerry grinned. "Any man that'll trust a Mormon is a dog-goned fool, that's all. And what's a safe conduct from Brigham Young worth? He's the worst damned killer in the bunch. You'd better go back home. We don't want nothing to do with you."

"I want to see Tarrant," insisted Lingo. "This is a matter of life or death."

"He ain't here," lied Jerry. "Now you git, you Mormon-faced whelp."

"Yes he is," cried Lingo in his high excited voice, "and I won't budge an inch till I see him!"

"Oh, let him come in," Tarrant said at last. "I can meet him down behind those rocks."

"Well, suit yourself," grumbled Jerry in disgust. "Ain't you all right, here with us?"

"Sure," agreed Tarrant, "but Jake is all right, too. Let's see what he's got to say."

"He's a Mormon," pronounced Jerry, "and that settles it with me. Now he'll soft-soap ye, mark my word."

Zachary crept down the gulch, keeping cover as he went, and, when at last Lingo saw him, he jumped down off his horse and came running with outstretched hands.

"Thank God," he cried, "you ain't dead, air ye! Brigham sent me out here himself."

"Why this sudden solicitude?" inquired Tarrant sarcastically. "Perhaps he's looking for another chance to kill me?"

"No, no," insisted Lingo, "that was all a mistake. You didn't need to leave town at all."

"And I suppose," went on Zachary, "I didn't need to hide when Ammon Clark and his Avenging Angels came after me?"

"No, indeed," replied the Mormon, "they weren't after you at all. I've been trying to find you everywhere."

"Well, here I am," answered Tarrant shortly. "Now what is this message from Brigham?"

"You must come back to Moroni at once."

"Thanks." Zachary smiled. "They didn't treat me so well there that I'm in any great hurry to go back."

"That was different," argued Lingo. "We thought you were a government spy."

"Well, what do you think I am now?"

"Why, a lieutenant in the Army, of course."

"Correct." Tarrant nodded. "But I might as well inform you that I'm not going back to Moroni. There are too many Avenging Angels in the hills. A safe conduct from Brigham Young doesn't appeal to me at all. I'm safer right where I am."

"Yes, but, Zack," pleaded Lingo, "you've got to come back. There are five troops of cavalry camped right by the temple, and the colonel sent word to Drake that, if a hair of your head was touched, he'd . . . he'd lay our beautiful temple flat."

"What colonel?" snapped out Zachary, bewildered.

"Your own colonel . . . Colonel Valentine. He's occupied Moroni and driven half the Mormons from their homes. Or at least, they've fled, and Bishop Drake along with the rest. The marshals are trying to arrest him."

"How do I know all this is true?" demanded Tarrant suspiciously, although his eyes were beginning to shine. "Have you got any word from the colonel?"

"Why, yes," answered Lingo, beginning to grope through his pockets, "but this letter from Brigham is enough."

"Not for me," returned Zachary. "I believe he's perfectly capable of ordering his Avenging Angels to kill me."

"Oh, no," expostulated the Mormon, "you mustn't misjudge him on account of this little mistake. He telegraphed Bishop Drake under no circumstances to interfere with you, but when his message came you had gone."

"And when was it," inquired Tarrant, suddenly beginning to see light, "that the colonel sent his message, threatening to raze your beautiful temple?"

"Right before that," confessed Lingo, finally producing the colonel's note, and Zachary smiled as he read it.

"All right," he said, "I'll go with you, Mister Lingo. If the colonel is there, I'm the safest man in Utah . . . because he'll do what he says, every time."

CHAPTER THIRTEEN

The sun was just setting, touching the temple with a golden light when Tarrant rode back into Moroni. As he headed for the vacant block where the 3rd Dragoons were camped, he heard the trumpeters sounding "Retreat". Then the roar of a mountain howitzer woke the echoes of the cliffs, and the flag came fluttering to the ground. Never before had the American flag been saluted in Mormon Moroni, but now the times had changed. Long picket lines of horses stood before long rows of tents and five hundred men, armed and equipped for war, were camped by the temple grounds. A new era had begun in this last stronghold of Mormonism—the Army had occupied Zion.

When in 1847 the Mormon pioneers had crossed the Rockies and beheld the Promised Land, it was only a neglected province of old Mexico. Driven out from Ohio and Missouri and Illinois, they had turned their faces westward in a last, desperate attempt to escape the persecutions of the Gentiles. The memory of many a bloody deed still rankled in their hearts, and, before they left Nauvoo, they had taken an oath in the temple to avenge their wrongs on the nation. Divinely led, as they believed, to this refuge in the desert, they had founded the Mormon State of Deseret, and, except for an accident, they might have built up an empire. That accident was the discovery of gold. Two years after Brigham Young drove his stake for the temple the first rush of the gold seekers arrived, and the embittered Saints now discovered that Mexico had ceded Utah to the United

States as a result of the Mexican War. After all their attempts to escape what they called tyranny, they were back beneath the Stars and Stripes. But if the flag waved over them, it did not rule their hearts or gain more than the formality of submission. The men who had taken that oath would never be citizens of any state but Deseret.

Wave after wave of gold-mad 'Forty-Niners came to Salt Lake and passed on west, and, after levying a tariff on all sales and purchases made by Gentiles, the Mormons made the most of the situation. If the gods had decreed that their empire in the wilderness should be invaded by this horde of miners, it gave them an opportunity to sack the Philistines, to trade horses for goods from the States. Old horses for young, pack animals for heavy wagons, hay and vegetables for furniture and supplies— never before was there such trading, such giving of much for little in order to reach the land of gold. A blooded horse with a sore shoulder was exchanged for a dish-faced mustang that was able to carry a man. Jersey cows, sore-footed from their journey over the rocks, were bartered for what they would bring. And when Brigham found the gold seekers winter-bound, he levied a tariff on all they possessed. He had cause to hate these men, for many came from Missouri where the Saints had suffered their martyrdom, and all were from a nation that he loathed and despised and had taken an oath never to acknowledge. But where many passed through, some stopped from time to time and tarried in the fertile valley of Salt Lake. The railroad came pushing west, bringing a horde of construction men who didn't fear man, devil, or Danite, and sullenly the Gentile-haters moved southward. There the Western rush passed them by, but only for a while, and then the Southern Trail was opened up.

Turned aside by the snow that blocked the northern passes and held them winter-bound at Salt Lake, the restless Western emigrants broke a road to the south and crossed the Mojave

Desert to Los Angeles. Even the Mountain Meadows Massacre had not stayed the huge wagon trains in their search for the Land of Gold and, more sullenly still, the Gentile-hating Mormons retired to the desert itself. Cutting a road over the Black Mesa, they settled at last on the Río Virgen, and, as trouble with the Americans made northern Utah too hot for them, the worst of the Mormons joined them. So Moroni had waxed and grown, a community to itself, owning allegiance to no man but Brigham Young, no nation but the State of Deseret. They had planted vines and fig trees and reared a mighty temple in which to worship the God of Israel, but after twenty years of quiet a ghost had risen to plague them—the ghost of the Mountain Meadows Massacre.

Deny it as they would, the story rose up to haunt them, and in many a Mormon home there was a fear never stilled—the fear of a belated retribution. They had done the deed at the orders of their church, perhaps of Brigham Young himself, but would the church uphold them if they were brought to trial, or would it offer them up as a sacrifice? For twenty years they had asked the question, still fighting down their fears while they intimidated any weaklings that seemed to waver, and now with the soldiers encamped by their temple the old fear rose again. As Tarrant rode down the street with the dejected-looking Lingo, they gazed after him, the question still in their eyes.

All the way across the desert the apostle to the Lamanites had been sunk in gloomy thought. As they approached the soldiers' camp, he reined in his horse and broke the silence of hours.

"Do you reckon they'll arrest me?" he quavered.

"What for?" demanded Tarrant in surprise.

"Well . . . for being a Mormon, say."

"That's no crime," responded Zachary bluffly. "That is, unless. . . . Say, what do you know about this Mountain Meadows Massacre?"

"Nothing. Nothing at all," answered Lingo hastily. "I was out of the country at that time."

"And you never took part in any of these killings, did you? Then I don't see why you should be worried."

"I'm a missionary," protested Lingo with a fanatical gleam in his eyes, "sent forth for the conversion of the Lamanites. The Lord's work comes first in all my goings and comings, but this colonel has set his heart against us. He has brought men and cannons to destroy our beautiful temple unless we offer some Saint as a sacrifice. We are innocent of this crime. It was committed by the Indians because the emigrants had poisoned their spring. They gave them a poisoned ox, which killed four of the Pahvants and made all the rest of them sick. But the Mormons did nothing. Brigham warned us against it, because he knew we had suffered much. These people were from Missouri, where the Saints were martyred and killed, and they boasted they had helped kill Joseph Smith. They said they were just waiting for Johnston's army to reach Salt Lake and then they were coming back to hang Brigham Young and steal all our wives to boot. They deserved to be killed, but we spared them. Those were our orders from Brigham Young."

"Yes, but what about Lot Drake?" inquired Zachary, and Lingo eyed him searchingly.

"He's as innocent as I am," he declared.

"Is that so?" observed Tarrant. "Well, have it your own way. Shall I report to the colonel by myself?"

"Whatever the Lord wills, I will do," responded Lingo, "and Brigham ordered me to deliver you in person. Our Prophet suffered death for the building of the kingdom and I will not turn back from this. But your colonel hates our people, Mister Tarrant."

"He hates a liar," answered Zachary shortly, and fell in behind his guide.

It was one thing for the dour missionary to defend his own people—and himself, if he was innocent of the crime, but when he defended Lot Drake, he proved himself a liar and merited the colonel's honest resentment. Tarrant was carrying to this same colonel in the lining of his shirt a paper that would prove the bishop's guilt. Deseret had seen her own mother killed by this man that Lingo dared to defend. What a damnable religion it was, making liars and sycophants and murderers out of men still in the image of God. He shook his head angrily and only the challenge of the sentry brought him back to the business at hand.

"Corporal of the guard!" called the sentry, after Lingo had given his name, and Tarrant drew his hat over his eyes. He was no longer the smart lieutenant, returning his men's salutes as he strode up the company street, but, as he stood there in the darkness, the old love of the Army came over him and he envied even the private on guard. He was a soldier, yet not a soldier, a man consenting to disgrace for the good of his country, a sinner, serving out his just penance. But when he had paid the price for his dalliance with Tamar Young, he would again don the Army blue. At the door of his colonel he stood now like a suppliant, ignored by the scornful sentry, but, as the adjutant ushered him in, the colonel came bounding out and clasped both hands in his.

"My God, boy," he said, "we thought you were dead." And then he spoke roughly to the guard. "Take this man out of camp!" he ordered, pointing to Lingo. "He's a Mormon . . . disloyal to the government. They're all disloyal, all traitors at heart." He dragged the lieutenant inside. "Well, Tarrant," he said, looking him fondly in the eye, "I never hoped to see you again. Were you surprised to hear that the old Third was here?

We started south on the day of your arrest. But before I left, I sent this bishop a message . . . and I meant every word of it, too. I've been reprimanded more than once for my outspoken methods, but what these Mormons need is the truth. They are in the United States and amenable to our laws, and any man who stands up against our government should be dealt with as a traitor. I promised Bishop Drake that I would lay his temple flat if a hair of your head was touched."

"Your message may have saved my life," answered Tarrant, "but it came a little late, even then. After the captain of the Avenging Angels had made an official call, picking his teeth with the point of a Bowie knife, I decided I'd better leave town."

"And were you driven, as this Mormon says, across the line into Arizona to seek protection among those outlaws and cutthroats? By heaven, you must have been desperate."

"I met four of the bravest men that the West has ever produced," answered Zachary with a gleam of pride. "The Wamsutter boys, over on Rustler Mountain, and I want a guard sent to their mine. They took me in when it meant a fight with all the Mormons in Utah. But as old Dick said . . . 'In this Western country we white men have got to stand together.' "

"These men are miners, then?" commented the colonel admiringly, after Tarrant had finished his story. "Of all the men in the West the prospectors are the bravest . . . they'll go anywhere, endure anything for gold. Perhaps it's sordid but to me it seems great. It's not the gold, it's the getting it, the game. We'll send them a strong guard at once."

"Not that they need it," assured Tarrant. "They can whip all the Avenging Angels in the world, but it will give these Mormons a lesson."

"Yes, a lesson they dearly need!" exclaimed the colonel vehemently. "But before I get through, they will know we have a government, and that it is prepared to protect its citizens. No matter who he is or what his antecedents, every American citizen passing peaceably through this country is entitled to protection from these Mormons. And when a lieutenant in the Army is marked for death as a spy, it is time the United States interfered. Have you any information to report?"

"I have a paper here," answered Zachary, and laid Porter's bloodstained letter on the table in front of his chief.

"The very thing. This is conclusive," pronounced the colonel as he ran his eyes over the tattered document. "But that reminds me . . . do you know Drake by sight? You do? Then you're the man we want. When we occupied the town, Bishop Drake made his escape, and so disloyal is the populace that we can't find a single man to accompany the marshal's posse. Not a man, you understand, right here in the United States, who will identify this traitor to our government. Why, of all the Mormons we've questioned, not one would even admit that he knew such a man as Lot Drake. We've been tied up from the start, because the United States marshal had no way of identifying his prisoner."

"I'll never forget Lot Drake," replied Tarrant, smiling ruefully, "but I'm afraid he'll be a hard man to catch. When does the posse wish to start?"

"Right now," said Colonel Valentine. "They want to visit his numerous homes and surround them under cover of darkness. It seems he has nineteen wives in different parts of the country. But, Lieutenant, we must get that man. The success of this whole venture depends on one thing . . . whether we can capture this renegade and punish him."

"Give me something to eat and I'll go," agreed Zachary, and once more the colonel took him by the hand.

"Lieutenant Tarrant," he said, "you have merited my confidence. I shall report your success to Washington."

CHAPTER FOURTEEN

Not until he took the trail with the United States marshal's posse did Tarrant realize the coherence of the Mormons. They were one people, set and united to resist the invaders and to protect their fighting bishop, Lot Drake. At the first mountain village where the posse began its search an unforeseen difficulty arose. No one would show them where the bishop's wives lived or admit that his home was in their town, and it was only by questioning the children, too young to have learned guile, that his house was at last located and searched.

Bishop Drake was not at home and his two tight-lipped wives disclaimed all knowledge of his whereabouts. He had fled—that was all they knew. Town after town where Drake had established a home was visited and his dwellings searched. They were easily discovered, now that the marshal had the key—Drake's houses were the best in each town. They were even built on the same plan—large, two-story stone houses, well-made and well-maintained, and always with a horde of children. By his own confession Drake was the father of sixty-four, each of whom would help to exalt him in the celestial kingdom to come. It was only after he had visited one family after the other that Zachary sensed the shuddering abhorrence of Deseret. To be married to Lot Drake was merely to become a brood animal, the mother of more children—for his kingdom.

The posse had worked north into the small mountain towns that lined the great highway to Salt Lake and a week of bootless search had convinced everyone except the marshal that Lot Drake would never be found. Every movement they made was reported to the authorities until at last in desperation the marshal quit the roads and took to the mountain trails, yet how he hoped to capture his man was a mystery to Zachary Tarrant. Drake had had full warning, he had been absent two weeks, and, if rumor was true, he had more wives and families, hidden away in the desert of Arizona. The Paiutes and Navajos had known his power for a generation, while he was acting as Indian farmer in Utah, and neither bribes nor threats would induce the lowliest Indian to indicate where he might be found. Yet the marshal pushed doggedly north, never far from the great highway, and one day, as they rounded a corner, the posse spied a long procession. First a squad of armed men came riding around the point and behind them a row of carriages, each drawn by four horses and followed by baggage wagons in the rear.

"It's Brigham," stated the marshal, as the first carriage drew near. "What the devil is he doing down here?"

In a big open landau, gleaming with paint and polished metal, the president of the church and revelator of the Lord's will sat in state with his favorite wife. A guard of eight men, the pick of his fighting Angels, rode beside him to defend him from attack. As the big posse of the marshal suddenly appeared down the road, they drew their repeating rifles and spurred close. But, though he bore them no good will, it was not the purpose of the United States marshal to molest this long procession of church dignitaries, and, reining off to one side, he gave them the road at which Brigham waved his Avenging Angels aside.

They passed then, face-to-face—prophet, apostle, and bishop and the hard-eyed officers of the law, women in dainty silks with tiny parasols above their heads, and unshorn posse deputies in buckskin. Each eyed the other curiously, the deputies

looking for their fugitive, the churchmen scanning the faces of their enemies. As the third carriage passed, Tarrant suddenly found himself gazing into the eyes of Tamar Young. She was riding with Hyrum Paine, the young secretary of her father who Zachary now knew to be her husband, yet, when she saw him, she rose up and smiled. He looked back, astounded, unable to understand why she should suddenly be waving her hand, but strange as it seemed she was beckoning him to her and he could only shake his head.

Had she forgotten the occasion that had resulted in his being there, a humble deputy in this marshal's posse? Had she forgotten that he had lost his commission in the Army because of her Circe-like wiles? Perhaps she did not know that he had discovered her deceit, that he had gazed with his own eyes on a copy of the record that had sealed her as Hyrum Paine's third wife. It was a marriage against the federal law, then being strongly enforced, which forbade the practice of polygamy, but to him it was more than that, it was a denial of the love for which he had sacrificed everything. For her sake, and the spell that her love had cast over him, he had forgotten the first duty of a soldier—just for one more dance with her, and that night as a final punishment Colonel Valentine had shown him the record of her marriage. Yet now she still smiled and waved her handkerchief.

The rest of the procession became a blur before his eyes. Love, anger, and regret all strove at once to master his surging heart. Then, as he rode on, one of the Avenging Angels galloped after him and handed him a hasty note.

I must see you on a matter of great importance. Will you call on me as soon as possible—at Moroni?

He crumpled it in his fist and straightened up stiffly. "Convey my regrets to Miss Young," he said, "and tell her I shall be unable to see her."

Then he waved the man away, scowling hatefully into his eyes, and on his lips there was a muttered curse. Not for Tamar—although she had flouted him and given him a wound slow to heal—but for the whole Mormon church, which could countenance such things, and her father, who himself was the church. He married and gave in marriage, he sent men on lonely missions or banished them to the ends of the world, and, when it suited his purpose, to pay for some knavery, he gave his own daughter into polygamy. He it was, and men like him who made the church what it was—a curse on all that fair land, but the time would soon come when even the church must stand and answer, for the Army had brought the law. They must answer for their sins before the bar of judgment—and Brigham Young with the rest.

As the posse moved on, still pursuing their hopeless quest, a sudden dissatisfaction came over Tarrant and he brought his horse to a stop. Of what use was all this force of deputy marshals—would they ever come up with Lot Drake? And if not, if their search would never succeed, why travel along in their wake? He reined out of the road, following some impulse newly born to cut loose and work by himself. The rest of the deputies were only time servers, content to ride and draw their pay, but he had more at stake, more to love and more to hate, and every hour that passed was precious. He had gone through Moroni like a thief in the night without even a glimpse of Deseret, and now, seeing Tamar, old memories were roused up, though his love for her was dead. He remembered the anguished longing that had haunted him against his will as he rode resolutely out from Salt Lake, and then the long days when, twisting and turning like a fugitive, he had made his way to Moroni. All had been like a hideous dream and life itself had meant nothing to him, until at last he awoke from his madness in the presence of Deseret.

Then another dream had come, a dream so sweet and different that the other seemed never to have been, and through one mad day and night he had moved in an exaltation with Deseret by his side. Then once more he had fled to the desert, to escape the murderous Avenging Angels until, at last, he had returned, only to be seized in the great whirligig and snatched from her presence again. And now, when he was free to return if he would, Tamar Young had gone before him. How could he explain, if Tamar saw them together? What could he say to Deseret? All the world seemed out of joint—stark mad.

It was evening when Tarrant rode back to the road, still pondering on which way to go, and, as he paused and looked both ways, he saw another procession, slowly wending its way from the north. In the lead rode a man in a cheap, homespun suit, and behind him at some distance there came a long train of wagons, loaded high with household goods. Women and children walked beside them, a herd of milk cows trailed behind, and farther to the rear the patiently plodding ox teams seemed hardly to move at all. It was an emigrant train of Mormons, being sent forth to some colony, and, as Zachary sat watching them, the leader approached and gave him a friendly greeting. He was a sturdy, bearded man, well-mounted and armed, and despite a certain grimness his face had a kindly look and Tarrant responded with a smile.

"Which way are you traveling?" he asked.

"To Moroni," answered the Mormon, stopping his horse and looking back, "and then to the Little Colorado."

"You'll have a rough trip," predicted Zachary.

The wagon master nodded his head. "Know anything about the country?" he asked.

"Not much," responded Tarrant, "except what Jake Lingo

told me. We were out by Rustler Mountain last week."

"Is that so?" exclaimed the Mormon, suddenly looking at him again. "I thought I'd seen you somewhere. My name is Moses Stout, from Provo."

He held out his hand, and Zachary shook it warmly, though with a certain feeling of deceit. He could see that this honest Saint had mistaken him for a Mormon and instantly he assumed his old part.

"I'm Zack Grey," he said, "out looking for some horses." He rode along beside him.

"I'm sure glad I met you, Brother Zack. What does Brother Jacob think of this trouble with old Kuchene?"

"It looks bad," replied Tarrant, "but you know Brother Jacob . . . he won't hear a word against the Lamanites."

"No, he won't," agreed Stout. "He has been called by the Lord to carry His word to these people. But what do you think about the matter?"

"Well"—Zachary shrugged—"I'm afraid you'll have trouble. Everybody tells me that the Indians are on the rampage, running off ponies and cattle by the thousand, and, if they come clear into Utah to get their revenge, what chance have you got in their country?"

"Mighty little," grumbled Stout, "but don't tell these people. They've been called for this mission, but their hearts are not in it. I'm afraid they don't respect the Lord's will. This is the third time our people have tried to settle in Arizona, but the hand of the Lord has smitten us. The first mission turned back after they had crossed the Colorado, and all the good land that they might have had has been taken up by Gentiles. The second wagon train went through and took up land along the river, but the Little Colorado is subject to floods, and their houses and fields were swept away. The next year they moved and got washed out again, but President Young has set his heart on colonizing that country, and we are the first to be called. I have sold all my land and everything I own and my wife and family are behind. Brother Zack, I'd feel better if I could leave them here in Utah. I don't like this Indian war. But it's the will of the Lord, and Brigham has given strict orders on no account to weaken and turn back. We are the first of many who will follow in our wagon tracks, and it's all to build up the kingdom."

He sighed and shook his head, then after a long silence he inquired about Brother Jacob. "There's only two men," he said, "that can pacify those Indians . . . Jake Lingo and Bishop Drake. Brother Lot is out there now, building a dug way down to the ferry, but I'd feel a lot better if Jake was in his place, because he knows the hearts of these Lamanites. Bishop Drake is wonderful when it comes to handling men, and building these ferry boats and such, but he don't love these Indians and live with them like Jake . . . and that's what counts, every time."

"Yes." Tarrant nodded and his narrowed eyes gleamed, for at last he had located his enemy. He was hiding at Mormon Ferry, a hundred miles from the posse that was following so stubbornly on his trail. Zachary bade his friend good bye, carefully remembering to call him Brother Moses, and turned off on some horse tracks that he found. Then, keeping to the trails that criss-crossed the country, he rode like the wind for Moroni.

CHAPTER FIFTEEN

If "Brother Zack" had been a Mormon, believing fully in signs and omens and the promptings of some monitor within him, he would have assigned the stroke of luck that had led him to talk with Stout to a secret admonition from the Lord. But his Lord and theirs were two different beings, for the God of the Saints was a man like themselves in everything but his transcendent power. He was a God who dwelt among them in one form or another, eating and drinking and living like men, and their tabernacles were full of stories of the Apostles Peter, James and John and their appearance in some humble abode. To some, Brigham Young himself was the Godhead—God Almighty in the form of a man. They were a people far removed from practical life, a people whose whole lives were molded by revelation, a people who lived by faith. They had given up their wills, for to believe absolutely is to cease thinking, and for thirty years they had placed their lives in the control of Brigham Young and the priesthood. To pay their tithings and obey the bishop was the sum total of their duty, and even the blood atonement, the killing of apostates to save their souls, was accepted as the will of the Lord. The massacre at Mountain Meadows had given their faith its supreme test, but, when the priests had ordered the massacre, the people had responded, doing their bidding like men in a dream. But now, after twenty years, the power of the church had been challenged and the country was in a state of war.

Riding by cow trails through the hills, avoiding houses and skirting highways, Zachary spurred on toward the south, until at last, just at dawn, he found safety in the colonel's tent. He had learned his lesson well. Although the Avenging Angels were watching the roads, no one knew he had returned to Moroni. His eyes drooped with sleep as he reported to Colonel Valentine the secret of Lot Drake's hiding place. Then, his duty done, he fell asleep in an Army tent with the colonel's commendations in his ears. But when the evening gun finally roused him, his thoughts went back to Deseret.

Darkness was falling and no one noticed him as he strode down the road toward the hotel, for a change had come over Moroni. The streets were hung with banners, flags and bunting were everywhere, and in the churchyard near the temple a huge bowery had been built to shelter the visiting crowds. Brigham Young had come to town while Tarrant was sleeping and the whole countryside had swarmed in to greet him. But though he saw the flags, and the banners of welcome, Zachary's mind was on Deseret. Was she still there in the old hotel, and would she know him in the crowd? And would her eyes light up at the sight of her lover, or would they be downcast and sad? A month had gone by since she had kissed him in the churchyard and told him her fear of Lot Drake—would she be the same smiling Deseret?

He entered the dining room unnoticed and, after a quick glance about, took a table in one corner of the room. Deseret was nowhere in sight. Flushed women hurried to and fro, serving a gay party behind a curtain that had been hung across one end of the room, but the main dining room was almost vacant except for some countrymen who sat waiting, impatient to be served.

The great crowd had come and gone, leaving the tables a waste of dishes for the young Mayberry children to carry out.

Zachary brushed back his hair, stroking the week's growth of beard that made him no less rough than the rest. Sister Rachel, Mayberry's first wife, who had glared at him before, now went by without a glance. The party behind the curtain seemed to demand all their attention—but where was Deseret?

As he watched the kitchen door, hoping to see her dainty form, a sudden fear like a faintness swept over him. Had Lot Drake carried her away? Had he taken her by force, knowing he could never win her heart, and borne her away across the desert? He sank back in his chair, his brain reeling at the thought, when suddenly she appeared before him. In one hand she bore a pitcher, filled bumper-high with Dixie wine, but her errand for the moment was forgotten.

"Why, Zachary," she breathed, speaking low and tremulously, and a wineglass smashed on the floor. He rose up, trembling, and, as he smiled into her eyes, all the world might know he was her lover.

"I . . . I thought you were dead," she stammered, and then the curtains down the room were parted. For an instant Zachary saw a woman's face peering out, attracted by the crash of glass. Then, as Deseret blushed and remembered her duties, the curtains dropped back into place. Deseret hurried on, the tray of glasses all a-tremble as she carried in the wine to their guests, and, when she came out, Zachary avoided her eye, for the curtains had been parted again. Some inquisitive woman, half-concealed behind their folds, was watching him with hazel-gray eyes. As he returned her stare, he recognized with a start the pouting countenance of Tamar Young. Then the curtain dropped back.

When the party broke up, she brushed past him without a glance. Behind her, with his round face and staring, bespectacled eyes, came Hyrum Paine, her husband. Zachary turned his head away, muttering curses at the fate that had thrown them together at the start. But his heart was set on a word with Deseret, and he lingered on, watching the door.

It was then that Mother Rachel, the Gorgon-eyed wife of Mayberry, finally recognized the man beneath his beard. As she slammed the door behind her, he rose up reluctantly and passed out into the night. Along the street old Mormons in homespun jeans and cowhide boots were chatting and passing the news, while their womenfolk put the children to bed. Over at the bowery the young people were gathered in crowds, impatiently awaiting the dance. On their lips, as he passed, he heard the one word: "Brigham." The Lion of the Lord had come back.

There was no fear now in the hearts of these people, not even of the soldiers destroying their temple. Brigham himself had come down to protect them by his presence, and when had the Prophet ever failed? Had he blenched when the U.S. Army of ten thousand soldiers had marched across the plains on Salt Lake? Lot Drake and the ex-members of the Mormon Battalion had delivered his answer to the nation. They had burned the supply trains and run off the cattle, leaving the Gentiles to starve at Fort Bridger. In the spring, after their hard winter, when the Army entered Salt Lake, they found the whole city deserted. Streets were vacant, houses tenantless except for a hardy few left to fire the great city and burn it down. The Army had marched through, taking their hats off as they passed, in salute to Brigham Young. He had warned them not to stop, not to loot or occupy houses, and, rather than see the city burned, Johnston's army had passed through and camped across the River Jordan. Then, seeing them keep their word, the bold Brigham had returned with all his people behind him. So the bearded Mormons said—and believed it, too—for to them Brigham Young was a god. Every act of his, every word that he uttered, was inspired by the Spirit of the Lord.

There was music up the street, the loud braying of a brass

band, and the beat of militant drums. While the Saints made way, a procession approached, made up of the leaders of the church. Here were councilors and apostles, high priests and bishops and presidents of Mormon stakes. In their midst, stepping off confidently, marched Brigham and his wives, with Tamar and her sisters behind. Hyrum Paine was absent now and Tamar walked alone. As he gazed at her from the crowd, Tarrant felt his heart leap and old memories rushed up like a flood.

After a sonorous prayer the dancing went on apace, outdoors beneath the shelter of boughs. Hiding in the shadows of the pomegranate hedge, Zachary waited and watched for Deseret. She came out at last, closely guarded by Mother Rachel, and, as they entered the bowery, Tarrant edged through the crowd until he stood where he could look inside. Once more, after long weeks in the solitude of the desert, he gazed upon women in silks, women beautifully gowned, dancing with men clad in broadcloth, who bowed as they offered their hands. Among them, almost fairy-like in her pink and white prettiness, danced his temptress, Tamar Young. But Deseret was lost in the crowd.

Some perverse star must have ruled his fate that night, casting its influence against his happiness, for as he moved from place to place, peering about for Deseret, it was Tamar who saw him first. If she had read his secret from behind the curtains at the hotel, there was no trace of jealousy now. As their eyes met in passing, she beckoned with her fan, glancing back as she whirled down the bowery. In spite of his rebuffs she still wished to see him, though perhaps it was only to chide him. Zachary shook his head and, pushing back into the crowd, continued his futile hunt for Deseret. Tamar did not know—and how could he tell her that he had seen the record of her marriage? It was better to avoid a meeting, yet some madness took possession of him and he stayed until he found Deseret.

She was sitting alone, although Mother Rachel was very near. When she met his questing eyes, her face lighted up with a smile that was at once radiant and sad. She shook her head slightly, looking dreamily away as if to ignore his presence. Tarrant glanced about the bowery. Joel Mayberry was there, dancing gallantly with Sister Mary, the youngest and most attractive of his wives. Brigham Young, too, was dancing as spryly as the best of them though he was now nearly seventy years of age.

Tamar Young was there, also, a petite figure in floating silks, but Deseret was fairer by far. Her gown was of white dimity, but it fitted her dainty figure as if made by a French modiste, and her eyes, though they seemed to look far away, had taken on the soft glow of love. Perhaps she was dreaming of that evening, long ago, when he had taken her heart by storm.

Zachary felt unseen hands drawing him gently toward her; his feet bore him without any volition. Before he was aware of this new indiscretion, he stood, bowing and smiling before her. Her dark eyes wavered a moment as he offered her his arm and requested the pleasure of a dance, but in an instant the old mischievous twinkle had returned. She leaped up and gave him her hand. He slipped his arm about her, and they danced away down the bowery, their feet hardly touching the ground as they yielded to the sway of the waltz. It was a madness for both of them, yet neither regretted it, and they lived on from minute to minute regardless of the future, each moment an ecstasy in itself. But, as they passed the raised stand where the priests of the church sat, Tarrant felt their searching eyes upon him. He glanced up, suddenly recalled from the dream world of the dance, and there was Brigham Young, watching him.

The music stopped, too soon, and, as they halted before the stand, Hyrum Paine came hurrying toward them. The fat-faced young man with his staring brown eyes had a bustling air of importance. Without recognizing Deseret, he spoke directly to

Tarrant, as if he were alone on the floor.

"Miss Young would like to see you," he said, and his voice had the ring of a command.

Zachary drew himself up, glancing reassuringly at his partner as he bowed in acknowledgment of the request.

"Kindly ask her to excuse me," he said, and led Deseret to a seat. He had given the retort courteously, but, as he turned his back on Tamar's emissary, he saw the anger in Hyrum Paine's eyes. And Deseret, too, had seen the signs of a gathering storm, for suddenly there were tears in her eyes.

"Do you know her?" she asked under her breath.

"Yes," he said. "I knew her well, in Salt Lake. May I take you for another walk?"

"Oh, do," she entreated.

As they hurried out of the bowery, Tamar Young came flying after them.

"What do you mean?" she demanded, catching Zachary by the arm and snatching him away from Deseret. "Didn't you receive my request? Then what is your reason for refusing it?"

"The reason," answered Tarrant, "is one I need not mention. You know better than I do why it is we can never be friends."

He turned to go, but in that one, brief moment Deseret had stepped out of sight.

"If you mean," taunted Tamar, "this affair with a waitress. . . ."

"You know what I mean," flared back Zachary. "Do you know why I was dismissed from the Army?"

"No, I do not," answered Tamar angrily, and for the first time Tarrant met her eyes. They were black with jealous rage.

"It was for going to that ball . . . with you," he said, and instantly her manner changed.

"Why, Zachary?" she cried. "Why did you never write me? Was it nothing if I suffered, too? And when we met you on the road . . . why did you answer me so rudely? I think that was very unkind."

"Unkind or not, that is my answer," he said. "I never want to see you again."

"But why?" she pleaded. "What is the reason for this change? Is it something I have done? Tell me, Zachary."

"You know, better than I do," he answered, choking, and she gazed at him, smiling inscrutably.

"Oh, well," she said at last. "I need not reproach myself too much, whatever the reason may be. I see you have found someone else, to bind up your broken heart. Some waitress, I believe, at the hotel."

"Yes," retorted Zachary, stung to the quick in Deseret's defense, "her father and mother were killed by the Mormons . . . that's why she has to work. They were killed in the Mountain Meadows Massacre."

"Oh," said Tamar, still watching him with a smile into which a new cunning had crept, "so that's why you're making love to her. She might come in handy as a witness. I understand that's what you're here for."

"Yes," acknowledged Tarrant defiantly, "that's just exactly why I'm here. I'm a deputy United States marshal, getting evidence to convict those murderers, and, if half that I hear is true, it was your own father who ordered the massacre. That is why Deseret is an orphan."

"You lie!" she snapped back, her eyes furious with anger. "My father did nothing of the kind. You're so hateful you'd believe everything, but the Mormons never did it . . . those emigrants were killed by the Indians."

"I know a whole lot better," answered Zachary stubbornly, "and I'll prove it, before I get through. We're down here to punish the murderers of those people, no matter who they are."

"Oh, but Zachary," she cried after a frightened moment, "you surely don't suspect my father!"

"We certainly do," he said. "These men did the killing, but their orders came from Salt Lake."

"Why, Zachary," she retorted, drawing away from him reproachfully, and then her proud head dropped. The little shoulders that had stood so straight suddenly lost their defiant set and her dainty body was racked by a sob. "Oh, I hate you!" she cried, and ran blindly away from him, dashing the tears from her eyes as she fled. But when Zachary turned around to look for Deseret, she, too, had disappeared in the crowd.

CHAPTER SIXTEEN

It was late when Tarrant gave up his search for Deseret and retired to his tent for the night. At breakfast she was still missing, although Mayberry and Mother Rachel both guarded the kitchen door. Zachary went out and returned, lingering about uneasily, until at last his fears overmastered him. Deseret was a witness against Lot Drake, although he had kept the fact a secret until that night. As he racked his brain for some reason for her absence, he remembered his quarrel with Tamar. Like the fool that he was, he had blurted out his secret, simply to spite her for putting him in the wrong. He had told her all he knew, led on by some madness as fatal as it was now inexplicable. He could not understand what had prompted him to such folly, but the time for repentance was past. The deed was done, and, if Deseret was in danger, it was necessary to act at once.

Striding back through the kitchen, he discovered Mayberry and his wife busily beheading a crateful of chickens, but the hard-eyed Mormon only glared at him.

"I don't know where she is," he snapped. "We thought you might be responsible . . . you were with her."

"Yes, and I warned you, young man," spoke up Mother Rachel accusingly, "to leave my daughter alone. This is all your doings and the doings of that colonel . . . he hates our people like pisen, and now here we are, with our hotel full of people, and Deseret not home to help."

She heaved a great sigh and Tarrant turned away, his heart as heavy as lead. Something terrible had happened to Deseret, he could tell by the look in their eyes. These Mormons who had kept her as a bound slave for years blamed the loss of her services on him. Deseret had been taken away, by orders of the church, perhaps to keep her from him. But which of his enemies was responsible? There was Lot Drake and the Avenging Angels and Ammon Clark, Tamar, and Brigham Young. The great conflict was on between the forces of the government and the powers of the Mormon church—what was a single witness, more or less? What was a woman's life and happiness to the men who by word or deed were responsible for the Mountain Meadows Massacre?

Zachary hurried back to camp, and the colonel listened patiently, though his mouth had a grim, set smile.

"Lieutenant Tarrant," he said at last, "we have lost an important witness. Why haven't you mentioned her before?"

"Well, because . . . because I thought it was much better to keep her out of sight. If it became known, she might be spirited away."

"True enough," agreed the colonel, "that is just what has happened, not only to her but to all the other witnesses that the United States Attorney had in mind. But are you sure, Lieutenant Tarrant, that you have told the whole truth? Were you not slightly in love with this girl?"

"No, sir," denied Zachary, but, as the colonel eyed him steadily, a guilty flush mantled his cheeks.

"My boy," said the colonel, "your looks belie your words. We have encountered your old weakness again. Achilles had his heel, and you have a heart that goes out to fair maidens in distress. Have you forgotten Tamar Young?"

"No, sir," responded Zachary doggedly.

"Perhaps I am misinformed, but I have reason to believe that you met her at the dance last night."

"Yes, sir, I did," admitted Tarrant.

"And I am still further informed that in a heated discussion you mentioned this and that and the other . . . things which any loyal daughter would speedily make note of and hasten to convey to her father. This is too bad, my boy, too bad. You have spilled the beans again. All our witnesses are gone, the U.S. Attorney is crazy . . . and Brigham Young and his advisers have gone, too. There is no chance now of the U.S. marshal arresting any of them, for they have crossed the line into Arizona. What possessed you to talk as you did? Haven't I warned you, time and again, whatever you do not to match your lovesick wits against a woman's? She was playing you, sir, wrapping you around her little finger, making a fool of you to find out what you knew. And now about this new flame, has it ever occurred to you that Tamar may know something of her whereabouts?"

"Why, no," answered Zachary, startled.

"Tamar is jealous, no doubt, though why she should be is a question, since we know she is married to Paine. But, putting the reason aside, we know that she was angry when she saw you at the dance with Deseret. She sent her husband to summon you, to pluck you away from this new charmer. When you refused, she followed along after you and snatched you bodily away. Then you quarreled back and forth, and, when she had finished with you, you discovered that your new love had fled. Or, more correctly, she had disappeared. Now I'll wager anything that, right there in that crowd, she was seized and carried away. These Mormons are adept at that."

"My God," burst out Tarrant, starting up in astonishment. "Are conditions as bad as that?"

"They are as bad as they can be, and the reason is not far to seek. Brigham Young has come down here to handle this situation himself, to match his wits against ours. Within twenty-four hours we discover our witnesses gone, as well as the leaders of the church. They say it is Brigham's boast that in all his life he has had only eleven days of schooling, but that man has a genius for strategy and intrigue that would do credit to a Talleyrand or a Richelieu. Within one day after his coming, we find every move checkmated and the Prophet across the line in Arizona."

"Then what can we do?" demanded Zachary, and Colonel Valentine shrugged his shoulders.

"Keep on fighting," he said at last. "No matter if we are defeated a hundred times, we must fight our way through to the end. If our witnesses are stolen, we must get them back, and the same thing applies to their leaders. They are hiding in the mountains but, fortunately for us, we know where one is to be found."

"You mean Lot Drake," suggested Tarrant, and the colonel nodded impressively.

"Bring that man back," he said, "and I will overlook this affair of last night."

"By the Lord, I'll do it!" cried Zachary, rising, but the colonel held up his hand.

"One thing more," he continued. "While we are fitting out a detachment to go on this scout, I have a final commission for you to perform. I want you to ride over to Hurricane and observe what is going on. If you can pick up any information regarding the whereabouts of these witnesses, it will help to dispel the gloom. Only keep out of trouble . . . that's all."

He dismissed him with a gesture, and Tarrant saluted and went out, grinding his teeth with rage at his plight. It was no fault of his that Tamar Young had come south, and why she should be jealous of Deseret was something inexplicable to him. She was a Mormon, like the rest of them, and according to their custom she had become the plural wife of Hyrum Paine. Then why should she be angry if, driven away by her inconstancy, he had found another love?

At Salt Lake she had led him on to commit a thousand indiscretions, the last of which had resulted in his dismissal, and all the time, while she was appealing to him for sympathy, she was the third wife of Hyrum Paine. While she was weeping in his arms and protesting against polygamy, she had accepted the very fate that she denounced, and mingled with her sobs she had slipped in artful questions, playing the spy while she professed to be his sweetheart.

Tarrant rode off to the south, his brain hot with the fever of mingled anger and despair—anger at one woman who had ruined his career, and despair at the loss of the other. Deseret had disappeared as if the earth had swallowed her up. She had been merged in a moment into the sea of Mormon life that surrounded them on every side. While he turned his head, she had been snatched away from him—and Tamar Young had abetted it. She had taunted him purposely, leading him on with her sharp retorts while the agents of her father and the Mormon church had snatched his sweetheart away. He rose in his stirrups and, looking back at the gleaming temple, called down a curse on Brigham Young and his spies.

There was a furor in Hurricane, the same flaunting of banners and parading of notables that Moroni had witnessed the day before. From the two-doored Mormon houses in that city of sealed wives, women came out to greet long-absent husbands. Zachary looked on from a distance, lingering beneath the huge cottonwoods where he had first met good-natured Jerry Wamsutter. But Jerry and his brothers were now washing out their gold, well protected by a guard of soldiers, and no one passed by that he knew. The long cortège of carriages bearing the Prophet and his advisers had filed away toward Brigham's castle. As Zachary sat watching, another procession approached, toiling in across the desert from the north.

First a lone man appeared on the brow of the last rise, and then, team by team, the slow procession of emigrants that Tarrant had met farther north. While the heads of their religion were driving on from place to place, bowing and smiling to the plaudits of the crowds, these lowlier folks were proceeding on their mission to the settlements on the Little Colorado. Four hundred miles still lay between them and the struggling Arizona colonies, and Hurricane was the last town on the trail. Barring their way stood the Navajo chief, Kuchene, demanding vengeance for the deaths of his sons. Yet their orders were to go. They had been called for this mission and with the simplicity of their kind they went forward, never questioning.

Somehow Tarrant's heart went out to these poor, misled people and to their leader, the sturdy Moses Stout. But as they drew in by the canal and made camp on the open desert, he hesitated to renew the acquaintance. In the guise of a Mormon boy out hunting for horses he had scraped acquaintance with the wagon master—and learned, by an accident, what the marshal had not discovered in a fortnight. He had located Lot Drake and the following morning, if all went well, he would be riding across the desert to arrest him. If he resisted arrest, as he undoubtedly would, he might even have to kill him—and to Stout, Bishop Drake was a god. So Zachary lay where he was in the shade of the cottonwoods until Stout rode by, going to town.

"Hello!" he hailed as with the quick eye of a frontiersman he recognized Tarrant's horse. "What are you doing down here?"

"Watching the world go by," answered Zachary evasively, and the wagon master laughed to himself.

"Seems like that's all you do," he jested.

"Well, I got this far," bantered Tarrant. "How are you folks getting along? Did you pick up Brother Jacob?"

"He's in town," replied Stout, "jest riding in to see him. Well, here comes the old rascal, right now."

He pointed down the road where at a shambling pace Lingo's piebald mustang was shuffling through the dust, and Zachary stepped over to his horse.

"I've got to be going," he said, and tightened the girth with one jerk.

"No! Wait a minute!" protested Stout. "Brother Jacob won't bite you . . . unless you've been talking ag'in' the Lamanites. Then you will git into trouble."

"I've been doing worse than that," answered Zachary jestingly as he swung up into the saddle, but Stout caught his horse by the bit.

"Hold on here, young man," he said, "I want to talk with you myself, jest as soon as I see Brother Jake. I been thinking about you and . . . there's Jake waving, he wants to see you, too."

The apostle to the Lamanites had suddenly gone into action as he saw Tarrant mounting to go, and now, swinging his spurs at every jump like an Indian, he came galloping up the road.

"Bless the Lord!" he exclaimed, riding up and shaking hands cordially, but more particularly with Zachary. "Another of my visions has come true. Do you remember, Zack, the first time I met you, when you were riding down the road to Moroni? I had a vision then of you and me, standing together on the bank of a strong-flowing stream. That river was the Colorado and I knew it well, having crossed it often before. But what I did not tell was that Brother Moses Stout was standing right there beside us. We stood together and the people went by and they looked up at you and smiled. That was why I always knew you were our friend."

"Yes, sure," assented Tarrant, speaking hurriedly. "I remember your vision well. But I doubt very much whether we'll stand there together, because I'm not called in on this mission."

He reined away again, but Moses Stout still held his bridle.

"I've got a word to say there," he stated. "Zack, I don't know you, more than to pass the time of day, but when we met by those cedar brakes, the Spirit suddenly revealed to me that you would be one of our company. That is why I stopped your horse when you started to ride away, and I call on Brother Jake to support me. I say he is called, by your vision and mine, just as much as if the bishop had read his name. What do you say, Brother Jake?"

For a moment the deep-set eyes of the prophet glowed, and then he glanced back down the road. "Someone is coming," he said, "who will settle this for you. Jest wait . . . it is the will of the Lord."

He turned in his saddle and gazed fixedly toward Hurricane. As Zachary sat staring, a woman came galloping toward them, mounted on a high-bred and mettlesome steed.

"It is the daughter of the Prophet," announced Lingo, and Tarrant saw it was Tamar Young. Yet so furiously was she riding that she had almost passed by them before she caught sight of Tarrant's face.

"Why, Zachary!" she cried, bringing her horse to a stop and reining back to join them.

Without a word Lingo jerked his head at Stout, and they rode off together into town.

"Miss Young, I believe," greeted Tarrant, bowing low in the saddle with an air of mock gallantry. "This is an unexpected pleasure, like meeting those two worthy men, one of whom has taken me for a Mormon."

"You could do worse"—she smiled—"than become one of the Saints. Is this the camp of their wagon train? I was just riding out to see it." She glanced at him expectantly.

"I am sorry," he said, "that I cannot accompany you, but I am riding back to Moroni."

"Will you gallop?" she challenged. "Then I'll ride along with you."

Zachary shook his head. "I know now that you are a dangerous woman to deal with. So please allow me to ride alone."

"Oh, Zachary," she coaxed, "would you deny me that small pleasure, when perhaps it will be our last ride? I know why you are angry, but it is all for your own good. You will never see her again."

She glanced at him, half defiantly, and at a touch of her whip his horse started and stepped off with hers. As for Tarrant, he sat thunderstruck, hardly believing his ears, and so they rode away up the road.

"What do you mean?" he asked hoarsely. "Has Deseret been killed? My God, what a devil you are."

"I am your friend," she answered, "though why I cannot tell, after the way you have broken my heart. But that girl was not for you and she has been taken away. You will never see her again."

She spoke with such assurance, such confidence in what she said, that Zachary could hardly disbelieve her, and yet, if that were so, she was confessing to him that she knew where Deseret had been taken. She was admitting, without saying so, that she herself was responsible, since she said it was all for his good. Yet she rode by him calmly, her eyes resolute and unwavering, and he set his mind to think. Always before she had outwitted him, playing alike on his anger and the sympathy her sufferings evoked, but now they were matched for one final bout of wits and he remembered the colonel's rebuke.

"I did not think," he said, "that you would go so far, and still claim to be my friend. But I have discovered once more that there is method in your madness, that you carry all you learn to your father."

"Oh, indeed," she expostulated, raising her eyebrows sarcastically. "Then what are you yourself but a spy? If my father's life is threatened is it any more than natural for me, his daughter, to inform him? But you have hired out as a spy on my people. Except for an accident, and this friendship that you flout, you would have suffered the punishment you deserve. Do you remember when you were arrested by Bishop Drake in Moroni and he telegraphed to Salt Lake for instructions? I happened to be in my father's office when this message was delivered and I dictated the answer myself. That is why you were given your horse and released, so perhaps I am not as heartless as you think."

There was a mist in her eyes as she met his questioning gaze, but Tarrant had learned his lesson and he shrugged his shoulders and said nothing.

"Oh, I hate you. I hate every man in the world," she burst out as he turned his face away, "and you are just like the rest. You have destroyed the last particle of faith that I had, but I never thought you'd descend to turn spy."

"Well, what are you yourself?" he asked, turning back. "And what were you all the time? You were a spy when you invited me to meet you in secret, and like a false fool I was a traitor to my government. I would not believe this, Tamar, even when I was dismissed, until the colonel showed me papers to prove it. He showed me reports that you yourself had written. . . ."

"I did not!" she interrupted spitefully.

"Yes, you did," he went on steadily yet with a tremble of anger in his voice, "but what hurt me most, and turned me against your people, and made me hate you, too, was another paper I saw. It proved beyond a doubt that you had been using me all the time, that you had never loved me at all."

"Oh, but, Zachary, I did," she insisted, "until you. . . ."

"Do you love your husband?" he demanded, and she faltered and looked away.

"Why, I am not married. What do you mean?" she quavered, but he could see her flushed cheeks go pale.

"You were married all the time," he answered sternly. "You were married to Hyrum Paine."

"Oh, no, no," she protested. "You have just heard some rumor and used it as a pretext to disgrace me."

"In what way have I disgraced you?" he inquired, and Tamar was quick to see her chance. They were treading on dangerous ground.

"By making love to this waitress," she burst out, feigning a passion. "But you'll never see her again. And if you do, it will be too late. She is given to be married to a Mormon. But what a common thing to do, after all your sweet words and promises. To come down to Moroni and make love to a common waitress, the first woman you met at the hotel. That is when I lost faith in. . . ."

"*You* lost faith," he scoffed. "My God, what a woman. You were married all the time. You were the one that was faithless. You were married to Hyrum Paine, and yet you allowed me to ruin my life."

"I was not," she answered vehemently, but her voice had lost its passion and her face was suddenly gray and desperate.

"You're a Mormon, like the rest of them," he responded bitterly, "you're all liars, all cheats, all polygamists, and your hearts are black as hell. I know you're the third wife of Hyrum Paine. I have seen the record myself. You were married on the Twenty-Second of May and your own father performed the ceremony. And now you come here and look me in the eye and try to tell me I lie."

"Well, you do . . . ," she began, but, when he looked over at her, she faltered and bowed her head. A tear splashed down on her daintily gloved hand, then with a last imploring look that smote him to the heart, she turned and galloped furiously ahead.

CHAPTER SEVENTEEN

Zachary had told Tamar Young that her heart was black as hell, but, as she turned away, her eyes wet with tears, something told him she was still a woman. There had been a poignancy of grief in that last, beseeching glance that had startled him, even caused him to doubt. Yet how could he doubt when her own actions admitted that everything he had said was true? She was the plural wife of Hyrum Paine, and had been all the time. The kisses she had given him were not honestly hers to give, but belonged to her polygamous husband. Yet Tarrant sighed as he turned away from watching her and somehow he felt in the wrong.

He had won their battle of wits and routed his fair enemy before she could do him further harm, but the barb of one shaft still rankled, for she had told him of Deseret's fate. She had been carried away to wed some Mormon, carried away where she could never come back, and the instigator of this deed was Tamar herself. Her heart was black as hell. In this she was no shrinking creature, but a woman as stern and ruthless as Brigham Young himself. As she had told him Deseret's fate, there had been a look in her eyes that had reminded Tarrant of her implacable father. Blood will tell, and despite her prettiness she was the daughter of the man who held all Utah in his hand.

Deseret was gone, as far removed from his search as if transported to another world, and, as he galloped back to Moroni, Tarrant promised himself to take vengeance on the

Mormon church. It was the hidden power that had snatched his love away and taken her where no Gentile could follow. Until it was smashed and brought to its knees, what hope was there of getting her back? But a quick dash to Mormon Ferry and the swift arrest of Lot Drake might strike terror to their arrogant hearts. Then the same power that kept Deseret concealed could be invoked to bring her back. All it needed was one blow—and back in Moroni the dragoons were waiting to start. Mules were packed and rations issued, and that night under cover of darkness Zachary led them on their dash across the desert.

All night they traveled eastward across a hard-baked plain and then up a cedar-covered ridge. At dawn they looked down into a broad, level valley, almost illimitable in its sweep to the east. To the north, vermilion cliffs caught the sun's first rays, turning rosy and then blood-red. The south walls of the valley gleamed white in the distance until they were lost in a jumble of crags. In the crystal-clear air a hundred miles was nothing, and far away across the river they could see the painted cliffs that gave shelter to Kuchene and his Navajos. But between them there ran a line, blue and shadowy and cavernous, where the Grand Cañon of the Colorado barred the way.

Only by circling the long, red cliff and following up into a wedge-shaped valley where the river came out into the sunlight could the great barrier of the cañon be crossed. And there, at the very apex, where the river flowed out of the blackness, the Mormons had built their ferry. It was in a spot wild and hazardous, with shattered crags on both sides and a sandy shore barely wide enough to pass, but here the tumbling waters, after escaping from Cataract Cañon, could spread out sweetly in the sun. Yet not for long, for around the next bend they were sucked into a greater abyss, the Grand Cañon of Arizona.

Tarrant had looked the country out from the summit of Rustler Mountain, with Jerry Wamsutter to show him the landmarks, but as he gazed across it now, after their forced march from Moroni, his heart sank at the immensity of their task. Below them in the broad valley a thousand black specks showed where the cattle of the church herd grazed, cattle taken from the people as tribute or tithing and now held by Brigham himself. He and the church were one, for he gave no accounting of the wealth that passed through his hands, and to question his title to the vast properties he had acquired would be to court the death of an apostate. To make his hold on this herd more secure, he had consigned them to the care of the Avenging Angels.

Here in this lonely valley, beyond the cedared mountains that cut them off from the last of the settlements, Ammon Clark and his mysterious followers, the night-riding Angels, sought seclusion after their daring raids. Here they raised their blooded horses, with hoofs as hard as flint and muscles toughened by long journeys to water, and never before had their solitude been disturbed by such an invasion as this. Even the war parties of the Navajos had learned to ride around them, although their race horses tempted many a savage thief, for the Avenging Angels were desert-bred, inured to hardships, picked to fight, and they could trail a barefoot horse for weeks. Only the Mormons knew the country and the trails that led into it, but from the summit of the mesa Tarrant could see the big corrals that had been built at House Rock Springs. They lay at a bend of the floor-like valley, close against the southern wall, and now that daylight had come the cattle in long lines were stringing in across the plain. On the rocky slopes above them the Mormon horses could be seen, cropping the rich grasses that grew among the stones. There was no smoke from the chimney, no riders faring forth—the valley was deserted. But why?

The all-seeing eye that looked down upon the Mormons had taken cognizance of the Gentiles as well, for not only had the departure of the soldiers been noted but their destination had been guessed. When under a broiling sun they rode down to House Rock Springs, they found the stone buildings deserted. Only the tracks of men and horses, still fresh in the dust, told the story of their hasty flight. The troopers, dead beat, put their horse herd out to graze and took shelter in the vacant rooms. Nothing was left but the bare furniture—beds, tables, and chairs. In this ordered retreat Tarrant recognized the ancient tactics by which the Mormons had always conquered their invaders. Their flight was like the Parthians', designed to draw their pursuers on and lose them in the desert sands, and, although they had no proof of the hostile intent of the soldiers, they left nothing to comfort the enemy. There was no food, no bedding, no wood to make fires, only the endless lines of cattle, shuffling in to drink, and the spring with its big flow of water.

The Mormons had retreated east toward Jacob's Pool, the last good water on the road. Shortly after noon the commander of the detachment summoned his men and followed after them. Zachary rode on ahead, traveling by landmarks across the country, but, as he dwelt on its immensity, his courage almost failed—what a wilderness in which to search for one man. And yet he must make the attempt. The Mormons were forewarned, Lot Drake would be vigilant, and his Avenging Angels would be watching every pass. Yet they must push on to Mormon Crossing and, taking his trail from there, follow after him until he was captured.

It was almost dark when the weary column of troopers came in sight of Jacob's Pool. After a hasty reconnaissance they rode in to the abandoned water hole, which lay close to the north wall of the valley. Once more they found stone houses, stripped of all they contained, and tracks leading on into the desert, but no wood for their fires and no feed for their horses, for the grass near the spring had been fed off. Only out on the broad plain, where the cattle had not congregated, was there pasture for their jaded mounts, and shortly after dark the horse herd was sent out, for another forced march lay before them.

From House Rock Springs to Jacob's Pool was little more than twenty miles, but the road to Mormon Crossing lay through alternate rocks and sand, a distance of forty miles. A guard was posted and the tired soldiers slept. But as the morning star was rising, they heard a rumble that spelled disaster—the horse herd out on the plain had stampeded. There was a clatter of flying hoofs as the relief rode out after them and then for weary hours the little detachment waited and watched, for the dawn had shown no trace of the herd. Wherever they had fled, the herders had ridden after them and the sun was blazing hot before they returned, driving the dispirited horses before them.

"Something scared them," they reported, and the captain and Tarrant exchanged glances. It was Mormon tactics again. The Parthian retreat, a furtive watching from the crags, then, as the horse guards dozed, a sudden rush at the herd and a stampede across the limitless plain. Now their mounts were gaunt and jaded, the day was half gone, and an unknown trail lay before them. The horses were watered and their legs rubbed down, and then, leaving behind that ill-omened spot, they pressed on into the unknown.

Plodding along at a slow walk, they passed through the drifting sand that kept them in a smother of dust, then up over stony mesas and a thousand cross washes and down into cañons again. The red cliff drew in closer, throwing its black shadow upon them as they approached the entrance to the gorge, and at last they came out within sight of the river, gliding along against the opposite cliffs. The cañon walls drew together, forcing them down into the bottom where the sand was being whipped up by the wind. Darkness was upon them when they came to a freshly made dug way, leading along the steep slope of the bank. Here at last was the road that Lot Drake and his men had been building for the emigrant train, but it would take a stout heart and a steady hand to guide the cumbersome wagons up this grade. It began at a sand wash, leading straight up a tremendous pitch, then, scaling to new heights, it slid down to a dug way above the river, barely wide enough to hold the wagon wheels. The jaded troop horses snorted as in column of twos they came out above the raging flood, and the stars were all out before they rounded the last point and came suddenly upon the Mormon camp.

It was more than a camp; it was a large and well-kept ranch with log houses and fenced fields of hay. But the cañon in which it lay was so black and mysterious that the captain commanded a halt. Scouts were thrown out in advance, the houses were hastily searched, and then, finding the headquarters of the Mormons deserted, the command made camp in the yard. Fires were lighted, supper cooked, and horses groomed and fed. Morning found them sleeping under a grove of huge cottonwoods, their mounts turned into the hay.

This was the cañon of the Pahreah, or Muddy Water, first charted by the explorers of the Grand Cañon, and on a broad piece of level ground the Mormons had led out the muddy stream, planting hay and a big orchard of fruit. There were barns and corrals, a stove-in skiff under a tree, and beneath the largest of the cottonwoods Lot Drake had built a house, big and strong and two stories high. Tarrant knew at a glance what hand had laid it out for he had seen a dozen just like it—it was the kind of house that Drake always built to shelter his plural wives. Everything that he built had the stamp of good workmanship and this was no exception to the rule. But Drake himself had fled, and his followers with him, although no doubt they were watching from the heights.

On both sides of the Pahreah there rose high and jagged cliffs, gleaming red in the morning sun, and to the west in bold outlines appeared the silhouette of the Sleeping Chief, swathed in blankets except for his head. He lay on the high cliff, his head toward the river, his bold features well cut and clear, and the full stretch of his body covered half a mile of crags, the south wall of Pahreah Cañon. From their camp beneath the trees the ferry was not in sight, but the roar of the rapids came to their ears like distant thunder and they knew that the crossing was near. But now that they had got there, after crossing the desert sands, the troopers were too exhausted to do more than lie down and rest.

The air was sweet with the smell of green things, and of hay and of cottonwood smoke, and even Tarrant was content to remain in camp that day, for the Mormons had fled across the river. At daylight he had been up and inspecting the rugged country into which the fugitives had fled, and half a mile up the river he had discovered the Mormons' ferry, its boats moored against the opposite bank.

A shelving ledge of limestone, tilted up till it mounted the cliff, gave a foothold on the other side, but the dug way that led up from it was so breathtaking in its height that its passage seemed practically impossible. To drive a loaded wagon up that track way along the cliff face would be to risk a terrible death. It mounted from shelf to shelf, riding the tops of the ledges, then shooting up a steeper incline. The first driver who lost his head and allowed his team to swerve would fall three hundred feet into the stream.

Zachary traced the road in silence, awed by the audacity of the man who had deemed such a dug way possible, and at the thought of Moses Stout driving his cumbersome wagons along the precipice he felt a thrill of fear. Except by a miracle the Mormons could never mount it without losing some wagons

146

and lives, yet even now they were pressing forward, men, women, and children, breaking a road across the desert as they came. They had been called for this mission, to cross the Painted Desert, and settle on the Little Colorado. The Prophet had given them orders on no account to turn back, not even in the face of death.

Behind this eastern cliff, on the mesa that stretched off endlessly, the savage Navajos were lurking, waiting to take them by surprise and wreak vengeance for the slaughtered sons of their chief. At its base, in treacherous quicksands, the strong current of the river swept past to the rapids below. What courage, what blind faith and unthinking obedience were in the hearts of these Latter-day Saints. They set forth like the Children of Israel, led on by their lesser Moses, to make their way to another Canaan, and like them they must suffer thirst and the scourge of heat and serpents, before they came to the Promised Land. They were brave and uncomplaining, but their minds were enslaved and they bowed down to Brigham like a god. It was pitiful, and at the same time sublime.

Tarrant had ridden out to capture the master mind who had conquered this river and its cliffs. He had been sent to arrest Lot Drake, pluck him forth from his desert hiding place, and put him on trial for his life. Yet what chance in a million did he have of accomplishing such a mission? Did he have any chance at all? He rode back despondently, racking his brain for some expedient to lure this man of iron into his power, but even the Indians avoided them, and it soon became apparent that their search was foredoomed to failure. The Mormons had fled into another *terra incognita,* the land of the savage Navajos, and, after scouting along the river until their rations ran low, the detachment turned back toward Moroni.

In that vent of the Grand Cañon the wind was never at rest— either it blew up the river, driving a storm of sand before it, or it blew down, driving it back. The Pahreah was in a pocket, protected by the high cliff upon which the sculptured Indian chief was sleeping, but when the dragoons rounded the point and turned their horses' heads toward home, they met the west wind, blowing strong. At each blast the feathery sand rose up like startled birds that have suddenly sensed the swoop of a hawk, and, after a swift leap forward, it fell back in tiny waves, as regular as the rollers of the sea. It buffeted the column of troopers like the blows of some mighty hand, invisible but stinging with fury. As they wavered, it snatched the dust of the leaders and hurled it into the teeth of the rest. Their whole trip had been full of buffets, and, as they turned back, defeated, they sensed the sinister nature of the land.

It was a country whose every aspect spoke of treachery and violence, a land of drifting sand and poisonous waters where hidden enemies were always waiting to strike. Since they had entered House Rock Valley and the refuge of the Avenging Angels, they had not seen a living man—only their tracks in the dust, the houses they had lived in, and the boats they had built to cross the river. Yet night after night their horses had broken and run, stampeded by skulking men, and only the utmost vigilance and a doubled guard had kept them from losing their mounts. Now, as they rode away, they felt Mormon eyes upon them, malevolently planning more mischief.

Riding beside the captain at the head of the command, Tarrant still plotted some desperate coup—a sudden return after dark, the surprise of the Mormon camp, a battle to the death with Drake. But as they swung down off the dug way, they encountered a Mormon wagon, stuck fast on the first steep pitch. Behind it, up the wash where the road led down, the other wagons of the train were stopped, and team after team of horses were coming forward to pull the stalled leader up the hill. Women and children were huddled in hollows to escape the fury of the wind, and from the openings of covered wagons little heads were popping out as the youngsters sensed the presence of the troops.

Every face lit up with hope, but a long ride lay before the troopers and they were returning in an ugly mood. These were part of the same people who had stampeded their horse herd and put them afoot on the desert. They were an alien sect, the natural enemies of all Gentiles and especially of United States troops. They were fleeing from Utah to escape the very government that these soldiers were sworn to serve, and without even a word of greeting the captain rode by them. But Zachary reined out and stopped.

"That's a bad grade you've got ahead," he said to Moses Stout who was directing the work of the teams. "Any word you want to send to Moroni?"

"No," answered Stout, looking him over curiously, "I reckon we'll git through somehow. What are you doing, away out here?"

"I'm guiding that detachment of soldiers . . . out scouting for Navajos," replied Zachary as he started to go. But the wagon master held up his hand.

"How far is it to the ranch?" he shouted above the wind. "We're pretty near out of water."

"About a mile," returned Tarrant. "There's no wind around the point. You might send the women and children ahead."

"See any Injuns?" Stout called after him, and, as Zachary stopped again, the last of the troopers filed past. A cloud of dust, stirred up by the horses, obscured their rapid march, but as Zachary was held in talk it suddenly came over him that he was alone with a hostile train. By this time Stout knew his history and his errand among his people, for Jake Lingo was standing near. Roused to his danger, Tarrant suddenly reined away, waving his hand as he spurred up the wash.

"Good luck!" he called back, but they only stood, staring, a look of startled wonder in their eyes. Zachary looked back again and they were still gazing after him. Every man on the job had stopped work, and, as he passed a certain wagon, they seemed frozen in their tracks, as if fascinated by what was taking place. Yet to him there was nothing unusual. This wagon was like the rest, only no heads popped out of it to stare at the passing Gentile. As he looked again, the canvas cover was thrown back and a woman's face peered out. He stopped short. It was Deseret.

CHAPTER EIGHTEEN

Tarrant's brain worked lightning fast as he spurred up to the wagon from which Deseret had shown her scared face. Here at once was the answer to the Mormons' concern and the hints of Tamar Young. Deseret was a prisoner, sent out with this wagon train to be buried in the heart of the desert. But for his stopping, he would have lost her forever—even now she had disappeared. The wagon cover had been jerked back as if to hide her from his eyes, but he had seen her and he tapped on the canvas.

"Deseret!" he called, and a huge woman looked out, blocking the interior of the wagon with her bulk.

"What do you want?" she demanded sharply.

As Zachary looked for Deseret, he heard a horseman come galloping up. It was Moses Stout, but now his eyes were gleaming and he had drawn a long pistol from his belt.

"Git back from there!" he ordered. "What are you doing in my wagon? You go on now, and leave us alone!"

He was angry and tremendously excited, brandishing his weapon as he talked, but Tarrant did not give way. "Deseret Mayberry is there," he said, "and I'm going to see her. I don't care what you say."

"You're not . . . she is not," denied Stout. "That's my wife you saw inside." Then, as Deseret struggled into view: "Suppose it is her . . . what then?"

"Is she a prisoner?" demanded Zachary. "Why have you got

151

her shut up here? This doesn't look right, Mister Stout."

"Now you keep out of this," advised the wagon master as his men came up behind him, "or you'll find yourself in trouble. I don't want to hurt you, but Sister Deseret is in my care, by order of Brigham Young. You'd better leave things alone."

"No," said Tarrant stubbornly. "I won't move an inch until I talk with Deseret. If she wants to go, all right. But if. . . ."

"Don't give me orders!" broke in Stout defiantly. "The soldiers have gone, understand? And by the time you get them back here Deseret will be gone, too. She'll be lost up there in those cliffs."

"Then I'll stay right here," declared Zachary, "no matter if you kill me. But it will be a serious matter if you do."

"I don't intend to kill you," answered Stout. "That is, if you mind your own business. But President Young has entrusted this girl in my care, and I want you to leave her alone."

"Let me talk to her," coaxed Tarrant. "I won't go till I do. Come over here a minute, Deseret."

He smiled as he met her glance, but her face was set in a mask of stony-eyed grief. She seemed deadened and numbed, like a person in a trance or held under the influence of some spell.

After meditating a minute and conferring with his men, Stout lifted her out of the wagon.

"Remember where you are," he said, and she shrank from him like a frightened child. All her old fire was gone, and, as Zachary led her aside, she moved stiffly, like an automaton.

"How did you get here?" he asked when they were out of hearing. "And where did you go that night?"

"I was called," she answered, as if surprised at his asking. "When we are called for a mission, we have to go."

"Yes, I know," he replied. "But didn't they kidnap you? I hunted for you everywhere."

152

"Why, no," she said, "you were talking with . . . her. And so. . . ." She faltered and her eyes filled with tears. "Why didn't you tell me?" she asked.

"Tell you what?" he demanded. "That I knew Tamar Young? What difference did that make, Deseret?"

"She . . . she told me you loved her. And she warned me against you. She said you just treated me . . . like a waitress!"

She bowed her head and wept and Zachary stood helpless with the hard eyes of the Mormons upon him. He could not explain to her now.

"Are you a prisoner here?" he asked at last.

She glanced fearfully at Moses Stout. He was watching her, his face stern and menacing.

"Why, no," she said, "I'm just called. You'd better go," she added hopelessly.

"Will you go with me?" he demanded eagerly.

She looked up, a gleam of light in her eyes. But before she could answer, Moses Stout came striding over and motioned her back to the wagon.

"That's all," he said to Tarrant, and stood waiting for him to go.

"All right," answered Zachary, but, as he went to his horse, he stole a last glance at Deseret. She was gazing after him through her tears, her eyes big with a new-born love and solemn with a last farewell.

"I'm going to stay right here," he said, "until you let Deseret go. I summon her as a government witness."

"You what?" cried out Stout.

When Tarrant displayed his badge, the crowd of rough Mormons laughed. But Stout was thoroughly enraged and his pent-up anger burst forth.

"You government spy," he yelled, "you keep out of this affair! It's none of your business at all. Didn't she tell you she was called? Didn't she say she wasn't a prisoner? Then you git or we'll plant you right here."

"You kill me," answered Zachary, "and those soldiers will come back and wipe you off the map. They saw me stop here to talk."

"Well, git out of here," ordered Stout. "We don't want you around. Ain't we got enough trouble, stuck on that hill in this wind, without you trying to make us more? What do you say, Brother Jacob?"

He turned to Lingo, who had been listening gravely, and the prophet shook his head. "He won't go," he said. "I know him."

"Then what are we going to do . . . let them soldiers come back and kill us? I'm responsible for the safety of this wagon train!"

"Let him stay," advised Lingo, "because that is the Lord's will, as revealed to me in a vision. But the soldiers are our enemies, so have him write a letter, saying he joined us against our will. Then send it by one of our boys to that detachment that jest went past, and ask them to deliver it to the colonel."

"I'll write you a letter," offered Tarrant, "and give you another one to keep. But I'm an officer in the Army and a deputy United States marshal, and I'm going to stay and protect this girl."

"She don't need no protecting," spoke up a big, bearded Mormon who had been watching him with jealous eyes, but Stout shook his head and pushed him back.

"Write the letter," he said to Zachary, "and let's git back to that wagon. You know you ain't welcome, but I'll submit, under compulsion. We don't want no trouble with the troops."

He called for pen and paper, and in the lee of a wagon Tarrant dashed off a hasty note. Then, as a Mormon boy rode off with it, he wrote another for Stout to keep, in case he was called to account. After that, he watched the wagon as it jolted down the rocky wash and up over the newly made dug way, until at last, toward evening, they rounded the last point and saw the green fields of the Pahreah before them.

The wind ceased as if by magic, and the sting of the flying sand. As the dirt-grimed teamsters urged their horses to one more effort, the women cried out for joy. For a week they had walked by the side of the wagons or sat huddled among their household goods, but as the slashing wind suddenly ceased, they gazed entrancedly on this new Elysium. Every wagon flap was thrown back; children stuck out their towheads and mothers held up their little ones. Beneath the cover of Stout's wagon, Zachary caught a glimpse of the girl he had watched for all day.

Since he had left the soldiers and attached himself to the wagon train, the Mormons had ignored his presence. No one offered to give him food or a drink from the half-empty barrels that were slung on both sides of the wagons. Stout was too deeply occupied with the Herculean task of dragging his heavy wagons up the dug way, and the Mormon men, tugging and sweating in the dust, were ready to drop with fatigue. In the wagons the weary women had resigned themselves to their fate, sitting listlessly behind the flapping covers, but at sight of the Pahreah, every head had come out and Tarrant stole another look at Deseret.

She had changed again since he had beheld her that morning, so different from her former self. Now the look of despair had given place to a desperation that made her eyes gleam and dance. She had come to herself again, after giving up all hope, but if her mask of grief was broken, it had not made her less unhappy, and, as she saw him, the tears came again. She shook her head warningly, gazed deep into his smiling eyes, and bowed her head in a paroxysm of sobs.

There was something strange and sinister about this taking away of Deseret. If she had gone willingly, it was only because Tamar had told her that Zachary did not love her. She had been like a fragile leaf, suddenly seized by contending winds that swept her away, willy-nilly, into the desert. But at sight of her lover, following devotedly beside her wagon, the scales had fallen from her eyes. Deseret knew now that Zachary truly loved her, for he had turned back and joined the wagon train, even though in that wild and desolate country, swarming with outlawed Avenging Angels, he was powerless to give her aid. He had thrown away his life without helping her—and death would soon snatch him away.

As they drove up the narrow road to the popping of whips and the shouts of the Mormon teamsters, Tarrant saw a band of horsemen trotting rapidly down the cañon, and in their lead was Ammon Clark. The Avenging Angels were returning to their camp. Driven out by the soldiers, they had retreated far up the cañon and rimmed back along the cliffs, until, seeing the troopers leave, they had ridden back and followed down the valley to Pahreah. Nor were they his only enemies, for as the cavalcade came closer Zachary spied the huge form of Lot Drake. He, too, wore the black hat of the Danite destroyers, and he rode close behind Ammon Clark, but, when he recognized Tarrant, he spurred into the lead and came thundering down on the caravan.

"What's that man doing here?" he demanded of Moses Stout, pointing a threatening finger at Tarrant. "Don't you know he's a government spy?"

He paused and gazed at Zachary as if half doubting his own eyes, and the Avenging Angels came galloping up behind.

"Well, I warned him," defended Stout, "but he came back anyhow, and now he can take the consequences. He's following along after that girl."

"What girl?" demanded Drake, glancing hastily around, and his eyes fell on the shrinking Deseret. "Oho!" He nodded, and he gazed at her a moment before he turned to Ammon Clark.

"Take care of this man," he said.

"No, hold on," protested Stout. "I'm responsible for his safety because those soldiers saw him stop at our wagon train. Jest let this case wait a few days."

"But the soldiers have gone," argued Drake. "If we wait, they're liable to come back."

"We'll talk that over later," replied Stout, "after we've camped and had something to eat."

"I want that man right now!" stormed Drake. "And I'm going to have him, too."

"You'll never take me alive," flashed back Zachary, and whipped out his pistols as he spoke.

"We'll take you dead, then," blustered Drake, glancing back at his men, but none of the Angels moved.

"You kill me," warned Tarrant, "and you'll have a war on your hands. I'm an officer in the United States Army."

"And there's that colonel," broke in Jake Lingo anxiously. "He hates our people like pisen. He'll lay our temple flat. He said so. Didn't President Young himself send me out to Rustler Mountain with a safe-conduct to bring this boy back? And, brethren, I've had a vision, a revelation from the Spirit. Brother Brigham is sending us a message. Great changes have taken place since we left Moroni, and I saw in a vision a messenger riding swiftly on Brother Laney's big roan horse. Then the Holy Ghost came over me and I heard a voice saying . . . 'Do nothing with this man till he comes!' "

He turned his eyes to heaven as if seeking some further message, and Lot Drake laughed and spat.

"You talk like a fool," he said.

"No, no," insisted Stout, "Brother Jacob has the gift and the Spirit has spoken unto him. We will wait until the messenger comes."

"Yes, and suppose he don't come?" sneered Drake.

157

"He will come," responded Lingo impressively.

"So you say," scoffed Drake, but, as his men began to murmur, he shrugged his broad shoulders impatiently. "Well, we'll wait a couple of days," he said. "But, listen," he went on, turning fiercely on Stout, "I want this man kept in his place. He's a Gentile and a spy and the first thing you know he'll be interfering with the customs of our people."

"I won't interfere," promised Tarrant, and Stout nodded his head approvingly. But when Zachary looked around, he saw that Deseret was weeping—and Drake regarded him with an insolent smile.

CHAPTER NINETEEN

Through a night that seemed endless, Tarrant lay on the bare ground and watched the closed wagon of Moses Stout. While the Great Dipper wheeled and sank and rose up again, he could hear Deseret softly crying. She was afraid—afraid of Lot Drake. But toward morning she slept, outworn by her grief, and Zachary dozed off, too. It had wrung his heart to hear her stifled sobs and the scolding of fat Mrs. Stout. When her weeping ceased, Nature had drugged him to sleep, and, when he awoke, it was dawn.

The first early risers were out after their horses, walking stiffly after the labors of yesterday, but the rest of the emigrants lay just as they had dropped after their beds had been spread on the ground. Little children were sprawled in rows on the thick Mormon blankets that their mothers had put down by the wagons, and the faded blue of the men's overalls with which the quilts were covered spoke eloquently of their economy and thrift. Nothing was wasted with these women, except their own narrow lives, given wholly to building up their husbands' kingdom, a kingdom in the world to come when each mother would be a queen, each child a star in her crown. But in this life they must pay in hard, laborious toil for the celestial reward to come.

The mothers roused up one by one to start the breakfast, the husbands to attend to their horses. As Zachary sat watching, Deseret stepped out at last, as pale and thin as a ghost. Grief had quite overmastered her, leaving her broken and wan, but now all her tears were shed. She was dry-eyed and listless and suddenly old beyond her years, and she kept her eyes fixed on the ground. The sight of Lot Drake had destroyed her last illusion—she knew she was doomed for the sacrifice. Yet, as Zachary turned away to beg his breakfast from Jake Lingo, her eyes followed after him wistfully.

The apostle to the Lamanites was kneeling by his fire, absently stirring corn meal into a can of smoky water while his glazed eyes were fixed on space. Unlike the other Mormons he had no woman to cook for him, no wagon to haul his food. His life had been spent in the camps of the Indians until at last he had taken their ways. The one blanket behind his saddle was a cloak by day and a cover for his bed at night, and his commissary was contained in the one greasy flour sack that went inside the pack. Yet withal he seemed content, for his thoughts were on other things.

"Good morning," he responded as Zachary greeted him. Then, while his porridge cooked, he stirred it over the coals, gazing at the cliffs with unseeing eyes. He was living in his dreams, conversing with the monitor that guided his daily life, and, when their meal was done, he stalked off without a word, leaving Tarrant to wash the dishes.

Something ominous was afoot in the camp of the Mormons— there was no preparation for the crossing of the river and the leaders had conference after conference. First Lingo and Stout stepped off to one side and talked together in low tones. Then Bishop Drake, striding arrogantly out, shouted their names and beckoned them to the house. They returned, glum and dejected, to another conference by themselves. As the day wore on, they visited Drake again, but nothing was said to Tarrant. His fate hung in the balance, and the fate of Deseret as well, but he waited impassively, and along toward evening Stout led him away from the rest.

"Tarrant," he said, "Brother Jake and I have done our best for you, but Bishop Drake is ag'in' ye. I reckon you know what that means. It's time for you to go."

"Can I take Deseret with me?" asked Zachary.

"You know that's impossible," responded Stout. "Brigham Young himself, for purposes of his own, has placed her in my care. She has been sent on a mission and it is the will of the Lord that she shall stay here, to build up His kingdom. You will never see her again. But if you leave right now, I can promise you protection. We don't want any trouble with the troops."

"Can I see Deseret?" requested Tarrant at last, but the wagon master shook his head.

"You will never see her again," he said.

"Then I won't go," answered Zachary resolutely.

"But why not?" flared up Stout. "Don't think for a minute you can run any blazer over us. I've been talking all day to get Bishop Drake to the point where he'd agree to spare your life. These men want to kill you, and they have reason enough for doing it. So you'd better make tracks right now."

"What does he say?" shouted Drake, coming to the door of the house. When Stout did not answer, he stepped out and came over, his eyes as baleful and dangerous as a rattlesnake's.

"Won't go, eh?" he snarled. "You leave him to me. I'll soon put a ring in his nose. What do you mean," he demanded, glaring intolerantly at Tarrant, "pushing in where you know you're not wanted? Don't you know this girl has been sent by Brigham Young in the care of Brother Stout? Then why can't you leave her alone? What is she to you, anyway?"

"She's my promised wife," answered Zachary, "and I won't leave this camp without her."

"Oh, you won't, hey?" jeered Drake, rolling his eyes at the people who had gathered to witness their quarrel. "I venture to say that you will. You'll leave here tomorrow morning, a sadder and wiser man. I'm the boss here . . . understand?"

He stood looking at Tarrant, his lips drawn to a grim line, then turned and swaggered away, leaving Zachary to face a battery of hostile eyes. For a man to oppose their bishop, and the will of Brigham Young, was to them the unpardonable sin; it was a sin past all forgiveness, and many a man for less had had his blood poured out on the ground. But Zachary had made his choice the day before, when he had turned back to follow Deseret. Now the soldiers were far away and the Avenging Angels of Lot Drake would never let him reach them alive. He must fight it out to the end.

The day dragged on, and, as the hush of evening came, Zachary sat by the fire with Lingo. Their meager meal was over and, furtively dabbing at his nose with snuff, the prophet of the Lord scanned the cliffs. Like a giant shrouded for death the Sleeping Chief lay outstretched, his grim features showing sharply against the sky. As the dying sun turned the rocks a deeper red, the prophet began to mutter to himself.

"I see a vision," he said at last, his eyes gleaming with prophetic fire, and pointed to the blood-red cliff. "I see visions," he went on, "but these men of little faith see nothing. Their eyes are blind and sealed. The Lord has not given them His blessing and the gift of the Holy Ghost. But His will is made manifest to me by the revelations of His Spirit. Do you see that face on the cliff? That is not the face of a Lamanite. It is the countenance of Bishop Drake." He paused and sat silently, his lips working rapidly as he muttered to himself, and then he turned solemnly to Zachary. "Our bishop is going to die," he announced. "His days on earth are numbered. I see him in his coffin, and the blood runs out of his breast. There are soldiers standing near and their guns give forth smoke. There is no one there that is his friend."

He shook his head regretfully, and turned back to the titanic form, stretched so grimly along the summit of the cliff, but the ruddy glow had vanished. Somber shadows had taken its place and the prophet blinked, turning inquiring glances at Tarrant. "Was I talking?" he asked, speaking low. "Tell no one . . . it is the will of the Lord." And he bowed his head in prayer.

Zachary rose up quietly and left him to his dreams and his communion with his inner spirit, and yet he was not unimpressed. Jake Lingo had prophesied the first day they had met that they would stand on the bank of a river and watch his people pass by. Only the day before that prophecy had come true, except for one unimportant detail. The people had not smiled as they passed. And now, as they gathered for their evening prayer meeting, they regarded him with alien eyes.

All day the hard-worked women had been washing clothes in the muddy creek and tidying up their children after the journey. As Zachary followed the crowd to the light of the big campfire, he saw they were all dressed in their best. The men had washed and shaved and put on their Sunday suits, the women were many of them in white. Close by Mrs. Stout, Deseret sat with the rest, attired in her dimity gown. It was her one good dress, the gown she had worn before when Tarrant had met her at the dance, but now she was overly pale, her girlish beauty had vanished, and her eyes were haunted and distrait. She was afraid, and Zachary watched her closely. What was it that she feared—was it Drake?

The bishop came late to the fire, his bull neck confined in a starched collar, his broad shoulders bulging the sleeves of his coat. Although he bowed his head in prayer and took part in the singing, there was an angry, dominating look in his eyes. Elder Stout in sober black took charge of the meeting, leading off in the singing and prayers. After the service was over, he rose up and cleared his throat, then summoned a perfunctory smile.

"Brethren and sisters," he began, "you all know the Bible saying . . . 'It is not good for man to live alone.' The God of Abraham has commanded us to marry and bring forth children to build up the heavenly kingdom and we are gathered on this occasion to celebrate the wedding of our good bishop, Brother Drake"—he bowed toward the bishop, whose eyes never changed their set stare, and cleared his throat again—"to Sister Deseret Mayberry."

Zachary felt his heart leap and stop. "Why . . . what's that?" he cried, struggling to gain his feet, but two burly men had suddenly seized him from behind and were holding him like a vise.

"You shut up!" ordered Drake, rising up and coming toward him. As their eyes met, Tarrant saw he was trapped. The men at his back were Avenging Angels and their pistols were pressed against his body. "I won't stand any interference with the customs of our people," announced Drake as he turned to the company. "Are you ready to go ahead, Brother Stout?"

He strode over before the elder and every eye in the company was fixed on the trembling Deseret. She sat huddled like a child against the ample bosom of Mrs. Stout, who was patting her and urging her to rise. Other women gathered about her, raising her gently to her feet, and still Deseret hid her face. But as the loud voice of Lot Drake suddenly called her by name, she struck them aside and faced him.

"I won't marry you!" she cried defiantly.

"Yes, you will," he answered. "You have been given to me by the Lord, by the hand of his Prophet, Brigham Young. He holds the keys to seal for time and all eternity, and he has sent you to be my wife."

"I don't care," she sobbed, "I won't marry you. And if you make me do it . . . I'll kill you!"

"Kill me!" he exclaimed, squinting his keen eyes down threateningly, and then he laughed in his throat. "All right,

Elder," he said, "I'll risk it."

He caught her in his arms and led her before Stout, who stood waiting, book in hand. As Tarrant struggled against his guards, he felt a knife against his side and the sweep of a flowing red beard. Ammon Clark was stooping over him, ready to kill him with one thrust if he broke in on the marriage ceremony. Like a man in a nightmare, where he cannot move a hand, Zachary sat awaiting the inevitable. And suddenly Deseret ceased her futile resistance and stood quietly by the side of Lot Drake. Not for nothing had he dominated the lives of his people during thirty years of strife—he swayed her against her will by the touch of his hands and the power of his masterful eyes.

"We are ready," he announced to the elder, and a hush fell upon the audience. They had known from the first what her destiny must be, and Deseret had known it herself. Now as the time came for the fateful words to be pronounced, they held their breath and stared. Only Jake Lingo stirred, raising his head in a listening pose, and Drake drew his brows down and scowled.

"I hear a horse," announced Lingo, holding his hand up for silence.

Drake turned quickly to Clark. "Take that crazy fool away," he ordered.

"It is the messenger!" shrilled Lingo. "He's coming up the road . . . the messenger from Brigham Young!"

He flung his arm up imperatively, and, as they craned their heads to listen, there was a patter of hoofs down the cañon.

"It's a loose horse!" burst out Drake. "Take this crazy loon away! And go ahead, Elder Stout. . . ."

"There he comes!" shrieked Lingo as a horseman hove in sight. "It's Ed Haskell on Brother Laney's racer!"

"It's the roan!" shouted a voice, and in an instant all was clamor, for Jake Lingo had foreseen this in a vision. The circle by the fire suddenly broke up in confusion. As the rider trotted up, his horse shying at the fire, they rushed forward to see what he bore.

"Here's a letter for Elder Stout," announced the messenger, and a silence fell on the crowd. Here was prophecy, revelation, the holy power of the Spirit made manifest in their midst, and they turned reverently to Jacob, the prophet.

"Open the letter!" he commanded with a gesture to Stout. Even Bishop Drake felt his power. He had changed in that moment from a ragged desert guide to a man who communed with God.

The elder tore open the letter and scanned it hastily by the firelight. As he read, he looked up in amazement, then he leaned over it closer and read it through to the end.

"It ain't possible," he muttered at last.

"What ain't possible?" demanded Drake, reaching angrily for the letter, but Stout snatched it hastily away.

"This is a letter from the Prophet," he said, and passed it on to Lingo.

"It's the Lord's will!" responded Lingo after a silence. "Shall I read it aloud, Brother Stout?"

"Give me that letter!" broke in Drake, suddenly asserting his authority.

Lingo handed it over, though reluctantly. Then every eye was fixed on the face of the bishop as he began to read by the fire. After fumbling in vain for his glasses, he held the letter at arm's length, squinting his eyes down in order to decipher it. As he made out the first words, a muttered curse escaped his lips, and he looked up angrily at the messenger. "Where'd you get this letter?" he demanded.

The Mormon boy avoided his eyes. "From President Young," he said at last.

"You're a liar!" shouted Drake, suddenly beside himself with rage. "He never sent no such word. What? Me cut off from the church . . . after all I've done for it? You wrote this thing yourself!"

"No, sir," denied the messenger indignantly.

"Cut off!" exclaimed Drake, squinting again at the letter. "All my property taken away? My women divorced? My God, it can't be so!"

"That is what the letter says," stated Stout.

Drake raised his lion-like head. He was still a master of men. "He don't dare to cut me off," he declared. "I've done his dirty work too long. Suppose I'd tell what I know . . . what would happen to Brigham Young? I'll fix this up, damned quick."

He paced back and forth, and glanced at Ammon Clark who responded with a loyal nod.

"My enemies have been at work," said Drake. "But I am still the bishop, and don't you forget it. Go ahead with the wedding, Elder Stout."

He turned on Stout, his eyes stern and menacing, but the elder shook his head.

"No," he said, "you can't marry her now. You've been cut off from fellowship with the church."

"But Brigham Young sent her to me. She's mine and always has been. I'm going to have her, no matter what you say."

He caught Deseret by the arm and drew her toward him, but Stout did not shrink from him now.

"You didn't read the whole letter," he said. "The Prophet has placed you under the curse."

"The curse!" cried Drake. "After all that I've done for him. It ain't reasonable. What was my offense?"

"The letter says," stated Stout, "that you were the leader of the Indians in the Mountain Meadows Massacre. You killed all those innocent people."

"Innocent people!" raved Drake. "They were guilty as hell. And Brigham Young ordered them killed. He told me to kill them, and thanked me for it afterward. I had orders . . . from Brigham himself!"

"You did not," returned Stout, "and I warn every Saint that Lot Drake has been cursed by the church. He is no longer our bishop. He is cut off!"

"Cut off?" muttered Drake, and, as the people gazed upon him, he suddenly realized his fate. In one day he had been stripped of everything he possessed—his bishopric, his property, his wives. He had fallen from the heights and one stroke of the pen had cut him off from all hope. Even his celestial kingdom had been taken away from him, and in the world to come his women and children would not be his own. The Prophet had cut him off.

"My God," he sobbed, and, as the people moved away, he bowed his head and wept.

Chapter Twenty

When morning dawned on the camp of the emigrants, Lot Drake and the Avenging Angels had vanished. During the night they had ridden off into the fastnesses of the mountains, leaving the missionaries to shift for themselves. For these wild riders of the desert acknowledged no man as their master, unless perhaps it was Lot Drake. When he was cursed and banned, their light allegiance snapped and they had abandoned the wagons to their fate. The ferryboat had been built and the dug way that led down to it, but the one man who was capable of making the crossing a success had been cut off from the fellowship of the church. Strong man that he was, he had broken down and wept when the letter that excommunicated him was read. Brigham Young had been his friend, his leader, almost his God, since the death of the Prophet Joseph. He had obeyed him in everything and at the end of thirty years he found himself under the curse. No Mormon could harbor him on pain of death, or give him food and drink. He was an outcast, a fugitive, in worse stead than an apostate, for he still remained firm in the faith. The Mormon doctrine was in his blood, it colored his every thought, and now he was cast out of the kingdom. But after his burst of grief, he had gone grimly on his way and the Avenging Angels had dispersed to their hiding places.

The Mormon teamsters had risen early and caught up their horses, for Stout's orders were to prepare for a start. But now their hearts were not in it and they harnessed slowly, while the women piled their goods into the wagon. There was grass here and shelter from the wind, which was roaring across the mouth of the Pahreah. Before them lay the terrors of the treacherous crossing and the perils of the dug way beyond. It mounted up from the ferry, a hairline against the cliff, a road to daunt the stoutest heart. Beyond lay the poison water holes of the Painted Desert and the warriors of old Kuchene. With Drake and his men to help, to pilot them over the river and up the road they had cut, the emigrants would have followed their lead. But the same hand that had sent them forth on this mission to Arizona had cut off their trusted bishop. Lot Drake could have pulled them through.

The men lagged at their work, talking low among themselves. Then as Moses Stout called them sharply to task, they grew bolder and murmured openly.

"We can't climb that hill," cried one, pointing his whipstock at the dug way, "so what's the use to cross?"

"We can't cross!" chimed in another. "Who knows how to work that boat? We ought to have Lot Drake."

"Lot Drake has been cut off," answered Moses Stout sternly. "There's nothing to do but start. The Prophet has ordered us on no account to turn back. The rest is in the hands of the Lord. He has guided our people through greater perils than this. All that is needed is a little faith."

He climbed up into his wagon and kicked off the brake. When the lead wagons failed to start, he swung out and drove past them, for there was no turning back for him. Only the night before he had seen the anger of the Prophet as it was visited on Bishop Drake, and rather than share his fate he was prepared to risk everything, even the loss of his wife and family. His orders were explicit, on no account to turn back, and, if he died, it was for the upbuilding of the kingdom. They were pioneers of the church, for other wagon trains would follow them. But, as he pulled out, only one man went with him and that was the Gentile, Zachary Tarrant.

As, with Ammon Clark's knife pressed threateningly against his heart, he had witnessed the ordeal of Deseret, Zachary had conceived a greater hate than ever before of the Mormons and all that they taught. He had seen an innocent girl sent out by Brigham Young to be made the wife of their brutal bishop. When the bishop had been cursed, he had seen her droop like a flower and fall to the ground in a faint. Now she lay in the jolting wagon, barely able to lift her head. Where she went, he would follow. It was not for love of Stout or for loyalty to Brigham Young that he pressed on where others were afraid, but because Deseret was there. She had been saved by the same hand that had sent her to her fate, although not from any eleventh-hour repentance. The Prophet had sacrificed Drake as he had intended to sacrifice her, in order to protect himself. Brigham Young had fled across the borders of the State of Deseret to escape arrest at the hands of the marshals, and now, seeing the net of the law closing in, he had thrown out a bishop as a sop. He could not rule Utah and retain his prestige while he dwelt like a fugitive in Arizona, but if the leaders of the church could be supplied with a scapegoat, his kingdom might yet be saved. So he had struck again, boldly, and Bishop Drake had fallen, like Lucifer cast into hell. He was a pawn in a mighty game, like this party of frightened emigrants sent to break a new route of retreat. If one or both were lost, there would still be more bishops, and more leaders like Moses Stout.

Stout led off now alone and, crossing the muddy Pahreah, swung around a rocky point to the ferry. But, as he went bumping and grinding over the washed boulders to the boat, the Mormons came dragging along behind. They dared not turn back, after witnessing the fate of their bishop. Although the Indians were gathering on the opposite cliffs, they followed along after Stout. Jacob Lingo was in the lead and they put their trust in him, for he had prophesied that no harm would befall them.

Near the base of the high cliff where the river, leaving its dark cañon, suddenly turned to a placid stream, a broad flatboat made of driftwood was moored to the shore, awaiting the crossing of the emigrants. Coils of rope lay on its deck and two skiffs were hauled up. But Moses Stout was not a river man, nor were any of his men, and the wagons came to a halt. A boat was sent across, seeking an anchorage for the long towrope. The women and children climbed out to watch. But as the skiff touched the opposite shore, a yell greeted them from the cliffs that suddenly were alive with Navajos.

They were stripped and painted for war, brandishing lances and long muskets, and with high, defiant whoops they stood out boldly on the summit and motioned the Mormons to go back. The boat returned immediately, but Moses Stout was determined and, with Jake Lingo as his interpreter, he rowed across unarmed and held up his hand for peace.

"Ah-hah-lah-ney!" he shouted, but they screamed back words of abuse.

"Go back!" they motioned.

When the Mormons started forward, they threatened them, then sullenly withdrew. They wanted no talk with the hated *Gomelays*, not even with their friend Jacobee, and Lingo shook his head as they returned to the boat, for he knew that their actions meant war. To begin crossing their wagons would be to invite attack, and at a time when their forces were divided. There was a long conference among the leaders, and then the Mormons camped where they were, without attempting to cross.

Although there were some who still held out against the orders of their leader, there could be no turning back without braving the wrath of Brigham Young. The next morning they ac-

172

cepted the inevitable. The skiffs put off, leading swimming horses across the river, and, as the first wagon was run aboard, they towed the cumbersome ferryboat until it touched on the other side.

Driftwood was thrown in to bridge the treacherous quicksands, the wagon was dragged to high ground, and soon wagon after wagon was being ferried across and landed on the broad, shelving ledge. A chute was built to guide their loose stock into the water. and the horse herd and milk cows were crossed, and still the lurking Navajos held off. Not an Indian was seen, which to some seemed a good omen, but Jake Lingo kept his eyes on the cliffs.

The Navajos were treacherous and, with their eyes on the rich plunder of the train, they were biding their time to strike. But strike they would and only a miracle could save the Mormon emigrants from destruction. Always before, old Kuchene and the western Navajos had been the friends of the peaceful *Gomelays.* They had come to the river to trade blankets for ponies and buy tobacco and trade goods at the stores, but the death of Kuchene's three sons and the return of his youngest, shot through the back and almost dead, had roused the chief to a fanatical hate.

He had declared war on the Mormons, though nominally at peace with the *Belikanas,* as they called the Americans to the east. Three peace missions on the part of Lingo had come to nothing, although each time he had risked his life. They had motioned him away and ridden off into the desert, and Jake had been too wise to follow. But now, with their women and children, their cattle and their horses, the emigrants were invading the Indian country. If the Navajos withdrew, it was only to tempt them further, beyond their last chance of help. Jacob Lingo was not alone in his knowledge of Indian warfare and of the strategy of the crafty Navajos, for Zachary Tarrant had spent his life in the frontier forts of the West, and he, too, watched the cliffs. If there had been any escape from the murderous Avenging Angels, he would have snatched Deseret by force and ridden away with her in the night, but Deseret was weak from the shock of her fright and the Avenging Angels were guarding the water holes.

When the detachment of dragoons had ridden in to House Rock Springs, the Avenging Angels had fled before them, but the footprints of a lone stranger would invite a swift pursuit, and the desert would do the rest. There was no escape, and so Tarrant followed on, although he took no part in the work. The Mormons put up with him, but only Jacob Lingo would give him a place by the fire. He was a Gentile—a government spy.

The broad ledge of rock upon which the emigrants had landed was really the beginning of the new cañon wall that farther west became the Grand Cañon. It led up at a rugged pitch to the base of a higher cliff, and then there began the tenuous line of the dug way, three hundred feet above the stream. The first wagon pulled up the pitch, and, while the women and children walked, the driver essayed the ascent. With not six inches to spare between the crumbling edge and the solid face of the cliff, he drove out with a steady hand. His four draft horses pulled evenly, every move was auspicious until he came to the last steep descent. Then, despite his backing wheelers and squealing brakes, the wagon slipped, slid sideways, and rushed down, and at the foot of the hill, though he escaped unhurt, his wagon and team piled up.

Sweating teamsters ran in and disentangled the frightened horses, righted the wagon, and sent it ahead. Then, one by one, the less competent drivers moved forward to take their turn at the dug way. From the teamster's seat the outer wheels seemed riding on air, balanced precariously on the edge of the precipice, and, as the third wagon reached the middle of the dug way, the driver took fright and reined away. Instantly his front hub struck the bank, the wagon came to a halt, the horses cramped the wheels and backed. Before he knew it, the frightened German on the seat had one hind wheel over the edge.

Stout and the others ran to his aid as he threw on the brakes and jumped to save his life. As Tarrant rode up, he saw them stop and hesitate, for the wagon was trembling on the brink. Only a steady hand could save the panic-stricken horses from being dragged down the terrible descent. Zachary ran to the rescue. The instincts of a lifetime prompted him to seek the place of danger, but, as he blocked the hind wheel and started forward to take the reins, he met a big, bearded Mormon. He, too, had stepped forward, but at sight of the young soldier he drew back with a quick flare of hate.

"Go ahead, if you know so much," he sneered.

"Oh, no," retorted Zachary. "It's your outfit. Do it yourself. I couldn't tell you Mormons anything."

"Yes, go ahead," taunted another Mormon, "we was just waiting for some Gentile to show us how to handle these teams."

"Oh, you were, eh?" flung back Tarrant, suddenly stung into action. "Well, dig me out a channel to lead that wheel back on the grade, and I'll undertake to show you several things."

He snatched a pick off the wagon, and, while the Mormons held the team, he dug a ditch for the wheel. Then, stepping up into the seat, he unwound the long whiplash and motioned the Mormons away.

"Ho, boys!" he called as he tightened the reins and slapped the trembling wheelers across the rump. As they leaned into the collar, the long whiplash swung forward and cracked behind the scrambling leaders. They lay low as they set their feet and tightened the slatting chain, the wagon heaved forward and mounted up. It took the ruts again, and Zachary held it in the road until he came to the last fearful pitch. Then he threw on the brake and stepped down.

"Well, go on!" taunted the big Mormon, who had been following along behind. "What's the matter? Are ye afraid to drive down?"

"No, I've got too much sense," answered Tarrant. "Maybe you'd like to show me how?"

"Heh, we couldn't tell you nothing," jeered the Mormon, and Zachary turned to Stout.

"Bring me two yoke of oxen," he said, "and I'll show you how to go down this hill."

He unharnessed the useless leaders while the oxen were being brought up, and swung up into the seat.

"Now hook those oxen on behind," he directed, "and make them pull back with their yokes."

They came up, moving slowly, as placid and unafraid as the horses had been nervous and shy. When their chain was attached to the hind axle of the wagon, they set their splayed toes and laid back. The ox driver walked in front of them, striking their horns with his gad, and, as Zachary eased the brake, the huge wagon moved slowly down, reaching the bottom in a cloud of dust.

"That's how." Zachary nodded, throwing the reins to the German owner.

The teamsters gave him a cheer.

"All right, mister." The big Mormon grinned. "You showed us, and no mistake."

Moses Stout sprang forward to shake hands. "Tarrant," he said, "I want you to cross my team. I'd feel safer than driving it myself."

CHAPTER TWENTY-ONE

In the desperate venture before them the Mormons needed every man who could drive a team or carry a gun. When Tarrant came back and drove Stout's wagon across the dug way, they forgot that he was a Gentile. Better than any man there he could handle the heavy wagons as they followed the hairline of the grade for he had learned his business from the best freighters in the West—the regular Army teamsters. After Stout's wagon had been crossed, Zachary took another, and then another, and, when the last one had safely passed and the people gathered to resume their journey, they looked up at him, where he sat resting, and smiled. It was then that Jacob Lingo struck his hand on his knee and remembered his cherished vision.

"What did I tell you, Elder Stout?" he cried. "Do you see this scene before us . . . the wagons going by, the people passing on foot and looking up and smiling at Zack? This is the very scene I saw when the Holy Spirit came over me and I spoke with the voice of prophecy. I saw us three standing together on the banks of a river and the people looking up as they passed. From that day to this I have claimed Zack as our friend, though he is an enemy of Lot Drake and the rest. But the inner voice has told me he will do us a great service, so why should we not be his friends?"

"I remember," assented Stout, "this is that vision you spoke of when we met by the canal at Hurricane, but you said then that a woman would come riding down the road who would make Tarrant go with us."

"And so she did," declared Lingo, fixing Stout with his gleaming eyes. "It was the daughter of the Prophet, Tamar Young."

"True enough," admitted Stout, "but Tarrant was coming back when he stopped and joined our train."

"The way of the Lord is past understanding," defended Lingo. "The woman came and Zack rode off with her, and who knows what passed between them? Some word that she said must have turned him from his purpose, for he told us he would never go."

"Very likely," murmured Stout, gazing absently up the wash where the wagons were moving ahead, "but we must send forward some scouts, Brother Jacob. The Lord has blessed us in our passage across the river but there is a greater danger ahead."

"I will go," volunteered Lingo, "and Zack will go with me. The Indians will not trouble us today. Something tells me we will reach Navajo Springs in safety." And he rode off, smiling to himself.

To the others he was a dreamer, seeing visions at all seasons, only a small part of which ever came true, but to himself he was a seer, a prophet of the Holy Spirit, a man who dreamed better than he knew. Only his own unworthiness obscured the clarity of the visions that were sent by the Holy Ghost, and the inner voice was lost in the jangle of tongues raised by these men of little faith. They doubted his words unless proof was given as strong as Holy Writ, but with Zachary Tarrant the whole prophecy had come true and he regarded him with a benevolent smile. For, since his coming had been prophesied, he was under the direction of the Lord and an instrument of His will.

They rode up a rocky wash and across a high mesa where the wagons rolled smoothly along. As evening came on, the train was parked at the base of the cliff where a spring gave good water for all. The horses were hobbled and turned out to graze, closely guarded by well-armed men. The Navajos did not molest them, and, as they gathered around their fire, the Mormons sang songs of praise. Zachary gathered with the rest, to steal a glimpse of Deseret who had avoided his eyes all day. As she sat there, so meek and quiet, yet starting at every rough voice, he read what was in her mind. Even there she was afraid of Lot Drake.

For years she had been haunted by the fear of this man who had claimed her by a revelation of the Lord, and the perils of the dug way, the menace of hostile Indians, had not stamped out the memory of his threat. She was afraid because she knew him and the unyielding resolution with which he bludgeoned his way through the world. What he wanted he took, and, if he could not get her by marriage, he would seize her and carry her off by force. In the midst of this Painted Desert into which they were going Lot Drake had a hidden retreat. Some said he had a wife and a family of children among the Hopis, in their village at Moencopi Wash. For with Navajos and Hopis he lived up to his name—he was a man among men and a devil among women—a man without fear, or remorse. What he wanted, he took and few men there were who dared to say no to him.

While Deseret sat brooding, her mind still on the wedding that the Mormons had tried to force upon her, she saw across the fire the eyes of her lover and a wan smile lit up her face. Except for a premonition of greater terrors to come she could almost let her heart be glad, but Drake had claimed her, despite the church, and something told her he was not far away. Even now, while they sat there, he might be up on the high cliffs, looking down and marking her for his prey, or he might be far away, gathering the Indians to surround them and demand her as a ransom from Stout. She shuddered and bowed her head, and, as she turned away, Zachary saw the tears in her eyes.

Bitter Springs was the next stop on the old Mormon road

that led to the Little Colorado, and, after a wearisome journey over the rocks and up sand washes, they parked their wagons below it. The country was level now, except for the echoing cliff and the broken hills to the south. Without a break the long cliff stretched away, barring the way to the east and pushing them farther and farther south into the sands of the Painted Desert.

Huge stripes of red and black marked the face of this painted wall, with masses of white and green, and, above it, on the mesa, ranged the sheep of the pastoral Navajos and their herds of horses and goats. South from the rimrock there was nothing but desert, where not even an Indian could live. Its waters were poisonous, the soil barren and full of salts, and to the Mormons the land seemed accursed. Only the driving power of a will as implacable as death had sent them into this desolate land, and, as they tasted the acrid water of Bitter Springs, the women recalled their lost homes. They had left neighbors and friends, running waters and fertile fields at the call of Brigham Young, but, as their children refused to drink and the night shut down upon them, they gazed at their husbands with scared eyes. The sweet water in their barrels was reserved for drinking, though little by little it was drawn off furtively, and, after washing their children, the mothers sought their beds, leaving the men to take turns standing guard.

The stars pricked the sky with a million tiny tapers, wolves howled on the plains, owls hooted from the cliff, and then in the tense stillness the horses broke and ran, fighting their hobbles and snorting with fear. At the camp all was confusion, men catching their night horses and women silencing their frightened little ones. After the rush of the stampede the horses were brought back and the men returned to their beds. The word had been passed—it was Indians.

A naked form had been seen, running to windward of the horse herd and waving a Navajo blanket. All through the night there were stampedes and alarms, and men riding out from camp. The morning found them haggard and dead for sleep, the women excited and scared. But after a short conference the horses were harnessed and the wagon train moved on up the wash.

The limited flow of water from Bitter Springs was not sufficient to supply their horses and cows; the sparse grass had been fed off, there was no wood for their fires—they must push on to Limestone Tanks. There, from deep holes in the rocks, sweet water could be hoisted up and poured into troughs for their stock, but it was still twenty miles up the wash.

Night had saved them from attack, for the Navajos were superstitious, more afraid of *chinday* devils than the bullets of the white men—but at dawn the *chindays* had fled. They were back in their holes, in the cliff dwellings of the ancient dead, and Kuchene and his warriors became bolder. In the darkness their scouts had crept down the cliffs and harassed the Mormon invaders, but now, as the covered wagons pulled slowly up the wash, the hilltops suddenly swarmed with Navajos. Stripped to the waist and painted for battle, they were riding their fleetest ponies. Brandishing their lances and shouting defiance, they galloped from point to point, and all the time their numbers grew.

Pushing doggedly ahead to reach the water, the Mormons ignored their threats. The valley had opened out, there was room to maneuver, and the wagons could be parked for defense. Scouts rode on ahead and out at the sides to give notice of any attack, and every man carried his gun in his hand. So, hour by hour, they toiled steadily uphill, toward Limestone Tanks and safety. Once parked below the tanks, and with the provisions that they carried, they could stand off the Indians for weeks, but out in that desolate sand wash with the sun beating down on them they were suffering already for water. The tired horses, bathed in sweat, were weakening rapidly and the teamsters lashed them mercilessly; the slow oxen hardly flinched from the gad. Almost midway between the water holes the Navajos rushed upon them, and the order was given to park.

From a narrow side cañon, over a thousand naked warriors whipped out and swept down on the train. The Mormon scouts came fleeing before them, firing their guns to give the alarm. As the slow wagons spread out and swung in toward a common center, every man except the teamsters rushed out. They dropped down behind rocks and bushes, ready to fire if the Indians came too close, but, as the great wave of horsemen seemed about to break over them, the Navajos swept to one side. Riding their ponies at a gallop and waving their guns defiantly, they split as if on a rock and, swooping out around the Mormons, they made a feint to attack the teams. But it was only a preliminary, a savage parade to impress the enemy with their strength. After circling the wagon fort, they came to a halt, and the chief rode out for a talk.

Through an opening between two wagons the loose stock was driven in and the wheels chained together for defense. The draft animals were unharnessed and tied to the wagons and the women and children made safe. Then, with Lingo to interpret, Moses Stout rode slowly forth to hear the Indians' demands. They were outnumbered ten to one, without water and in an enemy country, but having met the show of force with a show of their powerful defense, Stout awaited the next move in the game. His men had not fired, nor had the Navajos fired at them, for the time had not come for battle. According to the code of savage warfare the game had just begun, and each side had shown itself prepared.

The Indians had halted the train ten miles from the nearest water and in the heat of a desert sun, but the Mormons with their rifles could shoot farther and straighter and they stood their ground, unafraid. In the open they could see their leader and Jacob Lingo, impassively facing the chief, and he, with arrogant gestures, pointing first at the ranks of his men and then at the Mormon wagons. He talked long and violently, waving his arms and shaking his fist. Then, very slowly, Jacob Lingo made answer, with few words and little play of the hands. The chief replied angrily, voicing his demands in loud shouts, and, as his warriors set up a yell, the Mormon leaders turned back to report to their waiting men.

"It's Kuchene," said Stout as a crowd gathered around him. "He says the Mormons killed three of his sons, and he wants three men to pay for them. And if we don't send them out right away, he says he'll kill us all."

"We didn't kill his sons," burst out Lingo bitterly, "and I told him so, a hundred times. It was done by that Gowdy gang of horse thieves and bank robbers . . . they were living in the country at the time. But no, he won't hear of it, and rather than give in I'm in favor of fighting to the last."

"I'd rather be killed myself," spoke up Stout, "than send out one of the brethren to be tortured. We're caught in a bad place, and I believe they intend to attack, but we've got to put up a bold front. I'm in charge of this wagon train, and, as long as I'm the captain, there'll be no man surrendered. But don't start the fighting, boys. Let 'em ride as close as they want to, and wait till I give you the word. Because if we kill one of these Indians, we'll never get through alive. What do you think about it, Brother Jake?"

"No, they'll never let up on us if we kill one of their warriors," assented Lingo with a lugubrious nod. "Best thing is to shoot at their horses."

He rode out into the open to make their reply, and, as he held up his hand, the Navajos all watched him—until he threw it to the right, palm up, the Indian sign for no. Then as they set up a yell, he pushed his right hand toward them, his thumb between the first two fingers. It was a sign of defiance, an expression of scorn, a dare for them to do their worst, and the Indians raised their weapons and charged. But their anger was not so great as to lead them to court destruction. When the defenders opened fire, they swung down behind their ponies and went by at a pounding gallop.

Again and again they charged, as if determined to take the wagons and shoot down the people behind them, but each time their courage waned and they went thundering by, a millrace of seething ponies and men. Then, as evening came on, they retired up the cañon, and the Mormons camped in their fort.

CHAPTER TWENTY-TWO

All night from their wagons the emigrants could hear the drums and the shrill, excited singing of the Indians. They were dancing the war dance, lashing themselves to a frenzy for the battle that would come with the dawn. On the point of the cliff a huge signal fire had been started to summon still more warriors to the fight, and from the summits of distant peaks other fires answered the call, until the horizon was dotted with lights. The whole nation was aroused and on the move to the west, to turn back the Mormon invaders.

At the wagons the women and children were bundled off to bed, and then by the fire the men gathered in a circle to decide what their next move should be. But this was no gathering of free American emigrants, able to turn back if they chose or to rebel against the orders of their captain—the missionaries were divided into tens, each commanded by a leader, and the will of Moses Stout was supreme. Lingo sat by his side as his guide and adviser and a huge Mormon named Amos Bush, who had opposed them from the start, sat opposite with his following of malcontents. But Zachary Tarrant, though he was trained in Indian warfare, was relegated to a seat in the rear.

Now that the dug way had been passed and his services were no longer needed, their old, deep-seated suspicions had returned. He was again the government spy, pushing in where he was not wanted and seeking to make trouble for their people. But for him Deseret might consent to marry another Mormon, now that Drake had been cut off from the church. When the Indians had first charged, he had sought to assume command and direct the defense of the fort. Even Stout had turned against him and rejected his advice, which was to push on to Limestone Tanks at any cost.

In the corral formed by their wagons the Mormons had all their horses, besides their oxen and cows, and unless they reached water they would soon be in desperate straits, if not too weak to proceed. But Stout had refused to listen, and, as he opened the meeting, his bloodshot eyes warned Zachary to keep quiet.

"Brethren," he said, after praying for divine guidance, "this is no time for backbiting and spite. We have been sent on this mission and you all know my orders . . . under no circumstances to weaken and turn back. Brigham Young has called this company to blaze the way for our people to escape the persecutions of the government. Even now the federal soldiers are camped by our temple and our leaders are hiding in the hills. But we have been sent ahead to make a road for them to follow, into Arizona and even into Mexico. We cannot turn back, so don't let me hear you ask it. The question is . . . how can we get through?"

"But why can't we turn back?" demanded Bush as his followers grumbled in their throats. "What good will it do the church to have us all killed, and our women and children tortured?"

"You won't be killed if you do what you're told," answered Stout with biting finality. "And Brother Amos, I'm going to report you to the council for punishment . . . you have forgotten your endowment oaths. But since you ask the question, I'm going to answer it for the benefit of the men that stand by you. If we turn back from these Lamanites, they'll think we're afraid of them and they'll follow and kill every one of us. There's only one way to handle an Injun, if you don't want him to run all over you, and that is to stand right up to him. We've got to meet these Navajos like we thought they're nothing . . . like we knowed we could whip a thousand of them . . . and any man that weakens or talks about going back I'll report him to the council for punishment. You have seen Bishop Drake, as brave a man as ever lived and a tower of strength against these Injuns, cut off by the word of the Prophet. He disobeyed Brigham Young, and, when the Prophet found it out, he cut him off from the kingdom. Now I want every man here to remember what happened, and why Lot Drake was cut off. He violated his oath, which calls for obedience to the Prophet, and for that he has been cast out and cursed. Brother Jacob, what do you advise?"

Jacob Lingo cleared his throat and sat in solemn silence after the manner of Indians in council, and at last he raised his head. "I will do what you say," he said.

"I know that," commended Stout, "and I call on the brethren to witness your strength in the faith. But you have lived among the Lamanites and understand their ways. Do you think they are going to fight?"

"They will fight," responded Lingo, "if we shed the first blood. But long ago, as you know, I was called by the Spirit to go and preach the gospel to these people. I was told in a vision I would never die by their hands as long as I did not thirst for their blood. They are the Lamanites of the Scriptures, the scattered remnants of the Children of Israel, but lost in their ignorance and sin. Yet their hearts are good and the Holy Spirit has made manifest to me that I am sent as a messenger of peace. I have laid aside my guns and I am ready to go among them, for I know that Kuchene is my friend."

"Is that so?" sneered Bush. "Then what makes your friend ask for three men to be burned at the stake?"

"Kuchene is my friend," reiterated Lingo after a silence, "but he is angry . . . his heart is bad. I went to him myself and told him the Mormons were his brothers, they loved peace and would be glad to trade. And so, to show his friendship, he sent over his four sons, and three of them were killed. The fourth came back, a bullet hole through his back, cold and hungry and nearly dead. He was thirteen days on the trail without a blanket, and then he laid down to die. But Kuchene was anxious and he rode down to meet his sons, and so he found this boy. Now his heart is bad and he blames it on the Mormons, but we know they were killed by Gentiles."

"Then you will have to fight him," concluded Bush, and Lingo fixed him with his piercing gray eyes.

"I am not afraid to fight," he replied, "like some who are sitting here tonight. But the Lamanites are our brothers and unless we thirst for their blood not a man in this company will be killed."

He lapsed into silence, gazing fixedly at the fire. As the Mormons murmured approval, Stout rolled his eyes at Tarrant.

"What do you think, young man?" he asked, and Zachary shrugged his shoulders. Stout knew as well as he did his views in the case, but at last he rose up and spoke.

"My advice," he said, "is to harness up right now and strike for Limestone Tanks. You're out of water and out of feed. Your animals are suffering already. If you wait till morning, your situation will be serious, especially if the Indians attack. But in the night they're superstitious, and, while they may stampede your horses, I doubt if they'll stand up and fight."

"Do you know more about these Indians than Jacob?" demanded Stout, regarding him sternly. "Well, you heard what he had to say. The Lamanites are our brothers . . . we don't kill them, like the Gentiles . . . and tomorrow Brother Jacob will make a peace."

He rose up abruptly, and, as the Mormons dispersed, Zachary caught the hostile glint of deep-set eyes. But he, too, knew Indians, and the loud whoops of the war dancers brought up pictures of naked, prancing warriors. Up the cañon the Navajos were acting out in pantomime the attack that they planned for the morrow, drawing their bows, brandishing their lances, leveling their guns at the enemy, and stabbing them to death with long knives. All night they would repeat it, shouting the war song in chorus and lashing themselves into a fury, and at dawn they would mount their ponies and sweep down on the wagons as resistlessly as the waves of the sea. But the Mormons still believed in miracles. They thought Lingo could turn back the tide.

As the night wore on, the corralled animals became more restless, the cattle bawling incessantly for water; children woke up crying and whimpered until their mothers dipped deeper into the almost empty casks. Zachary lay beneath a wagon behind the sandbags that he had filled, but which the Mormon emigrants had scorned, and listened to the sounds of the night.

In the hills on both sides Navajo scouts yelped like wolves or imitated the *whoo-whooing* of owls. Up the cañon, with the regularity of a heartbeat, the war drums repeated their *tum, tum, tum.* Singing, loud and shrill, like the high quavering of coyotes, the dancers made the night more hideous. But as Tarrant listened, he was suddenly reminded of another train of emigrants—at Mountain Meadows. Surrounded by howling Indians, cut off from the water, yet fighting bravely for their wives and little ones, they had made such a fort as this one. They had corralled their heavy wagons, letting their horses and cattle go, and fought for three days and nights. Men and women were shot down in their dashes for water to give to their children and the wounded, and all the time, over the brow of the hill, there came the measured *tum, tum* of drums. Many were killed, many wounded, and their powder ran low, and then, down the meadow there advanced a white man, holding up a flag of truce.

That white man was a Mormon, this same Bishop Drake

who had at last been cut off from the church. But as long as men lived to remember his bloody deeds, they would blame them on others besides Drake. They would blame the Mormon church, and every guilty man who had participated in that slaughter of innocents, and these men who now scorned Tarrant might yet pay the price of that crime of twenty years before. They, too, were surrounded by bloodthirsty savages, far away from all hope of help. If worse came to worst, they might see their wives and little ones struck down and left for the wolves. Was it Nemesis, or would Lingo save them?

The dawn broke at last, and on the ridges all about they could see dense masses of Indians. They were stripped to a G-string, riding their ponies bareback, and men and horses were painted for war. When Lingo stepped out with his hand held up for peace, they burst into discordant shouts. Kuchene rode out on his red-and-white war pony and began a long oration to his warriors. Then with a shrill yell the savage horsemen rushed upon them, while Lingo fled to the fort.

"Don't kill them!" he cried as the Mormons thrust out their guns.

When the horde was almost upon them, it broke like a wave on a rock and the Indians went flying past. But now, swinging low, they let fly a shower of arrows that struck against the wagons like hail. Sensing the Mormons' fear, they pressed nearer and nearer, daring the white men to open fire.

"Don't shoot!" commanded Stout, running from wagon to wagon.

Although the arrows fell among their animals, causing the horses to kick and squeal, they stood firm and reserved their fire. Then the Indians came riding back, almost obscured in the dust they had made, and the challenge was offered again. With one volley the Mormons could have shot down twenty-five warriors, for now they almost touched the wagons. The whole valley seemed filled with naked men on flying steeds, but Jacob still held up his hand. The Indians formed for another charge, and, as they massed themselves behind him, Kuchene rode out into the open. He was near them now. As he raised his voice, Jacob Lingo could hear every word.

"You Mormons are dogs!" he taunted. "You are afraid to fight, because you know my heart is bad. What are you doing in my country? Didn't I tell you to go back? Now my warriors are gathered to kill you. You pretended to be our friends, but when my sons went among you, you killed them. All but one. He told me who it was that had killed his brothers. It was the *Gomelays*, that pretended to be their friends. They shot them in their sleep as they lay in an old cabin, but my youngest son broke through them and escaped. He rode three days and nights in the bitter cold of winter with the *Gomelays* close behind. Then he hid in a deep cave and heard them hunting for him everywhere, and he knew from their voices they were *Gomelays*. But he escaped them at last and crossed the big river that separates our country from yours. I found him nearly dead and he told me how his brothers were slain. Now what will you *Gomelays* do, send out three men for blood vengeance? Or must we kill you all?"

He paused, and Jake Lingo stepped out to answer him, talking slowly, with few gestures, but speaking firmly. But hardly had he started, when Kuchene cut him off and repeated his demand for three men.

"We did not kill your sons!" replied Lingo. "Have I ever told you a lie? We did not kill your sons and so we will not pay, but we wish to pass through your country. Our cattle have eaten your grass and drained the water from your springs, and for that we will pay you ten cows. We are your friends and so we will pay."

"You talk with a forked tongue," answered Kuchene angrily, darting two fingers from his lips in the snake sign. "Did I come here to get ten cows? Send out three men, to pay for my sons, or I will come and take all your cows. Jacobee, you are worse than a dog!"

He made an insulting gesture, and turned to harangue his people while Lingo went back to the wagons.

"We have got to pay," he said as the men gathered around him, "or we will never get through alive. Kuchene is insulted because I only offered him ten cows, but I think he will take a hundred."

"A hundred!" exclaimed Stout. "I'll never agree to that. If we pay to go through, all the others will have to pay. I know these Injuns too well."

"The cattle will die anyway," contended Lingo. "We'll all die, if we don't get to water. Isn't it better to give up our cattle, and what horses we don't need, than to send out three men to be killed?"

"I'd rather be killed myself than to send out a man," declared Stout as the Mormons began to murmur. "Well, offer him twenty cows. And if he says he won't take them, we'll fight our way to the tanks."

"He won't take them," predicted Lingo as he went back to haggle with the chief, and then, as they argued and threatened and the hot sun rose higher and higher, the corral became an inferno of heat. Women and children begged for water, only to be told again and again that the barrels were dry to the bottom. The cattle and horses, thrashing about in a frenzy of thirst, stirred up the dust till it blinded and choked them, and still the wrangle went on. At first the old chief stood firm in his demand for the lives of three men and blood vengeance, but, as his men swarmed about him and argued for lieu payment, he consented to accept it in part. For each of his sons he would take one hundred cattle or horses, but only if one Mormon was turned over to him to suffer for the sake of the dead.

"No!" answered Stout, when Lingo came back to him to deliver the ultimatum of the chief. "I will never give up a man and I won't pay but one hundred cattle. The church will hold me to account."

Then, as he saw the angry gestures with which Kuchene received his offer, he shouted for Lingo to come back.

"We're going to water," he announced, "and, if these Injuns interfere, we'll fight till the last man is dead."

He turned to the teamsters and ordered the horses harnessed. As the wagons were unchained, he posted the rest of his men where they could protect the advance of the teams. Now that it was too late, he saw that Tarrant had been right when he had advocated a night march to the tanks, but since the Navajos were divided in their demands for indemnity, he counted shrewdly on a split in their ranks.

Only twelve years before, the soldiers from Fort Defiance had rounded up the Navajos like sheep, and for four years they had been held prisoners on the Pecos River until their war-like ardor had cooled. But these soldiers, to the Indians, were men of another nation—the Americans, or as they called them, the *Be-likanas*—for the *Gomelays* to the west had always maintained that they had a separate government. Now in their extremity, they were paying for the deception—and it was too late to appeal for aid. But the Indians of Kuchene, living far to the west, had for the most part escaped the roundup of their people. They had retreated into Utah or taken shelter in the Grand Cañon, and their spirits were far from subdued. For hundreds of years their people had lived by warfare and by raids on the herds of the New Mexicans, and, when they saw the first wagon begin to leave the corral, they seized the chance and charged.

The emigrants were in confusion, some wagons half hitched and the rest waiting the order to start. As the wagon corral was breached, the horses confined within made a rush and poured out the gap. That disaster saved the Mormons from total destruction, for as the Navajos saw the horse herd streaming out of the gap, the horse thief overcame the warrior. Like one man they swerved aside to cut off the escaping herd, while the Mormons parked their wagons and stood at bay.

The horses, that, if given might have bought off their foemen, were now the spoils of war, and with them had gone a good half of the milk cows, which the Navajos promptly turned into beef. But the Mormons had escaped with their lives at least. While Kuchene and his men sang and feasted by their fires, they prepared to defend their rude fort. Bags were filled with sand and piled up beneath the wagons as a protection against arrows and bullets, and shortly after the disaster a messenger made a dash to summon assistance from the settlements. Gaunt and parched as they were, the Mormons prepared for a desperate siege—but off to one side the apostle to the Lamanites sat brooding, for his plans and predictions had failed. The Lord had not softened the heart of Kuchene and the Lamanites had despoiled their Mormon brethren.

CHAPTER TWENTY-THREE

The day wore on in the grim misery of thirst and heat and all night the wailing of children made a ceaseless antiphony to the singing of the war-mad Navajos. Once more the bale fires blazed on the distant peaks to summon more warriors to the siege, and in the morning they swarmed forth to ride circles around the wagons where the Mormons lay sullenly at bay.

The Indians had no fear of the guns that were thrust out at them, for now they seemed as numerous as the sands of the sea while the emigrants were only a handful. Yet, if it came to a fight, many a Lamanite would bite the dust before the Mormons were overcome, and for all their jeers and taunts they did not attack, waiting for thirst to fight their battle for them. Not for twenty-four hours had the Mormons tasted water, and the dry wind cracked their lips till they bled. The wailing of babies had died away, although their mothers no longer soothed them with milk from the few remaining cows. Faces that before had been round and ruddy had suddenly become parchment-like and drawn, but still Moses Stout remained stubborn in his purpose to hold out and wait for help. The runner had set forth on the previous day, well-mounted and leading a spare horse, and by riding hard he could reach the river by dusk and House Rock Valley by dawn. Already Ammon Clark and his tireless horsemen might be galloping across the desert to their aid; at sight of him the Navajos would withdraw, for he feared no man in the world.

Since the Prophet Joseph Smith had blessed his beard, Ammon Clark had never weakened—he believed literally in the prophecy that one man could turn back a thousand and two turn back ten thousand. Joseph Smith had promised him that, as long as his beard remained uncut, he would never die at the hands of the Gentiles. To Clark and his Avenging Angels the Navajos were lower than any Gentile—they were less than the dust at their feet. They were horse thieves and petty murderers, ready to flee at the sight of that band that had ruled the Utah desert for years. Elder Stout still hoped and kept watch down the cañon for the bobbing black hats of the Avenging Angels.

Tired at last of their war-like maneuvers, the Indians withdrew to feast on the last of the beef, and the Mormon men were gathered in council when they heard a shout from the look-out. Far down the wash a single horseman could be seen, flogging his pony at every jump. It was a Paiute Indian, as they could tell by his appearance, and he would not cross the river alone unless he bore some message for the Mormons. A cheer went up as he came galloping toward them, but, before he reached their wagons, he turned suddenly into the hills and rode on to the camp of Kuchene.

"I know him," announced Jacob Lingo as the emigrants turned back sorrowfully, "that's Albert, Lot Drake's adopted boy. He's taking some word from Bishop Drake to the Navajos . . . our runner must have found them at the ferry."

"Lot Drake, not Bishop Drake," spoke up Elder Stout severely, but Lingo paid no heed. Nor did the Mormon emigrants, for two days without water had made them less bigoted in their religion. A helping hand from their one-time bishop would be welcomed by them, although he lay under the curse of the church. Their eyes were deep-sunk and haggard, their tongues swollen with thirst, and even the Prince of Devils, if he had come to their relief, would have received a measure of respect. Now, as they watched the camp and the confusion among the Indians, the most down-hearted suddenly plucked up courage.

"They want a talk," said Lingo as Kuchene held up his hand, and he made the sign of assent.

Having spoiled the enemy and driven off their stock, old Kuchene had declined to meet Lingo all that day, greeting his signals with angry-voiced taunts. The *Gomelays* were cowards; they were afraid to fight. They hid with their women behind the beds of their wagons, but the Navajos would trample them down. They would wait till they came out and stamp them into the ground beneath the feet of their swift-running war ponies, and then they would take their women and sell them for slaves and compel the Mormon children to herd sheep. But now, after the visit of the messenger, they were ready once more for a talk.

Jacob Lingo went out while from the wagons the emigrants looked on, trying to read what was said by the signs. To Tarrant it was evident that Kuchene's demand was still excessive, for Lingo threw out his hand to say no. Then they argued back and forth, Kuchene pointing to the wagons and speaking with increasing vehemence, until at last Lingo returned, his eyes on the ground, his gaunt face set like a mask.

"They want too much," he said. "He asks for one man to be killed for the death of his sons."

"But who was that messenger?" demanded Stout. "What word did he bring? Give us an account of what went on."

"I told you before," answered Jacob sullenly. "It was Lot Drake's Indian boy, Albert. But since the bishop has been cut off. . . ."

"That makes no difference," broke in Stout. "You are concealing something, Brother Jacob, and this is no time for trifling. Speak up. I want the truth."

"What?" cried Lingo. "Would you send out a man, to be

tortured by those Indians?"

"It may be necessary," replied Moses Stout grimly. "Isn't it better for one man to die than to have men, women, and children perish? But what I want to know is what word that Paiute brought. What message did Drake send to Kuchene?"

"He sent word," responded Lingo, "that it was all a mistake, that Kuchene's sons were not killed by the Mormons but by a gang of Gentile outlaws."

"We've told him that a hundred times," said Stout. "What's come over Kuchene, to make him ask for one man? Did he say what man it was?"

"Well . . . yes," admitted Lingo, glancing involuntarily at Tarrant, and suddenly the Mormons understood.

Although he was cut off from the church, Lot Drake was still their friend, still using this wonderful knowledge of the nature of the Indians to save his people from disaster—and since some man must be given to satisfy the blood lust of the Navajos, Drake had fastened the crime on the Gentile. They put their heads together in quick mutterings of approval, and then Elder Stout spoke up.

"What man did he say?" he asked.

"He asked for Zack, here," replied Lingo huskily, and every eye was fixed on Tarrant. All that day he had been clamoring for a small party of men to cut their way through to the water, for any kind of action instead of the passive waiting that was making the Navajos so bold. A swift dash through their lines, a stand at the tanks, and the death of a few of their warriors would break the fighting spirit of these Indians, so recently tamed by the soldiers. But Stout had refused him. As Zachary met his glance, he read what was in his mind. Stout was ready to become a party to Drake's plot for revenge and offer him up as a scapegoat.

"Tarrant," repeated Stout, feigning a measure of astonishment. "But why did he ask for him?"

"Because Lot Drake lied to him," burst out Lingo in a passion. "He sent word that Zack was one of the Gowdy boys that had killed old Kuchene's sons. But I know why he did that, and so do you. He has sold himself to the devil. He has been turned over for a thousand years to the cudgelings of Satan, and this is the devil's work. Zack is our friend. He has helped us in every way, and, if he goes, I'll go myself."

"No, no, Brother Jacob," protested the wagon master earnestly, "that would hardly be fair to the rest. We need you to protect us from the violence of these Lamanites, but with Zack here, things are different. He has forced himself upon us, making trouble at every turn. If he is guilty of this crime, as Bishop Drake says. . . ."

"Bishop Drake!" cried Lingo. "Have you sold yourself, too, to the devil that has entered Lot Drake? You know he is cut off and you know that Zack. . . ."

"Now, now," broke in Stout, laying his hands on Lingo's shoulders and looking him sternly in the eye, "remember where you are, Brother Jacob. And remember your oath of obedience to the church, and submission to the will of the Prophet. The Lord, by the mouth of his servant, Brigham Young, has put me in command of this company. If, after prayer, it seems best to give up Zack Tarrant. . . ."

"You don't need to pray over it," spoke up Zachary with biting scorn. "If I want to go, I'll go. And if I don't want to go, I'd like to see the man that can make me."

He slapped the pistol at his hip and placed his back against a wagon, where he stood with his face to the company. They were a poor, dispirited lot, utterly broken by their hardships and the thwarting restraint of their captain. He had kept them from fighting until the fight had gone out of them, and now they stood cowed by one man.

Dane Coolidge

"You know," went on Tarrant as Stout made no move, "that Lot Drake has only lied. I didn't kill Kuchene's sons, and I wasn't in the country when he claims the deed was done. But in a case like this, with your women and children suffering, I'm willing to do my share. So, if Lingo will go with me to interpret, I'll ride over and see Kuchene . . . and meanwhile you can go on to water."

He ceased speaking and looked around. His eyes met Deseret's as she stood on the edge of the crowd. As the women murmured their thanks, he strode over and mounted his horse. Deseret was still watching him, her eyes big with love as if she divined the purpose of his sacrifice, but he did not turn his head as, with Lingo by his side, he rode out to meet the chief. He was afraid even to speak to her, afraid he might weaken in the stern game that lay before him. Deseret was suffering, too—day by day she had pined away and become more fragile and downcast. She was too weak to wait on the tardy arrival of Ammon Clark and his men. Her ordeal at the river had sapped the last of her strength. Zachary had tried to protect her, and failed. But this he could still do—for her and for the rest—and he rode out to face old Kuchene.

Behind them the Mormons, roused at last from their apathy, were breaking up their wagon corral. The Indians, looking on, were apparently satisfied to let them depart undisturbed. Already at one swoop they had driven off their horse herd, and half of their milk cows as well, and every eye was fixed on the tall man with Jake Lingo who rode out to meet their chief. He still wore his guns—two pistols in his belt and a carbine under his knee—and, as he reined in before Kuchene, he met the glowering stare with a gaze as calm as Lingo's.

"Tell the chief," he said after the half minute of decorous silence that must precede every talk with the Navajos, "that I am the American he asked for."

200

Lingo lifted his hand, and, as a deep silence fell, he repeated the words in Navajo.

"Now tell him," went on Tarrant, "that I deny the false charge that Lot Drake has made against me. But if he will not molest the wagons and let them drive on to the water, I am ready to go and stand trial."

Lingo translated again, and after a long moment of silence Kuchene grunted consent. He was a tall, stalwart man with a nobility of features not uncommon among his race, but his eyes were set in a look of savage hate and his hair was fast turning white. Since the death of his sons, grief had aged him twenty years, but he still sat his fine pony like a warrior. It was the same red-and-white pinto that he had ridden in the first charge and across its white hip there was the mark of a bloody hand, Kuchene's declaration of war.

He had led out his warriors to kill the hated *Gomelays* who he held responsible for the death of his sons. Even now, as they broke the corral and drove away toward Limestone Tanks, he looked after them with glittering eyes. But the victim he had demanded had been surrendered into his hands and he turned and rode away. His men followed after him, casting back covetous glances at the plunder that was about to escape them, but the honor of their people had been vindicated by the outcome and Kuchene would have his revenge.

One by one the heavy wagons pulled away from the corral and took their place in the line of retreat. The Mormons had been defeated. They had feared to attack the Navajos, but the Indians had not pressed them too closely. For the *Gomelays* were white men and, though the American soldiers at Fort Defiance owned no brotherhood, they still might take their part. So they allowed them to proceed and rode away up the slope, looking back with regretful eyes. But, as they topped the ridge, a single horseman left the caravan and came galloping furiously after them.

"Who is that?" croaked Jake Lingo, reining in beside his friend, but Tarrant did not answer. The rider came closer. All the Indians turned their mounts to gaze at the unexpected sight, and then something familiar in the figure on the horse told Zachary that his subterfuge had failed.

"It's Deseret," he said.

CHAPTER TWENTY-FOUR

When Tarrant had ridden out to surrender to Kuchene and stand trial for the death of his sons, it was his final admission of defeat. Ever since he had turned back to protect Deseret from the Saints, he had been thwarted and put in the wrong. They had opposed him in everything, even when as on the day before he had advised them for their own good. They had hesitated and held back until their women and children were dying for lack of a few barrels of water, and yet, ten miles away, the water was waiting—all they needed was the courage to fight. But Stout had paltered with Kuchene until the Indians were spoiled, sensing the weakness and vacillation of their foes, and now they were bold and arrogant, demanding a white man for their blood vengeance—and he had been the man.

His arch-enemy, Lot Drake, had ensnared Zachary at last, playing with diabolical cunning upon the credulity of old Kuchene, half crazed by the death of his sons. Drake had learned, from the messenger that the Mormons had sent, of the perilous situation of the wagon train and at one blow he had disposed of his enemy and won the good will of the emigrants. Still Zachary had not been satisfied that the Indians were beyond control—with the aid of Jacob Lingo he hoped to win them over and escape the death that they planned. In any case, win or lose, he had departed with the thought that at least he had saved Deseret. Now with a madness that matched his own she had come galloping after them, throwing away the safety he had won for her.

"Go back!" he shouted as she came charging up the slope, cutting her way through the startled Indians.

Lingo, too, suddenly leaped into action, waving her back with his long, gaunt arm. But something had come over her, some return of her former fire, and she whipped on recklessly until she reined in by Zachary, who greeted her with a look of reproach. "My God," he cried, "do you want to be killed? Why didn't you stay with the wagons?"

"I was afraid," she panted. "I'd rather be here. Didn't you hear what they said . . . about Lot Drake? I'm afraid of him, Zachary, more than anything in the world. He's trying to get me. I know it."

"But how could he get you, if you stayed with the wagon train? He's been cut off from the church and Elder Stout would never consent. . . ."

"Elder Stout is a fool!" she burst out angrily. "He's nothing but a big bag of putty! Didn't he take me across the desert to give me to Lot Drake? Then how can we trust him now? Drake lied to these Indians to get you out of the way and win the good will of the Saints. I know how he works . . . the next thing he'd come riding in and demand me of Stout. He's made up his mind that he's going to have me and he'll never give up, till he's dead. . . ." Her voice trailed off despairingly, and, as she bowed her head, Kuchene rode up, glaring angrily.

"Who is this woman?" he demanded of Lingo. "Is she the wife of this man that killed my sons?"

"No," responded Lingo, "she is one of my people. But she wants this man for her husband."

"You tell her to go back!" shouted Kuchene in a fury. "This man is a murderer. We are going to kill him. You tell her I say she must go."

He waved his arms angrily, pointing back toward the wagons,

but Deseret shook her head. "You tell him no," she said. "Tell him I won't go back. You tell him those people will kill me."

She gave a reckless laugh and reined closer to Tarrant, and Kuchene grunted in disgust. But there was nothing he could do, for from their earliest infancy the Navajos are taught respect for women, the mothers being the head of the clan. Not even a chief dares to strike his wife, and, when she offends him, he must seek for some man on whom to vent his wrath. So Kuchene withheld his hand, although his eyes glittered dangerously, and the war party rode back to camp.

At the base of a sandstone cliff where, from a vent in the rocks, a spring of water gushed forth, the Navajos had made camp among the scattered cedars or sought shelter behind the rocks. Now they scattered in wild confusion, each drinking from the spring and hobbling out his horse for the night. After a great draft of water the three prisoners were led away and confined in a huge hogan. This was a circular affair, constructed of cedar logs, thrust into the ground, and daubed with mud. From a big hole in the top the smoke from the fire passed up into the clear night air. Darkness was falling already and a squaw crouched by the fireplace, grinding corn between two stones. A pot of goat's meat, mixed with corn, was stewing on the coals. After boiling a kettle of mush, the woman set the food before them, giving each a large iron spoon. She was slender and well-formed, with a red calico dress and buckskin moccasins on her tiny feet. As her guests began eating, she glanced shyly at Deseret, who had suddenly become her old self. It was as if some physical weight, which had been crushing her down, had been lifted from her shoulders. Her eyes, which had been so sad, were now radiant with a new happiness. Her frail body took its old, supple lines. As she met the woman's glance, she smiled and nodded a greeting, making signs that the food was good.

Tarrant and Lingo ate ravenously, now that their thirst was

slaked, and Deseret was not far behind, but from time to time she stole glances at the Indian woman who sat on a goatskin in the corner. Despite her greater height, the moccasins that she wore were no larger than Deseret's shoes. They had boat-like soles of rawhide with soft, red uppers, to the tops of which were attached long rolls of buckskin, to protect them from the bites of snakes.

Deseret watched the woman curiously, and at last she rose up and sat down close beside her. Then, as the men talked together, laying their plans for the trial to come, Deseret reached over and felt of the moccasins. They were made of the softest buckskin, stained red and fastened with buttons that the silversmith had beaten out of coins. As the woman returned her smile, Deseret admired the strings of beads that were hung about her neck. Some were made of ruddy coral, brought in trade from the distant seashore, others were of native turquoise, but over them all the woman wore a silver necklace, with beads shaped like pumpkin flowers. Deseret admired them and sighed, for she had no jewelry to show, not even a ring or breast pin, but, as she was turning away, the Navajo woman reached over and felt of her sturdy shoes. They were short and square-toed, made for service rather than beauty, but in her turn the Indian woman sighed. To her they seemed strange—and beautiful. Deseret took off a shoe and let her try it on, taking one of her moccasins in its place. After a long, delighted look, she made signs that she would trade, if the white woman preferred the moccasins.

It did not take long to make the exchange, for Deseret had ridden away astride a small boy's saddle, the stirrups of which chafed her cruelly. Boots and leggings she must have if she was to follow after Tarrant in the long ride that she hoped lay before them. As she fastened on the moccasins, she nodded joyously to the Indian woman, who suddenly was so smiling and kind.

Perhaps, to her mind, the donning of the moccasins had given Deseret certain privileges in the tribe, for as the chief councilors of the Navajos began to file into the hogan, she rose up and beckoned her to follow. The old men came in first, sitting to the left of the fire upon which the young men threw fresh fuel, but as Deseret divined the intentions of the woman, she stopped and shook her head.

The women of the Navajos, although they own their own homes and most of the sheep and goats, do not sit in the councils and this woman was preparing to go. The hogan was hers, but the making of war and trying of prisoners was the exclusive right of the men. Hence her insistence that Deseret should vacate the crowded house so that the talk of the warriors might begin. But with a final determined—"No!"—Deseret pulled herself away and took shelter behind Tarrant and Lingo. It was her trial as well as theirs, and, although the councilors demurred, she remained until the talk began. First, the old chief, Kuchene, rolled and lit a cigarette, blowing the smoke up and down and to the four points of the compass where the gods of the Navajos dwell. Then each man in turn exhaled the sacred smoke, after which they smoked a long time in silence. The close air of the hogan became thick with tobacco smoke and rank with the stench of sweaty bodies. Outside, the young men and the relatives of the murdered men pressed closer about the narrow door, but at last, when the silence had become almost unendurable, Kuchene began his talk.

Throwing back his blanket, he rose to his feet, his body gleaming like bronze in the firelight, and in stentorian shouts he hurled his accusations at Tarrant, at the same time demanding his death. Though he spoke in Navajo, his gestures were so significant that little was lost to the whites, for he acted out first the brutal murder of his three sons and finally the return of the fourth. It was then that his voice, which before had been so harsh, suddenly softened and trembled with emotion. He spoke with painful intensity, describing the boy's terrible sufferings and his own grief at the plight of his son. But when he had finished, his voice became loud again, and, as time after time he pointed accusingly at Tarrant, he drew his hand across his throat. Then he pointed at the fire, demanding by signs that Zachary be burned, and burst into a final denunciation.

Kuchene sat down and another chief leaped up, orating in the same savage strain. When all the older men had expressed their opinion, a hush fell in the crowded house. No one stirred. They hardly breathed for several minutes, and then with loud grunts they recommenced their smoking while Kuchene motioned Lingo to interpret.

"They say," began Jacob, speaking slowly and quietly, "that they know you killed Kuchene's boys. Lot Drake has told them and he has always been their friend. What he says has always been so. All but two or three have given their voice for your death, but the girl and I are to be spared. We are to witness your torture and go home on foot to bear witness that Kuchene is avenged. Now it is your turn to answer . . . but I will never desert you, Zack. If they try to lay hold of you . . . fight."

"Tell the chief," said Tarrant after a minute or two of silence, "that I know nothing of the killing of his sons. I am a Gentile, it is true, and for that reason Lot Drake hates me and wishes to have me killed. But if the Navajos, to please Lot Drake, kill an American citizen, the soldiers will come and kill them. I am an officer in the Army and I have fought the Utes, their enemies, but I have always been friendly with the Navajos. Still I am not afraid to die, and, if they decide to kill me, I will show them that I am a soldier."

He ceased, and, as the Indians waited in breathless silence, Jake Lingo picked up a pinch of tobacco. He applied it to his nostrils in place of a pinch of snuff, and sat in a long, dreamy silence. Then in his slow, quiet way he translated Tarrant's reply and reached for another pinch of tobacco. It was his way of showing that the white men had no fear, that, though outnumbered a hundred to one, they still retained their courage and that the battle was far from won. Zachary Tarrant was an American, as Lot Drake himself had said, and to kill him would bring back the soldiers.

One by one the oldest chiefs rose to express their various views, which now seemed to lean more to peace, but Kuchene interrupted them with loud corrections and accusations until at last he leaped to his feet.

"The *Belikana* lies!" he cried. "He says he is a soldier to keep the Navajos from killing him. But a soldier wears a cap and a long knife that touches the ground. This man is dressed like a trapper. My son who came back said the men who killed his brothers rode straight in the saddle, like soldiers, but that they wore buckskin shirts, so I know this is the man, and I will send for my son to prove it. If he says it is so, we will take this murderer and roast him on the coals of that fire. But if my son says . . . 'No, this is not the man.' . . . I am willing to let him go."

He shouted out the door, and, while Lingo was translating, his wounded son was brought in. He was tall but stooping, his body wasted by sickness and with a wild, crazy look in his eyes. After one look at the prisoners, he pointed at Tarrant and burst into a jabber of Navajo.

"He says you are the man," translated Lingo.

Zachary nodded briefly. He had sat through the ordeal without moving a muscle, as impassive and stoical as an Indian, but while one pistol was in his belt the other, unseen, was tucked into the slack of his shirt. When he had said he would show them how a soldier dies, he had meant he would fight to the death, but the time had not come—not yet.

Kuchene rose up, his eyes glittering with excitement, and commenced an impassioned harangue. In the midst of his speech he suddenly turned to his son and snatched away the blanket from his shoulders. There on his breast was the recent wound of a bullet and with a sudden access of rage Kuchene whirled him about and showed where it had entered his back. A chorus of angry grunts went up from the council as he described the cowardly attack—the death of his three sons, the escape of this wounded boy, and the treachery of the men who had shot them. Again and again he pointed his finger at Tarrant, and then at the wasted form of the boy. By signs and words at once, he demanded that Zachary should be seized and roasted on the fire.

When the Indians shouted approval, Jacob Lingo leaped up and motioned for Kuchene to cease. Suddenly casting aside his calm and measured speech, he spoke angrily, demanding answers from the chief. He asked if, in the twenty years since first Kuchene had known him, he had ever told him a lie. And then in quiet tones but deadly in earnest he warned the scowling Indians that their prisoner was an American Army officer and that his blood would be on their heads. As he talked, old Kuchene, his ferocious countenance working with passion, leaped up and laid a hand on his son.

What he said Tarrant never knew, but he saw the tide turn against him, and Lingo stepped back to his side. A hush fell on the council as they caught the significance of this act. Then as they came to their feet, Deseret reached forward and snatched the spare pistol from Zachary's belt. Nothing was said, but the three prisoners faced the angry crowd of Indians with a look that all could read. They were prepared to fight to the death.

In the pinch Kuchene hesitated, glancing angrily toward the door where there were shouts and a great commotion. Then as the crowd parted, the Indian woman rushed in and stood panting before the chief. She pointed at him reproachfully, appealing to man after man as she addressed the startled councilors. As Kuchene rushed toward her, she pushed him back with both hands and began an impassioned harangue. From the signs she made, it was evident that her speech had to do with misery and death, people gathered together and led away prisoners, women and children sick and dead. Although they grunted angrily, the chiefs listened to the end before they motioned her to go out the door.

"She says she knows you are a soldier by the way you walk," translated Lingo as Zachary glanced at him. "And if they kill you, the soldiers will come from Fort Defiance and the women and children will die. She says twelve years ago, when Kit Carson rounded them up and took the whole tribe to Fort Sumner, a thousand of them died in one day. Her own husband died and two of her sons . . . and she says Kuchene's son is crazy."

"I think he is," answered Tarrant, gazing closely at the man who had so nearly brought about his death.

At the sound of Tarrant's voice the boy, who had been watching him intently, suddenly jumped to his feet and ran forward. But now, although he pointed again at Zachary, he shook his head in denial. "This is not the man!" he cried. "I know by his voice. When the murderers pursued me, I hid in a cave and they camped just below me that night. There were six voices, all different, and I remember every one, but he was not one of that band. Their voices were loud and harsh. This man speaks softly, like a woman."

He approached and stared at Tarrant, then held out his hand. As Zachary reached to take it, Kuchene shouted angrily and motioned the crowd to be gone.

CHAPTER TWENTY-FIVE

The turns of Zachary's trial had been like a long run of cards, when the luck is against a man, but just as he faced either torture or a violent death, the run of the cards suddenly changed. The Navajo woman had broken in on the council, halting Kuchene in his rush on the prisoners, and then Kuchene's son, hearing Zachary's voice, had pronounced him not the man. One minute he had been lost and the next minute saved, but all from no virtue of his. The same fate that had pushed him to the edge of the abyss had snatched him back from the fall. But when it was over and the hogan was empty, Tarrant found himself weak and faint.

He stepped to the door, for the air was stifling hot, and, as he stood breathing the clean air and gazing up at the tranquil stars, he felt a presence beside him. Then his head was drawn down and Deseret was kissing him, while her body shook with sobs. They stood a long time in silence, staring out into the night where the Indians were moving about like specters. As his strength came back, Zachary gathered her closer and held her like a child in his arms.

"It has been too much for you," he said at last.

Although she sighed, she shook her head. "No, I am happy now. It is all past, like a dream, and at last we are together again. But tomorrow we must leave because . . . because he will be coming. Don't you hate the very thought of Lot Drake?"

"Yes, I do," responded Zachary, "and I've not finished with

that gentleman . . . not if I get you out of this country alive. And if I have to kill him . . . you've seen people kill a snake? Well, that's the way I feel."

"Oh, he's terrible." She shuddered. "It makes me sick just to think of him. Don't you believe he's sold his soul to the devil? You know the Mormons believe everything and. . . ."

"It's the Mormons that have made him into the devil he is," burst out Tarrant in a gust of passion. "They have made him the executioner of the church. He does their dirty killing, and then they turn him out and give him over to the cudgelings of Satan. But he's too dangerous to be at large, and when we get back to Moroni. . . ."

"Oh, no . . . let's not go back," she pleaded. "This Indian woman is so kind, let's get her to give us guides and ride east until we come to the railroad."

"And what then?" asked Zachary, puzzled.

"Why, then we'll be safe," she said. "Don't you know what I mean? Every minute we're here we're in danger from Lot Drake. And we're in danger from Brigham Young and the Avenging Angels. It's a terrible country. I can't bear to go back to it. And yet, I suppose we'll have to."

"Yes, we've got to go back," agreed Tarrant, "but it won't be for long, Deseret. You are tired out now, and you can rest at Moroni while I finish this affair with Lot Drake."

"Oh, can't you let him go?" she pleaded. "Let the soldiers and the marshals do that. We've had so much trouble . . . you've nearly been killed . . . don't you think that old colonel will let you off?"

"You don't know him." Zachary laughed. "He'll be choppier than ever when he finds I've come back without my man. But your friend here, this woman. . . ."

"Oh, yes," cried Deseret, slipping out of his arms as the Indian woman stood before them. "Why, she's got something to eat!" she exclaimed. "And it's late . . . Uncle Jacob has gone to bed already . . . so I suppose we'll have to go, too."

She followed after the woman, nodding and smiling and trying to thank her, and, after some porridge and a drink of goat's milk, Deseret kissed him good night and Zachary stretched out beside Lingo. But, tired as he was, he could not sleep at once, for death had come too near. Visions of naked warriors, drawing their hands across their throats and pointing to him and the fire, danced and flashed before his aching eyes. Every muscle of his body was cramped from his long wait while they decided between life and death. He had sat so long with his hand on the butt of his pistol that even now it seemed still in his grasp, and the particular spot in which he planned to shoot Kuchene was imagined with photographic distinctness. As he lay on the pair of goatskins the Indian woman had given him, the fantasy of death was stilled and the next thing he knew the dawn had come again, and Kuchene was standing at the door.

"*Ah-hah-lah-ney,*" he greeted with a placating smile.

As Lingo roused up, he spoke rapidly in Navajo, waving his hand to their horses outside. "He says," explained Lingo, "that the Indians have all gone except the young men of his clan. And to protect us from any harm they will escort us to the river, or wherever we want to go."

"You tell him," answered Tarrant, "that Lot Drake is my enemy, so we don't dare return by the ferry. But if he knows the trail, we'll go back by Ute Crossing and try to ford the river."

"He says all right." Lingo nodded after a brief colloquy with the chief. "But he asked me if you're really a soldier. Because, if you are, he's afraid they will kill him for what he did last night."

"You tell him," directed Zachary, "that I'm a lieutenant in the Third Dragoons and that I came to Mormon Ferry with that detachment. And then tell him that Washington will overlook what he's done if he'll protect us from Lot Drake and those Avenging Angels."

Lingo looked at him a minute before he interpreted to the chief, but, whatever it was he said, old Kuchene became suddenly solicitous and insisted upon shaking hands. A sober second thought in the cold gray of dawn had left him in a penitent mood. When his guests were ready to go, he rode up with twenty young men who were to constitute their guard to the river. They were savage-looking creatures with their half-naked bodies and their long hair bound back with gaudy handkerchiefs. Besides their bows and arrows, they were armed with new rifles that somehow had been smuggled into the country. Although they eyed the white men grimly, their mood was pacific, for they knew they had gone too far.

Kuchene's band of warriors were the irreconcilables of the nation, men who had for the most part escaped the roundup of the soldiers and still clung to the ways of their fathers. For centuries the Navajos have been men of peace and war—simple shepherds while at home and fierce fighters when on the warpath against the Utes and the distant New Mexicans. Unless all signs failed, these very men had lately been raiding into Utah. Some of their ponies had Mormon brands, but Lingo said nothing, for now it was Tarrant who led. Against the Mormons old Kuchene still cherished a grudge, for he blamed them for the death of his sons, and, although Lingo had acted bravely during the ordeal before their council, the Indians still viewed him askance. He and his people had been their friends and had traded them many rifles with which to make war on the Mexicans, but Lot Drake had deceived them and no protests on the part of Lingo could make them believe he was cut off from the church. To them the *Gomelays* were a people, not a religious sect, although like the Indians they believed in polygamy. Since now it was proven that Tarrant was not the murderer, the Mormons were again held to blame. With

Kuchene as he rode up was the same half-crazed boy who had
suffered at the hands of the killers, and, as he gazed at Lingo,
his wild eyes glittered wickedly for it was Jacobee who had lured
his brothers into Utah. But toward Zachary he was more
friendly. As they mounted to go, old Kuchene shook his head at
him sternly. On account of this boy and his own headstrong
rage he had narrowly escaped war with the Americans, and now
he was more than anxious to get them out of the country before
some detachment of soldiers appeared. For the first time in
their history the Navajos had seen dragoons in the heart of the
Mormon country, and the fact that Tarrant had been with the
command made the Indians apprehensive of war. They had
heard of the coming of the soldiers to Moroni and of the flight
of Lot Drake and his followers. If the white men were fighting,
it was best for the Navajos to be on the side of the Americans.
Above all it was desirable to escort their prisoners across the
river before their misdemeanor was discovered. Hence
Kuchene's daylight appearance and his anxiety to be gone—but
the white woman kept him waiting.

With the aid of Uncle Jacob she had learned the Indian
woman's name and inquired regarding the death of her sons.
Now, hand in hand, they sat together in the hogan, oblivious of
the fretting war chief. For it was Tall Woman's appeal to
Kuchene and the council that had saved Zachary from a terrible death. Divining Deseret's love, Tall Woman had told of her
own and described the death of her husband and sons. Then as
the tears came to her eyes, Deseret had wept with her, trying by
murmured words to console her. Only a nod from Tarrant
reminded her of her journey and the long trail that lay before
them. Before she left, she threw her arms about Tall Woman and
kissed her as she bade her farewell.

"Poor woman," she said to Zachary as she waved a last good
bye, "isn't it pitiful . . . she's all alone. And she gave me this

nice blanket to put on my saddle, so I can ride the way the Indian women do."

She exhibited a small saddle blanket made of fine German-town wool, such as the Navajos use in riding. As she tucked it under her, exhibiting the dainty red moccasins, the Indians grunted approving comments. To them this strange woman was one more enigma in an affair already complex, but they pressed forward at a fast trot, for it was far to Ute Crossing and Kuchene had begun to look back.

Two days before, while his young men were butchering beef and wrangling over the horse herd of the Mormons, a runner had left the wagons and escaped through their lines, riding back to the river for help. Lot Drake had responded first, taking advantage of ancient friendship by telling him an out-and-out lie, and the emigrant party had escaped, but Kuchene had saved his face by the horses they had stolen and the beef he had supplied for the feast. Yet the Mormons were not all as cowardly as Moses Stout, who had forbidden his men to shoot. If Ammon Clark and his Avenging Angels came riding after them, there would be another story to tell. And then there were the soldiers with whom Tarrant had come to the river—they, too, might be hot on the trail.

They pressed on rapidly over a barren, windswept mesa, ap-parently destitute of both water and life. As they approached the river, the country grew rougher, being cut up with innumer-able cañons. Huge walls of eroded sandstone reared up out of the sand, marking the entrances to long, boxed-in cañons, and at the mouth of one of these the war party halted while a scout ran up among the rocks.

"Enemy coming!" he shouted, pointing back. As he came bounding over the rocks, they mounted in haste and whipped off down the long, sandy wash. But the men who pursued them were better mounted and riding hard. As the cañon opened out,

Tarrant saw six bobbing black heads, then six horsemen galloping fast.

"Oh, it's Indians!" cried Deseret, following Zachary's eyes as he glanced back. Tarrant did not answer. The bobbing heads that they saw were the black hats of Avenging Angels, more dangerous by far than any Indians. Old Kuchene and his warriors had recognized them already and were preparing to put up a fight, for as they rounded a sharp point two men dropped behind and took shelter among the rocks. A minute later their rifles rapped out a halting challenge, and then they came flogging down the cañon. Each man wore a heavy quirt attached to his wrist—a plaited iron handle with double lashes—and at the sting of its thongs the Navajo ponies surged ahead, while the scouts protected their rear.

Deseret was flushed and frightened, clinging desperately to her blanket that had slipped out of place during the chase, but Kuchene hurried her on until they loped out of the cañon and beheld the broad river before them. Here, between walls of sloping sandstone devoid of vegetation, the turbid Colorado flowed over a huge reef that at low water made a passable ford. To the east the mighty river swept forth from its dark cañon and then, spreading out, it poured over the submerged ledge and swung back in another long curve. Escalante had crossed here in 1776, and many Indians before and since, but with their enemies close behind the Navajos made a stand, for it could not be taken on the run.

Only after a prayer and a sacrifice to the river god would they venture to cross it at all. As they awaited the attack, Kuchene massed his men and placed his prisoners behind. Against the Americans he would not fight, but the Mormons were his sworn enemies and he began a loud harangue to his warriors. Then on the heels of the last scouts, the Avenging Angels spurred into the open, reining in at the mouth of the cañon. Ammon Clark was in the lead, his red beard flying like a banner. After a few words with his men he rode boldly out, holding up his hand for a talk. Never since Prophet Joseph had given him his blessing had the Mormon captain held back. As long as his cherished beard remained uncut, he had no fear of the Gentiles. Other Mormons, almost as brave, relied on the efficacy of their endowment garments, but he felt the immunity of a special and particular blessing, and he rode out against them alone.

Kuchene was sitting his horse in advance of his men, with his wounded son beside him. Tarrant had dismounted on a ledge of rocks and stood with his rifle in his hands. Against a man on horseback he had a decided advantage, for the horse would whirl under fire. With Deseret safely hidden behind a boulder, he watched the insolent Mormon captain.

"I want that man," rasped Clark, jerking his thumb toward Tarrant, "and I want that woman, too. You tell him I said so, Jake."

He glanced arrogantly at Lingo who after a moment's silence interpreted his demands to Kuchene.

"*Doh-tah*," answered Kuchene, "no." As he raised his voice in an exhortation to his men, Ammon Clark began to curse.

"You old dog-eater," he shouted, "what do I care for your Injuns? Send out them prisoners, or I'll give you a taste of this quirt!"

He raised his quirt threateningly and jumped his horse at Kuchene, who reined aside, his eyes growing wild. But before he could retaliate, Kuchene's son thrust out his hand, pointing accusingly at Clark.

"That is the man," he yelled in Navajo, "that killed my brothers! He is the man that shot me in the back. I remember his voice . . . !"

"You're a liar," retorted Clark, who could speak Navajo when he chose. Swinging his quirt, he struck out viciously at the son, who whirled and fled back into the crowd. But as Ammon Clark plunged after him, Kuchene whipped up his gun and shot him through and through. For a moment he kept on, still brandishing his whip. Then, clutching at the reins, he fell slowly from his horse and hung with one foot in the stirrup.

The Navajos sat staring, looking first at old Kuchene, and then at the bloody form in the dirt. Then with one accord they whirled their ponies and charged the rest of the Avenging Angels. But a panic had seized them at the fall of their leader and they fled, pursued by the Indians. Kuchene rode at their head and in the rear followed his son, waving his arms and laughing wildly.

CHAPTER TWENTY-SIX

At the blast of Kuchene's gun Ammon Clark had fallen to earth like any other man, born of woman. The blessing of the Prophet on his flowing red beard had protected him not a jot. He fell slowly, his hand locked on one split rein, and his horse stood above him, trembling. At the rush of the Indian ponies, the horse jumped and flew back, but before he could run, dragging the body of his master, Tarrant sprang in and caught him by the bit. Ammon Clark's foot was hung in the stirrup. Although he had fallen, he was not dead. Jacob Lingo released him, shaking his head in silent wonder, and they laid the Mormon captain on the ground.

Like Achilles when the arrow of Paris had struck his heel, he had not escaped the stroke of death. The bullet had gone through him like any other man not blessed by Prophet Joseph. Although he stirred and opened his eyes, the blood was flowing fast and they could see he had not long to live. Zachary tore open his shirt and bound the gaping holes tight, and, while they watched him, his rugged strength ebbed back.

"Gimme some water," he ordered in his rough, harsh voice.

Jacob Lingo, still marveling at the miracle of his downfall, handed his empty canteen to Deseret. "Get some water from the river," he said.

She came back panting and, pouring the muddy water into a cup, held it out for Clark to drink, but even on his deathbed his nature had not changed. As he tasted it, he ripped out an oath.

"That water is dirty!" he cried, throwing the cupful into her face. "Go down and get me some good!"

"But it's all dirty," she protested as he glared at her intolerantly.

"Go on and get it!" He cursed. "Don't talk back to me!"

But Zachary went in her stead. From the horse tracks at the ford where the water had had time to settle, he dipped up a cupful of better water, and, when he offered it, Ammon Clark accepted it, for he felt his strength beginning to ebb.

"What's the matter, Jake?" he asked as he noticed the stricken look with which Jacob Lingo regarded him. "Do you reckon this is going to kill me?"

"You'd better say your prayers," advised Lingo. "You haven't long to live."

"Prayers!" scoffed Clark. "I ain't the praying kind. I serve God another way. And what's more, I ain't going to die. Didn't the Prophet say I'd never die at the hand of the Gentiles as long as my beard was uncut? It ain't cut is it, anywhere, Jake?"

"No," responded Lingo, after examining his beard carefully, "I can't find a mark, Brother Ammon. But you're shot through and through and you're bleeding inside . . . you won't live long, I know."

"I won't?" repeated the Avenging Angel as if scarcely believing it, and then he lay thinking in silence. "If it wasn't for that damned Injun," he burst out at last, "I wouldn't be laying here now. The red devils were stealing cattle and we started to wipe them out, but this crazy fool got away. We trailed him thirteen days over freezing ground before we finally give up. He got across the river, so we went back to the settlements and laid all the killing onto the Gentiles." A rush of blood came to his lips, following his raucous laugh, and, when the hemorrhage had passed, he found himself so weak he could hardly move his head. "Jake," he whispered hoarsely, "am I shore going to die?

That ain't according to the prophecy, and I can't die yet. I ain't killed all of Joseph's enemies. But. . . ." Another rush of blood sapped the last of his strength and at the end he beckoned Lingo closer. "Cut off my beard, Jake," he commanded. "You know what Joseph said . . . and I don't want to make him out a liar."

He gasped suddenly for breath, then with an agonizing scowl he looked up at Jacob, who stood hesitating.

Lingo whipped out his knife and cut off a corner of the long beard, and the next moment the stern spirit had fled. He died as he had lived, a man without fear and loyal to the Prophet to the end.

They were digging him a grave on the bank of the wash when Kuchene and his warriors returned. At sight of Ammon Clark, stretched out where he had fallen, the Navajos whipped back out of sight. Unlike the Apaches and the Utes they had a great fear of the dead, and, making signs for haste, Kuchene remained away until the body had been laid in its grave. Then, while Lingo filled in the dirt and said a prayer over Ammon Clark, Tarrant went to the beckoning Kuchene. Neither could speak the other's language, but they talked by nods and signs, after the manner of the Indians of the Plains.

Kuchene pointed toward the grave and made the motions of stroking a long beard, then, pointing to his son, he put his hand on his wound and glanced at Tarrant inquiringly. Zachary nodded his head, for the old chief had asked if Clark had really shot his son, and to make it more clear Tarrant snapped his finger away from his mouth, the Indian sign for: "He said so."

"Good," signed Kuchene and his strained face relaxed, for he had been in fear of further reprisals. But if Clark had really confessed that he had killed his sons, Kuchene had a better case, and with a friendly smile he pointed to Zachary and made a sign by pointing in different directions. "Where do you want to go?" he was asking.

Tarrant pointed across the river.

"Good," signed Kuchene, glancing up at the sun, and rode down to the crossing with his men. The white people followed, for the hour was late and a dangerous passage was before them. While the Indians stripped down for their struggle with the great water, they drew off to one side and waited. It was time for the sacrifice and the prayer to Nn-kliss, the great deity of the river. In its depths there dwelt other and lesser water gods, who must all be mentioned in the prayer, but the sacrifice was offered to Nn-kliss.

From four little buckskin sacks Kuchene took out four tiny chips of turquoise, white shell, cannel coal, and yellow abalone. He held them in the hollow of one hand while with the other he sprinkled them with sacred corn pollen. Then, closing his hand on them, he held it under water and prayed for a safe passage— over and back. At a tug from below, where the swirling currents surged, he released the sacrifice and stood up. The offering had been accepted.

With great solemnity he rode his horse into the water at the upper edge of the natural bridge, which gave a foothold for crossing the flood. Then, beckoning the white people to follow and rein their horses upstream, he led off across the swirling current. There was fear in every eye as his young warriors followed, for though they prayed to the river god, they considered it a devil that at any time might seize a man. As their horses slipped and floundered on the treacherous bottom, now stumbling against boulders, now stepping into potholes that threatened to immerse and drown them, they kept up a monotonous chant to protect them from the devil's power.

At every step the mighty river forced the horses downstream toward the lower edge of the reef, and beyond that the water was sixty feet deep with the roaring chasms beyond. To be swept down meant certain death for horse and man and the ponies set their hoofs against the rush of the stream, which every moment was edging them toward it. In the midst of the swirling waters their senses were confused, and they gazed with dizzy eyes at the sloping sandstone of the opposite shore, which seemed to recede before them. But Kuchene kept on, always reining his horse upstream, following the way that his fathers had taught him, until at last the sandstone wall rose abruptly before them and the horses waded out and stood dripping. They had crossed Toh Sin-nah unharmed.

Kuchene rested his horses while one of his scouts ran up to watch the trail beyond the rim. As he sat stolidly waiting, his eyes glowed with anger, or perhaps with the excitement of the crossing. Now he was on the Utah side, in the territory of the hated Mormons—a dangerous place to be found after the killing of Ammon Clark, and with Jacobee there as a witness. Since the burial of the Mormon captain, Lingo had not spoken a word, either to Kuchene or to Zachary and Deseret. He sat off to one side, his eyes fixed in a tragic stare, for he was conscious of Kuchene's resentment. Lot Drake and Ammon Clark had each added their quota to the grudge the Indians bore the Mormons, and yet they were the people he had gone forth to convert, the Lamanites of the Book of Mormon.

The scout on the cañon wall suddenly shouted and pointed west, before he came bounding down the trail, and Kuchene gave an order to his men. Then, as they sprang to their horses, he advanced to Tarrant and shook hands with an ingratiating smile. But when Lingo came forward, he grunted angrily and turned away, marshaling his warriors for their perilous return.

On the bank of the treacherous river he held up his hands and repeated the invocation to Toh Sin-nah. Then, his stern face set, he rode out into the water that separated him from the land of his fathers. Dusk was falling when he set foot on the opposite shore and turned to look back across the stream, and suddenly he threw up his hand in defiance. A column of dragoons, unseen by those below, had ridden out on the cañon rim, but Lingo bowed his head and turned away, for he knew that the sign was for him.

CHAPTER TWENTY-SEVEN

The scouting party of soldiers from which Kuchene had fled had been sent out to search for Tarrant, for Colonel Valentine had taken alarm at the prolonged absence of his lieutenant, knowing as he did the enmity of Lot Drake. After a week of fruitless search the column of cavalry had encountered Tarrant at the moment when he needed them most. Four days afterward, with Deseret beside him, Zachary rode across the desert toward Moroni. All their dangers and sufferings had come to an end when they fell in with the detachment of dragoons, and on this last day they loitered like happy lovers in the rear of their plodding escort.

Without their protection Tarrant would have fared badly on his return, for the Avenging Angels still guarded the water holes, but now all their difficulties had been miraculously smoothed away and the lovers rode hand-in-hand. Deseret's dark eyes, which before had been so sad, were radiant with life and happiness. Zachary, as he watched her, kept wondering to himself at the fate that had restored her to him. By what devious twists and turns that unseen, kindly hand had guided him to Moses Stout's wagon. And when he had left her, another miracle had matched the first, for she had followed him and escaped from the Mormons. Now at last she was free from the clutches of the church that had so ruthlessly ordered her life, for once in Moroni Colonel Valentine would protect her until she had served as a witness. After the trial they were going to be married.

The sun was sinking low as they rode down the road toward Brigham's Castle and Hurricane beyond, but, as they neared the stone fort with its huge gates and loop-holed walls and the tangle of trees below, a shadow came over Deseret. The joyous lilt left her voice and her eyes became fearful, although why she could not say. It was still the stronghold of Brigham Young, who had sent her as a present to his brutal retainer, Lot Drake, and only the lapse of time while the wagon train crossed the desert had saved her from the wretchedness of her fate. Because the Prophet had changed his mind—choosing rather to cut off Drake than to reward him with another young wife—she had escaped, but something still told her that the danger might not be past.

Trotting and walking in column of fours, the dragoons came to the castle, which now seemed wholly deserted, and behind them, still lagging, came Zachary and Deseret, staring curiously at the loop-holed walls. A great spring, over which the Mormon fort had been built, came rushing and gurgling down the slope, and below, terrace by terrace, were wooded gardens and miniature lakes, with paths leading under the trees. It was a beautiful spot, this oasis in the desert—too beautiful for the use to which it was put. For here, across the line in the no man's land of Arizona, Brigham Young brought his family and sealed wives. It was his place of refuge from the United States marshals and the law against polygamous marriages. From here the telegraph wire that connected him with the world could relay his messages and commands; it could warn him of danger, and, while he rested at ease, it gave him control of all Utah.

Deseret shuddered as she looked and turned her face away, for even its beauty brought up evil memories. But Zachary looked too long. By the edge of a quiet pool, half shaded by giant mulberries, he saw Tamar Young—Tamar Paine. She was watching them intently. As Zachary reined in, she beckoned to him, impulsively. For an instant he hesitated, with a quick glance after Deseret who had not yet missed him from her side. Then he shook his head, with a swift smile to save the hurt, and rode on with his own. Deseret was his loved one, and Tamar had betrayed him. And yet—Tamar had loved him, too. But he had hesitated too long, for Deseret caught the smile and the regretful shake of the head. Her glance followed his and she recognized Tamar, who replied with a disdainful smile.

"Come on!" burst out Deseret, her black eyes flashing fire.

Zachary followed, saying nothing. Anything he might say would make it worse. They rode forward in silence, Deseret suddenly conscious of her old clothes and her Navajo moccasins. When Tarrant glanced over, he saw tears in her eyes— tears that gathered and ran down her cheeks. But then he dared not speak. What he had to say to Deseret must be said at some other time, when the hurt of this encounter had passed, for now she was shaking with half-controlled sobs that soon would have their way. After the bitterness of her tears had assuaged the anger in her heart, then he would tell her again that she was the only one he loved and that Tamar Young was nothing. He would kiss her and hold her close, and Deseret would believe him, although the wound would be slow to heal. For Tamar had told her that to him she was only a waitress—the first woman he had happened to meet since he had parted with her at Salt Lake.

Deseret wept, while for the thousandth time Tarrant cursed the unhappy chance that had thrown him across the path of Tamar. From the first her wiles had brought him nothing but unhappiness—and disgrace, and the loss of Deseret, and now, by one look, one motion of the hand, she had destroyed their happiness again. It was as if she had the power by some magic enchantment to separate the happiest of lovers, to drive from their minds all kind and tender thoughts and plant the seeds of resentment and hate. Even the colonel had sensed the malevolent quality of her beauty, for he had warned Zachary more than once. She was a woman against whom a man must harden his heart, and in that Tarrant had failed again.

The long journey was nearing its end. As they passed through Hurricane, Zachary rode in closer to Deseret. But her eyes were downcast now and she avoided the hand that he held out in silent appeal. She was brooding over her hurts, feeling the pangs of the slow poison that Tamar Young had so artfully implanted in her heart, and Tarrant reined away. He fell back to the rear, looking at the crowd on the street. As he passed, he saw a familiar form come running from the Hurricane Saloon. It was Jerry Wamsutter, as drunk or drunker than usual, and he greeted Zachary with a cheer.

"Hel-lo, Zack," he shouted, rushing out to his horse and grabbing him by the leg, "come in and have a drink!"

"No, I've got to be going on," protested Tarrant as a sergeant fell back to guard him, but Jerry was not to be denied.

"Come in!" he urged hospitably. "I own the whole town. Didn't you hear what I did to Bill Crump? The Mormon-faced whelp ran for constable against me, and in some way he got the most votes. Anyway, they declared him elected and I came into town to put on a little show. Come in and have a drink with me, Zack! Oh, you won't, eh? Well, I want to tell you this story. I was up on the billiard table, dancing a hoe-down with my spurs on, when this one-eyed constable comes in.

" 'Be quiet,' he says, 'or I'll haf to arrest ye! And git down off that table,' he says.

"Well, sir, that made my blood boil, considering all that he'd done to me, and, when he jerked out his six-shooter, I jumped down and grabbed for my Bowie knife. But Zack, I'd been drinking and some way or other I got hold of it backside to. That's all that saved his life because I jabbed it behind his short ribs and fetched a half circle, clean around him. If the blade side had been toward him, it would've cut him in two, but, as it was, he jest felt the point.

"Nobody knowed that then, though, and it took two hours of hard work before we could get that poor fool to straighten up. He jest lay doubled over, holding his stomach with both hands and bellering like a calf. He can't stand up straight yet . . . and, as far's arresting is concerned, he's give up the idee entirely. The town is mine, Zack, and everything in it, so you might as well have a drink."

He caught Tarrant by the leg and, lifting him bodily from the saddle, dragged him laughingly into the saloon. Zachary, making a virtue out of necessity, tossed off a drink with very good grace.

"Now, Zack," continued Jerry, laying his hand on him affectionately and drawing him off to one side, "I've got something important to tell ye. No, now listen, and tell that sergeant he don't need to wait."

Zachary laughed good-naturedly and dismissed the grinning sergeant, sending word that he would follow a little later.

Then Jerry Wamsutter whispered hoarsely in his ear: "How'd you like to take Lot Drake?"

"Do you know where he is?" demanded Tarrant eagerly.

Jerry laughed exultantly. "Going to quit me, hey?" he taunted. "Ride right by your old pardner without sayin' . . . 'Howdy' or nothing . . . you bet your boot I know where he is."

He paused and nodded mysteriously, then knocked the neck off a bottle and poured out two foaming drinks.

"Now set down," he said, "and I'll tell you something good, only don't ask me how I know. Every man has got some secret . . . some woman he's bound to protect . . . but I know how you feel about Lot Drake."

He tossed off his drink and sat down at a nearby table, and Zachary was not slow to join him. Drunk or sober, Jerry

Wamsutter was a man full of knowledge, both of the country and the people around him, and the mention of Lot Drake had brought a gleam to Tarrant's eyes, for he knew what the colonel would say. Zachary had been sent to the river to arrest Bishop Drake and he had returned with a girl, instead. To be sure it was Deseret, and she was a witness against Lot Drake. But of what use was a witness while the man they sought to convict was still hiding in the heart of the desert? Zachary emptied his glass and moved closer.

"See that man over there?" muttered Jerry, glancing across the room to where a hard-faced man sat, watching them. "He's an apostate . . . been cut off from the church. Used to ride with Ammon Clark and his bunch of Angels, and he knows all Lot Drake's hiding places."

Jerry paused and looked around, and then he glanced back across the room. The apostate sat at a table, dealing solitaire mechanically, a tall, gaunt man burned mahogany red by years of desert sun. But his narrowed black eyes searched out every corner, and they were never long absent from Jerry.

"He's living in hell," confided Jerry sympathetically. "If anybody feeds him or puts him up for the night, they'll be cut off from the church . . . maybe killed. The Angels are after him, but they ain't got the nerve to jump him . . . he's considerable snaky himself. But he's got a special reason for coming to this town, and for two hundred dollars he'll lead you to Lot Drake and help you make the arrest. But he's got to see the two hundred dollars."

"Well . . . I've got that much," replied Zachary guardedly, "but he looks kind of bad, Jerry. Is he safe?"

"He'll sell his danged soul for two hundred dollars," returned Jerry, "but that ain't all of it. He's bad, I'll admit . . . one of Drake's Avenging Angels and took part in the Mountain Meadows Massacre. But he's got a good wife . . . or leastwise he used to have . . . and he wants to git her back. I don't know whether you heard that Lot Drake has been cut off. Well, he has, and Brigham Young has given his wives a divorce, only they're afraid to take it. Old Lot would kill 'em, sure. But . . . well, here's the idee . . . this man Frank's wife was taken away from him a little while ago and sealed to Bishop Drake, and he's game to take a chance on gitting killed himself to put the old dog out of the way. Fact is, he's still in love with this woman of his and they figure on making a quick gitaway. That's why he wants the two hundred dollars."

"I'll pay him," agreed Tarrant after studying a minute, "provided he takes me to Drake. But before I start, I've got to know, straight out, where he gets his information."

"You ought to know that," reproved Jerry. "Ain't I give you a pretty good hint? Well, he gits it from this wife, then . . . she's the favorite of old Lot, but she's kind of keeping company with Frank."

Jerry poured out another drink and nodded to the apostate who rose up and left the saloon.

"He wants to go after him right now," stated Jerry. "Before Lot picks up and moves."

"Yes, but I've got to report to the colonel," objected Tarrant, "and. . . ."

"You can report when you git back," retorted Jerry. "The thing to do is to ketch Lot Drake."

"You're right," decided Zachary, suddenly springing to his feet.

Jerry followed close behind him. "I'll go along with you," he said.

CHAPTER TWENTY-EIGHT

Mounted on one horse and leading another, traveling at a lope, trot, and gallop in the wake of the hard-eyed apostate, Zachary learned how the Avenging Angels rode. Every two hours they stopped and changed horses, braiding the halter of the tired mount into the tail of the rested animal and whipping on over mountain and plain. All night they rode fast, back across the eastern desert but avoiding the well-beaten trails, and at noon the next day they looked down on the Pahreah from the cliffs where the Avenging Angels had hidden.

From these same crags Lot Drake and his men had spied on Tarrant when he came with his soldiers, but the apostate knew the trails as well as they and no messenger had fled before him. With the dawn he had won the heights above House Rock Valley where no Mormon eyes could follow their flight. As the horses lagged and stumbled, he had pulled them to a walk, picking his way across high mesas to this point. Below them at the ranch house a Paiute Indian could be seen as he moved about, feeding the stock, but no white man appeared, and the apostate, well content, picketed his horses and laid down to sleep.

In the life of an Avenging Angel the nights were for riding and the days for watching and rest. While their horses grazed industriously on the rich grass of the high mesa, they slept and stood guard by turns. Frank Puter, the apostate, was a man given to silence—a man who thought much and said little—

234

and, as evening came on, he threw the saddle on his horse and led off down the trail to the ranch. Leaving Tarrant and Jerry to wait by the creek, he crept up across the fields to the house. After a few minutes of observation he returned, as silent as ever, and led the way up to the ferry. Two by two they swam their horses across the river at the stern of one of the skiffs, and the night was yet young when they passed the spot where Stout had parked his wagons.

Only a week before, surrounded by hostile Indians and still more hostile Mormons, Tarrant had laid inside the corral and heard the wailing of children and the demands of the women for water. Now, riding like the wind, they swept by at a gallop on the desert-bred horses they had bought, and at Limestone Tanks they saw the marks of the wagon wheels where the emigrants had camped and moved on. Up the long level wash they spurred on to a cedar ridge that formed the backbone of the divide. From there, still riding hard, they followed down another wash that drained into the Little Colorado.

All night they had traveled south at the base of a chalky bluff but toward morning they quit the road that the wagon train had made and skirted the bluff to the east. The country was sandy now and broken by square-topped buttes, which loomed up like houses in the moonlight. As the stars began to pale, the apostate stopped his horse and sat gazing at a dark spot ahead. The tops of giant cottonwoods showed faintly against the cliff, which here was broken by a cañon, and after a long look Frank Puter stepped down and motioned his companions to dismount.

"That's the place," he said, "right up under them big trees. He's got a house and everything. He's living there with Abbie, one of his old-time wives . . . and hellish scads of kids, of course. The old scoundrel ain't satisfied with nineteen different families, and God knows how many ketch colts among the Injuns. He's out to build up his kingdom, no matter whose woman he takes . . . but boys, if he's there, he's my meat. They all say he won't surrender, and I sure hope he don't, but we'll give him the chance when he comes out the door, and, if he runs, you leave him to me. We'll tie our horses here and sneak up through the brush, and I'll bet you old Lot is surprised."

He gave a bitter laugh, and, stripping the saddle from his horse, he tied him to a salt bush for safety. Then, rifle in hand, he glided silently through the brush until they came to the edge of a field. The first rosy dawn revealed rows of Indian corn, springing up from eighteen-inch holes, and under a spreading cottonwood its branches bowed to the ground. Puter showed them the outlines of a house. It was of stone, without windows— really a fort with one door and sinister-looking loopholes through the walls—and already the occupants were astir.

"Come on, boys." The apostate nodded, and, with his rattlesnake eyes gleaming, he crept up on the hiding place of his enemy. He seemed to glide, like a serpent, as he writhed up the long corn rows, holding his gun muzzle carefully out of the dirt. When the others came up, he was crouched behind some bushes, not forty feet from the door.

Smoke was rising from the chimney of the broad-throated fireplace on which the family cooking was done, and the voice of a woman was heard. Then at last the door opened and a tow-haired boy stepped out, searching the cliff with cunning eyes. Other children followed after him, scampering about with bare feet, as wild and wary as quail, and Puter shook his head. It was not working out as he had thought. But he stuck and at last a huge woman appeared, as tall and almost as broad as the door, a woman with the rugged, set face of a pioneer, and she, too, searched the heights.

"Breakfast!" she called at last.

As the children came running, the apostate muttered a curse and crept away. "He ain't here," he said, when they had gained the cover of the brush. "Old Lot gits up at dawn. He's the first man up, and he can't wait to git his coffee. Let's hide and watch the house."

They watered their horses at a spring and took shelter in a wooded cañon, watching the house by turns all day, but as evening came on Puter spat out an oath and went out and brought in their horses.

"He's gone," he complained. "The old scoundrel has sneaked away . . . but I know he was there last week. We'll ride up the wash to the Hopi village and tell 'em Lot Drake is our friend. Then I'll pull out a letter and ask 'em where he is. Tell 'em it's important . . . from Brigham Young."

He twisted his thin lips into a sardonic smile, and Tarrant glanced at Jerry. From the first it had all seemed too good to be true, this tip on the hiding place of Drake. Although Zachary had seen his wife and family and his refuge among the Indians, they had failed to take their prisoner. He had eluded them again, though their approach had been too swift for any word of warning to precede them, and now the dour apostate had suddenly become garrulous in his attempt to explain away their defeat.

"He's slippery," he said as they rode up the broad wash where the Hopis had planted their corn. "I've been out with him, hundreds of times. Never sleeps with the rest unless he's hid in some house, and then he bars the door. But we'll git him, mister, don't you never think we won't. We'll git him if we have to follow him to hell."

Jerry Wamsutter nodded grimly, and Zachary made no complaint, for Puter had demonstrated his worth. He had muscles that never tired, and, if Drake was ever caught, it would be by the methods he employed—the swift night ride, the silent approach, and the equally silent retreat. Drake's refuge in the wilderness had been watched all day, but this time no messenger was riding to bear a warning to its owner and sooner or later he would be trapped. Tarrant was tired and saddle-worn, but, as Puter explained his plans, he agreed to follow his lead.

"You watch me work these Injuns," ended Puter, and relapsed into his grim, watchful silence. They rode up the cañon to the Indian village, where the Hopis had for generations maintained a losing fight against the inroads of the hostile Navajos. It was stuck on the very edge of a high, sandy cliff, a huddle of stone houses overlooking the fertile fields to which they clung with Hopi tenacity. A thousand times the arrogant Navajos had ravished their cornfields and driven off their goats and sheep, but the Hopis had hung on, fighting waspishly to keep their hold on the water that to them meant life. Like most peace-lovers they were keen traders, and, when Puter asked for corn, they greeted him with eager smiles.

He bought feed for their horses and corn meal and meat for themselves. Then, squatting down against the wall of the old chief's house, he smoked and talked in brief gutturals. At last, as an afterthought, he drew a letter out of his pocket and asked if they had seen Lot Drake. The old Indian nodded gravely and pointed to the west, where a trail led off toward the river. "He went there . . . yesterday," he said.

"That is bad," responded Puter, slapping his leg impatiently. "I have come clear out here with a letter of great importance. Do you know which way he went?"

"No, friend," answered the old chief discreetly.

"This letter," explained Puter, "is from Brigham Young, the big chief of all the Mormons. He told me to put it in Lot Drake's hands myself, and not to trust it to anyone. That shows it is very important."

The Hopi gazed at him speculatively. The fact that Lot Drake was hiding from the soldiers was known to all the Indians. But what they did not know was that the bishop had been cut off, for to them a Mormon was a Mormon. Frank Puter had been excommunicated and put under the curse, also, but to the Hopi he was still a Mormon. If Puter was a Mormon, he was a friend of Lot Drake, who had been hiding near their village so long.

"I think," said the old chief at last, "he goes by Ute Crossing. The other place is watched."

"To be sure." Puter nodded, as if the news was nothing. "But where does he go, and for what purpose?"

"He bought presents," stated the chief, "to give to a woman."

"A woman," repeated Puter, rising up. "Boys," he said, swinging into the saddle and motioning them to mount, "the old scoundrel has gone back to Hurricane. Yes, and damn his black heart, I know what he went for . . . he's gone to see my woman."

Chapter Twenty-Nine

The conviction of Puter was so unqualified and absolute that it left no room for doubt. What the Indian had told him Tarrant did not learn till later, and they took the apostate at his word. He had leaped up like a man who had been stung by a knife thrust and, except for his curses, all they could hear was his statement that Lot Drake was after his woman. The curses were for himself as well as for Drake. It was the woman that he thought of, the woman he still loved but who had been taken away by Lot Drake, and now she was left unguarded, a hundred and fifty miles away, and Drake with a full day's start.

Puter rode at a gallop until his lead horse was winded, and changed until further change was useless. When they reached Drake's ranch, across the river at Pahreah, he commandeered the best mounts they had. At House Rock Springs he changed again, answering the protests of the cowboys with curses, and, seeing the killing light in his wicked black eyes, they let him have his way. Jerry and Tarrant were swept along like leaves in the wake of a whirlwind, worn and starving but game to the end. At dawn of the second day they came trailing into Hurricane, a quarter of a mile in the rear.

They had summoned every atom of their hardihood and endurance to keep up with this flogging madman, but at sight of the stone house where Drake kept his favorite wife, Puter left them as if they were staked. It was frenzy, a frantic fever of jealousy and hate that impelled him and his lagging horse ahead, and, when they came up, he was stalking the blank windows of the house with the savage restraint of a tiger cat. Was she there? And was Lot Drake there? They took their places in silence, one in front and one in the rear to block any attempt at escape. Then, his impatience overcoming his better judgment, Puter stepped back and charged the door.

It gave before his rush as if bolts and locks were nothing, and during a minute that seemed an eternity Tarrant and Jerry crouched and listened, expecting each moment to hear a shot. The silence was broken at last by the sound of a woman's voice and the harsh, accusing responses of Puter. Questions and answers followed swiftly, the voices becoming more excited, until suddenly the house was still.

"Something's wrong!" called Jerry, from the rear of the house, and with a sinking heart Zachary rushed in.

The doorway stood gaping, the shattered door lying to one side. As Tarrant entered the house, it was with a full expectation of finding the man or woman dead. But, instead, he beheld Puter holding the woman in his arms, and neither of them turned to look. With a muttered apology Zachary retreated to the door, where Jerry was waiting expectantly. His eyes were dilated with the sense of an imminent tragedy, and, when Tarrant motioned him back, he stood staring, unable to comprehend.

"It's all right," whispered Zachary, "Lot Drake didn't get here."

"We're in a hell of a fix," complained Jerry as the neighbors began to appear. "Dog-gone that crazy fool anyway. I'm kilt with the riding, and now he's in there with that woman. . . ."

"He'll be out," answered Zachary hopefully. "Say nothing and keep these people out."

He flashed his deputy marshal's star as an inquisitive woman came running over, then listened to the voices inside. Puter and the woman were talking, and a few moments later the apostate appeared, white-faced but with his eyes glinting dangerously.

"He's in town," he told them. "She locked the door against him. I'd give a thousand dollars for a drink."

"I'll git a bottle," proposed Jerry instantly, and went galloping down to the saloon.

"Lot has got another wife in town," went on Puter as Tarrant regarded him inquiringly. "Don't you never think, mister, that we won't git him yet. My woman jest knows he's in town."

"Where does this other wife live?" demanded Zachary with sudden interest, and the apostate pointed out the house.

"That big two-story house," he said, "over there by them corrals. They's something going on there right now!"

He mounted his blowing horse and went dashing down the street, and Tarrant followed closely behind him. Despite the fatality that seemed to attend the apostate's plans, he initiated every new move with such a certainty of success that Zachary was always convinced. Puter was surcharged with a restless energy, and his very lack of words made his promises seem all the more sure. Now with the reckless abandon he had learned as an Avenging Angel, he strode up and rapped on the door. As Zachary came up, he burst it in with his shoulder and plunged into the locked house, alone. Once more Tarrant stood guard, listening intently for the shot that would announce the discovery of Lot Drake, but, although there was cursing and a loud altercation with some man, the chase had not come to an end.

For an eternity of days and nights, each worse than the one before, Zachary had been following the lead of this daredevil of an apostate until he was ready to drop from exhaustion. But the search had come to naught and once more Puter strode out to offer some muttered excuse. It could not be said that he did not strike quickly but in some way his enemy eluded him.

"He's here," mumbled Puter, his hands working nervously as

he looked back through the door. "My woman heard him when he came to her place. She knew him, all right . . . knew his voice, you can't mistake it . . . but she ran away and hid. Then he came over here . . . must have come . . . right here, but them boys of his say no."

He glanced at two young men who were watching them from the windows and his face twitched spasmodically as he eyed them.

"F'r cripes' sake," he muttered, "what's keeping Jerry Wamsutter? I'm perishing on my feet for one drink!"

"Hey!" shouted a big voice, and, sighting Jerry down the road, Puter ran out and grabbed for the bottle.

"Have a drink," invited Jerry, after Puter had had his dram, and, as Zachary accepted, Jerry beckoned him aside.

"Keep your eye on that pen, behind the house," he whispered hoarsely. "Seen a woman looking in, kinder excited."

Tarrant nodded and stepped back where he could look around the corner. By the side of a log corral, obviously intended for a pigsty, he saw one of Lot Drake's wives. She was leaning over the top, throwing in an armful of hay, but at the same time she was talking rapidly. When she saw she was observed, she turned away. Then, changing her mind, she stepped back to the pen and spoke to someone inside.

"There's somebody in that pen," muttered Zachary to Jerry who had handed Puter back his bottle. "Let's go out and see who it is."

"All right," agreed Jerry, much heartened by his drink, and they walked back as if going to the barn.

"What do you want?" demanded the woman, coming forward to meet them. "My husband isn't around here at all."

"What have you got in that pen?" inquired Tarrant quietly, but, before she could think up an answer, a young man came out the back door.

"Here! What are you doing?" he demanded belligerently. "We don't want you around here, understand?"

"I'm a deputy United States marshal," answered Zachary. "I'm going to search that pen."

"There ain't no one there," returned the man, who was one of Drake's sons, "or, if there is, it's some of the children."

"We'll go out to the barn, then," said Tarrant with a glance at Jerry.

Walking past the pen, which had a hole near the bottom, he circled back and looked in at the top. There was nothing to be seen but a pile of loose hay, but, as he applied his eye to a crack lower down, he saw the side of a man's face, against the wall. That the man was Lot Drake seemed an absolute certainty and Zachary drew his pistol.

"Lot Drake," he summoned, "come out and surrender. I've got a warrant for your arrest."

The concealed man did not stir. As Zachary looked up, he saw young Drake running back toward the house.

"Come over here!" Tarrant called to Puter, who was still watching the house, but the apostate shook his head. With a pistol in each hand he was looking up at the windows that overlooked the yard and pen. Glancing up, Tarrant saw the flash of gun barrels and men's faces, looking out. Already he was covered, but it was too late to back down and Zachary shoved the muzzle of his pistol through the crack.

"You go in there," he said to Jerry, "and bring that man out. If he moves a straw, I'll promise to blow his head off. My gun isn't a foot from his ear."

"Hold on," spoke up a voice from the straw. "Don't shoot. I'll give up my gun."

"You drop it and put up your hands!" ordered Tarrant, who was expecting every moment to receive a bullet. Lot Drake rose up through the hay. A cocked pistol lay beside him. As he raised his hands, Jerry Wamsutter reached in and snatched it.

"Now come out of there," commanded Zachary, and Drake rolled out of the pen.

"Look out for the house!" yelled Puter from his hiding place.

Tarrant pointed both pistols at his prisoner. "The first man that shoots, I'll kill you," he said.

Drake held up his hand to his sons. "Don't shoot, boys!" he said. "They've got me!"

"You come with me," directed Zachary.

Drake obeyed without a word. It had been his boast that he would never be taken alive, but the early morning surprise had broken his courage and he seemed stunned by the appearance of his enemies. Fresh horses were commandeered for the short dash to Moroni. Without waiting for food or drink, Zachary motioned Drake into the saddle, for the street was swarming with men. Some were armed and some were not, but all were hostile in their attitude and an attempt at a rescue seemed imminent. Tarrant looked the crowd over as, with Jerry close beside him, he stood with his guns on the prisoner. As he was mounting to go, the apostate caught his eye, stepping forward from where he had been waiting.

"I'll trouble you for that two hundred dollars," he said, and at the sound of his voice Lot Drake turned. A gleam of hate passed between them. When Puter accepted his blood money, Drake burst into a fit of cursing.

"You damned apostate!" he raved. "So this is your work, is it? You sold me to get back that woman! Well, take her, the Jezebel, and I'll have you both killed as soon as I come clear on this trial. They'll never convict me. They ain't got the evidence. I'll spill your apostate blood on the ground!"

"Yes, you'll play hell," retorted the apostate evenly, and handed back the money to Tarrant. "Jest keep that," he said. "I'll go along as a witness. And when I get through, they'll shoot Lot Drake at sunrise. He can't call my woman a Jezebel."

CHAPTER THIRTY

There was a rush of affrighted Saints into the placid street of Moroni as the man who had been their bishop for twenty years came riding into town, a prisoner. He glanced up grimly at the gleaming towers of the temple that he had built for the glory of the kingdom. The Prophet he had served had cut him off from fellowship and laid him under a curse. He who had ruled these people with the power of life and death—collecting their tithings, arranging their marriages, calling them for missions—now returned to find himself an outcast and no one so poor as to do him reverence. But he rode on, huge and dominant, his narrowed eyes sullenly resolute, and the people gazed after him in awe.

Lot Drake had been captured, the forces of the government had prevailed, and the three haggard men who brought him in were taking him to the courthouse to stand trial. The word passed from lip to lip and the old fear, never absent, clutched at the heart of every guilty man. In the crowd that watched him pass were Avenging Angels who had done his bidding when he had ordered the emigrants killed. There were women who had grown old listening for the footsteps of officers, coming to arrest their husbands as murderers, and there were others, men too young for the massacre at Mountain Meadows, but with the stain of Gentile blood on their hands. They huddled together, muttering fearfully among themselves, and then every man turned his thoughts to the man who had never failed them yet.

Brigham Young was still with them, still inspired by the Holy Spirit to lead his people out of danger. When at last they dispersed, the old hope, never blighted, took possession of their hearts again. The Prophet would save them from their enemies.

In the crowd that watched their return after the long race across the desert there was one face that Tarrant missed—Deseret was not there with the rest. He delivered up his prisoner to the United States marshal and rode back past the old, familiar hotel, and his eyes, drooping from weariness, sought for her presence beneath the mulberry trees before he passed on to report to Colonel Valentine.

His racked body clamored for rest, for food and drink and the long, sweet oblivion of sleep. After the colonel had congratulated him on the success of his perilous venture, he tottered off without even asking for his sweetheart. There had been a rift between them on the day of their sudden parting and the colonel might not understand. Now that the long quest was over and Lot Drake was safely in jail, Zachary knew he had made up for the past. The whole power of the government had been invoked in this last effort to break the control of the priesthood—to destroy the invisible government of the State of Deseret and crush out the treason that was rampant, but until Tarrant returned with Lot Drake under arrest, the machinery of justice had stood still.

There had been courts, and United States Attorneys to prosecute the traitors, and United States marshals to hale them before the judge, but the hand of Brigham Young had swept criminals and witnesses away and no Mormon could be brought to trial. Now at last one man, the arch-murderer of them all, had been arrested and brought to bar. Even as Tarrant slept, the ponderous mill of justice began to turn, while all the world looked on. In the office of the marshal and the United States Attorney men were working far into the night—jurors were summoned, witnesses subpoenaed, papers made out and served—but Zachary slept through it all. He had been awakened at sundown by the evening gun, grim reminder of the government's power, but, after eating and drinking, he had gone back to bed, to sleep again until dawn. Then, back once more in the uniform of the Army, bathed and shaved and ready for the day, he saluted punctiliously the stern-eyed old colonel who even yet regarded him askance.

"Lieutenant Tarrant," he said, "I cannot commend you too highly for your success in this difficult case. The United States marshals have failed miserably in their efforts to arrest the leaders in this massacre, and, except for your assistance as an officer of the Army, our case would have fallen to the ground. We should have been compelled once more to acknowledge defeat at the hands of this traitorous Brigham Young who, by the way, so I am informed, has cut off Lot Drake and ordered the Mormons to testify against him. In any case his doom is sealed, provided no treachery takes place and our witnesses can be thoroughly protected. And in case he is convicted, he will be executed at once before some fresh treachery can be devised. We are still, as I have said, in a dangerous situation on account of the rampant treason among the populace. But, while I could use you very nicely, I am going to reward your services by as long a leave of absence as you like. I have wired your success to the Department of War . . . and also to your father, Major Tarrant. Unless my recommendations are totally disregarded, you may expect your commission as captain. You have done well, my boy. That's all."

He raised his hand perfunctorily, in token of dismissal, but Zachary stood his ground.

"Just a moment, Colonel," he stammered. "Can you tell me where Deseret, the young lady I brought back from the wagon train . . . ?"

"Miss Mayberry," broke in the colonel in frigid tones, "is in good hands. She is perfectly safe."

"Yes, but even then," began Tarrant with a deprecating smile, "I should like. . . ."

"Lieutenant," burst out the colonel, "you displease me very much in your conduct toward this young woman. With these rough miners like Wamsutter and men of that stamp I'll admit you have a certain success, but you have no conception of the delicate sensibilities of a woman, and especially of this poor, unhappy. . . ."

The colonel stopped and choked and Tarrant stared in amazement.

"Why, what do you mean, Colonel?" he asked.

"You know what I mean!" cried the colonel in a fury. "Here is this poor orphaned creature, as sensitive and delicate as a flower . . . carried away, I suppose, by your attentions. And then you have the effrontery to parade your conquests before her, to bow and smile to Tamar Young. Why, when I think what that woman. . . ."

"Now see here," broke in Zachary, "I think more of Deseret than of any other woman in the world. It was only by an accident, by one chance in a million, that I ever happened to see Tamar Young. We were riding by the castle, where I suppose her father still stays. . . ."

"And you bowed and smiled to her," accused Colonel Valentine. "My God, when I think what treason and disgrace that woman has brought upon you. . . . And then, with this pure creature riding along beside you, you turn back to scrape and smile. . . ."

"I did not scrape!" contradicted Tarrant hotly. "I merely bowed and smiled, as any gentleman would do. . . ."

"Now, listen," broke in the colonel sternly, "this is going a little too far. How many times have I warned you against this

Tamar Young? She is thoroughly unprincipled, as you know from your own experience, and, besides that, Lieutenant Tarrant, she is the third polygamous wife of Brigham Young's private secretary. But putting that all aside . . . though how you can speak to her is more than I can understand . . . have you no regard for the sensitive feelings of this poor girl you have sworn to love and protect? When she rode in here . . . alone, except for the escort and that treacherous old Mormon, Jake Lingo . . . she sat sobbing and waiting for hours. And except for quick work, she would have ridden away with Lingo, who knew she was a government witness. He intended undoubtedly to spirit her away to prevent her giving testimony against Lot Drake. But I ask you, Lieutenant Tarrant, how you can ever defend yourself for such despicable conduct toward a lady? Here she was, waiting patiently, while you stayed at that saloon, drinking whiskey with those barroom toughs."

"Colonel Valentine," said Zachary quietly, "it was two of those toughs who led me to the hiding place of Drake, and I won't hear a word against them. As for Deseret, let me see her just a minute and all this will be explained."

"No, sir," denied the colonel. "I owe a duty to our government to protect Miss Mayberry as a witness. You cannot see her now, nor till after this trial is over. And then, if you have a spark of manhood left, you'll go down on your knees and ask her pardon. Meanwhile, if you'll accept a word of advice . . . which I very much doubt, from the past . . . break off this affair with Tamar Young . . . who, I must remind you, is a married woman."

"My God!" burst out Zachary, grinding his teeth with helpless rage. Dashing out of the colonel's tent, he strode off through the hostile town, glancing in at each door as he passed. Through no fault of his own, except a superior call of duty, he had left Deseret at Hurricane. And he had left her, it was true, at the entrance to a saloon, with all his humble apologies unsaid. But was this a sufficient ground for the colonel's tirade, and his denunciations of his conduct toward all women? Only the tardy remembrance of his duty toward a superior officer had kept him from a biting retort. And who was the colonel to step in between him and the woman he had sworn to protect?

In the Army, as anywhere, a man can love who he will as long as his conduct is honorable. The pride of his life, before this unhappy affair with Tamar, was that toward women his conduct had been exemplary. But for that one mistake the colonel condemned him in everything—with such innuendoes and hints as made his blood boil, although he was powerless to reply. Yet surely there was one who still knew that his heart was all hers, and that he loved her devotedly and forever, and, if he could ever discover the hidden retreat of Deseret, he knew she would forgive his neglect. He had neglected her, it was true, but except for that swift turning and the wild ride across the desert, Lot Drake would still be at liberty. The case of the government would have collapsed—yet the colonel called his conduct despicable.

The trial of Drake began while Zachary, still distrait, wandered here and there in search of Deseret. Following the crowd to the courtroom, he looked on at the mighty drama that was being acted out before him. One by one the United States Attorney summoned his secret witnesses to prove the charge of murder against Drake, and, as friend after friend turned state's evidence against him, the chief of the Avenging Angels became bitter. Better than anyone he saw the hand that moved behind it all, bringing these puppets out to speak, yet, though he raged at and cursed Brigham Young, the confession never passed his lips. He was a Mormon still, and it was bred into his bones to remain loyal to the Prophet, right or wrong.

The end came when Deseret, accompanied by the colonel's wife, was ushered in through the side entrance of the courtroom.

As she told the halting story of the death of her mother, Lot Drake covered his face with his hands. It was too true, too convincing to invite cross-examination or rebuttal, and the attorneys for the defense offered no new evidence when the prosecution had rested its case. The instructions of the judge to the Mormon jury were as explicit as had been those of the Prophet. After a few minutes' deliberation, they returned a verdict of guilty, and Lot Drake was sentenced to death.

Given his choice, according to the laws of Utah, Drake elected to be shot rather than hanged. That same night, in order to forestall a rumored attempt at a rescue, he was led forth to execution. Heavily guarded by soldiers, he was taken to Mountain Meadows and on the spot where the emigrants had met their death he was shot as he sat on his coffin. No friend was present to witness his death or bid him a last farewell. As Tarrant saw him fall, he remembered the prophecy of Jake Lingo, when he had gazed up at the Sleeping Chief. For as Drake fell back, his grim features, so like an Indian's, were silhouetted along the top of the coffin. His huge body relaxed into the semblance of the sleeping form that Lingo had seen in his vision. He died, as the apostle to the Lamanites had foretold, without a friend to mourn him. He died as he had lived, a Mormon to the end, still hopeful of a reward in the kingdom. But on the spot where he fell, a cross had been raised, on which was written these words:

VENGEANCE IS MINE, SAITH THE LORD.
I WILL REPAY.

Tarrant rode home with the guard that he had accompanied to the meadows when there were rumors of a rescue by the Avenging Angels, but the town, which before had swarmed with bearded Mormons, was now suddenly deserted by the hosts. A victim had been found to appease the wrath of the United States and once more Brigham Young was free to set foot in Utah, for he had acknowledged the authority of the government. Once more in a time of stress he had saved his people, and the Saints had dispersed to their homes.

Zachary Tarrant, although he wore a captain's bars on his shoulders as a reward for capturing Lot Drake, felt no pleasure at the Mormon bishop's death. He had died without fear, declaring his mind at rest and conscience free from guilt, asking the god he had served, if his labors were done, to receive him into the kingdom. Right or wrong, he still looked for a reward in the celestial kingdom, for he had sacrificed his life for the Prophet. Against such a religion what were the laws of men? And of what avail was the killing of one fanatic? He had carried out the orders of those above him, slaying men, women, and children in the name of a god whose delight was in the shedding of Gentile blood. But what of Deseret and the children he had orphaned—and where was she now, so sad-eyed and downcast, with no one to give her comfort? Tarrant walked out at evening down the broad street of the old village where the clock chimed out the hours from its tower. In that churchyard, months before, he had promised to love and protect her, but fate had stepped between them. Tamar Young had dashed their happiness, and then the colonel had intervened, keeping her hidden until the day of the trial. When Zachary, watching eagerly, had stood, waiting, to follow after her, the colonel had summoned him to duty. Now once more he was free to seek her, but Deseret was gone.

At the end of the long day, while the milkers were calling their cows and the tranquil street was veiled in haze, he turned into the churchyard where, under the honey locusts, he and Deseret had plighted their troth. But someone was sitting on the well-remembered bench where they had hidden from the wrath of the Avenging Angels—a young woman, dressed in shimmering gray silk. His eyes dwelt on her dainty form—just for a moment before he turned—and, though the warnings of the colonel still rang in his ears, they lingered and he looked again. Yet who could be more dainty and appealing to the eye than Deseret, if she were clothed in silk? It was a weakness that he must conquer, this instinct to note the beauty of other women besides his betrothed—and now this woman was coming toward him. He made out her face beneath the broad Leghorn hat—it was Deseret, with a sad smile in her eyes.

"I knew you would come," she said, "but, oh, Zachary. . . ." And the rest was a rush of tears.

She ran into his arms, and, as he kissed her, she smiled, although she disregarded his protests of love. "I have been very unhappy," she sighed as he repeated them, and would not let him kiss her again.

"But Deseret," he pleaded, "I have hunted for you everywhere . . . haven't you ever seen me passing in the street? Then why didn't you come out and speak to me?"

"I . . . I couldn't do that," she said. "Because . . . it wouldn't be for the best."

"But why not?" he protested. "Oh, I know what's the matter . . . the colonel's wife has been talking. She's the worst old cat. . . ."

"She is not," stated Deseret defiantly.

"Well, what did she say, then?" parried Zachary.

"She was just as kind and thoughtful as she could be, when I came in off of the desert. And she was the one who helped me make this new dress. Don't you think it's very becoming?"

"Why, Deseret," he assented, "I couldn't believe it was you. And when I saw a strange woman, sitting there on our bench, I . . . I. . . ."

"Yes . . . I know," she said, and sighed.

There was a long silence. Then, as the clock chimed the hour,

Deseret turned away, smiling bravely. "I must be going home now," she said.

"May I go with you?" he asked. "That is, as far as the door? Of course, after all that Missus Valentine has said. . . ."

"She has been very kind," answered Deseret, but she did not tell him no.

They walked moodily along the road that led out beneath the cottonwoods, toward Hurricane and the desert beyond. Tarrant felt the veiled reproach of her silence, although he could not bring himself to speak. Perhaps it was true that he was better fitted for the camps and the company of hard-swearing men, but to explain to her now called for more delicacy than he could muster, and he allowed the precious moments to pass. They were approaching the old farmhouse where the colonel had installed his wife, when they saw a long procession approaching—a row of handsome equipages, gleaming with silver and polished trappings, and in the first carriage sat Brigham Young.

He sat up straight in the seat, his face resolute and calm, his linen and black broadcloth immaculate. As he passed the two lovers, standing hand-in-hand by the roadside, he did not give them a glance. The war was over, a scapegoat had been offered, and he was returning to the State of Deseret. But in the carriage behind him there rode one who watched them closely— and, when she caught Zachary's eye, Tamar Young smiled wistfully, then turned her face away. The carriage passed slowly on. When she looked back for the last time, there were tears in Tamar's eyes. Yet why should she not weep—was she any less a woman as the third wife of Hyrum Paine? But Zachary had learned his lesson. He did not look back, for Deseret was there at his side. They walked on in silence, then she looked into his eyes and smiled through a mist of tears.

"Do you love her so much?" she asked.

"No, Deseret," he answered, "I do not love her at all. Will

you believe me . . . and forgive what I have done?"

"Yes, Zachary," she faltered, "but. . . ."

"I understand . . . I understand," he said, and again took her hand gently in his.

ABOUT THE AUTHOR

Dane Coolidge was born in Natick, Massachusetts. He moved early to northern California with his family and was graduated from Stanford University in 1898. In his summers he worked as a field collector and in 1896 was employed by the British Museum in this capacity in northern Mexico. Coolidge's background as a naturalist is a trademark in his Western fiction along with his personal familiarity with the vast, isolated regions of the American West and its deserts—especially Death Valley. Coolidge married Mary Roberts, a feminist and a professor of sociology at Mills College, in 1906. In the summers, these two ventured among the Indian nations and together they co-authored non-fiction books about the Navajos and the Seris. *Hidden Water* (1910), Coolidge's first Western novel, marked the beginning of a career that saw many of his novels serialized in magazines prior to book publication. There is an extraordinary breadth in these novels from *Wunpost* (1920) set in Death Valley to *Maverick Makers* (1931), a Texas Rangers story. Many of his novels are concerned with prospecting and mining from *Shadow Mountain* (1920) and *Lost Wagons* (1923) based on actual historical episodes in the mining history of Death Valley to a fictional treatment of Colonel Bill Greene's discovery of the fabulous Capote copper mine in Mexico, a central theme in *Wolf's Candle* (1935) and *Rawhide Johnny* (1936). *The New York Times Book Review* commented on *Hell's Hip Pocket* (1939) that "no other man in the field today writes better Western tales than Dane Coolidge." Coolidge, who died in 1940, wrote with a definite grace and leisurely pace all but lost to the Western story after the Second World War. The attention to the land and accurate detail make a Dane Coolidge Western story rewarding to readers of any generation. *War in Lincoln County* will be his next Five Star Western.